The Disclaimer

Faith Moulin

Published in 2014 by FeedARead.com Publishing

First Edition

A CIP catalogue record for this title is available from the British Library.

Faith Moulin has lived in Somerset for 40 years tinkering with words
but only now getting round to serious writing –
if this can be called serious!
She was shortlisted in the 2013 Somerset Short Story Competition
and in 2014 received a Commended and a
Highly Commended for her entries.
This is her first novel.

This novel is entirely a work of fiction. The names, characters and events portrayed in it are the work of the author's imagination. Any resemblance to actual persons, events or localities is entirely coincidental.

To my long-suffering husband, who has supported me throughout it all.

FOREWORD

I was christened Katherynne Jannette Jones. My mother hated the name Jones and over-compensated for its ordinariness (for which she never forgave my father), by giving me forenames with multiple alternative spellings because the name Jones was common. I learnt early on that that C-word had two meanings. In the case of our surname neither of them was desirable. I was twenty-four before I understood that 'keeping up with the Joneses' wasn't just to do with her. As her maiden name was Smyth I totally get her obsession with name spelling but I wish she had just changed the spelling to Joans instead of taking it out on my future identity.

Once I was five I learnt that I had to emphasise all the syllables in my first name or people left out the E sound. With my second name I had to say '*Jan-nette*', not Janet or Jeanette. I learnt to spell both my forenames out loud while still without my front teeth. It over-rode my natural shyness, so there is something I should be grateful for.

I was about eight or nine when I read 'What Katy Did' and realised that I could effectively change my name. From then on I loudly said, "But I'm called Katie" whenever my name came up and pretty soon I was known as Katie Jones.

My mother was horrified. She thought it was the start of the slippery slope and I would start eating in the street, wearing too much make-up and smoking cigarettes. Those things came much later – I don't think I was at all common until I turned thirteen.

I am who I am and I lay it out for you as baldly as a boiled egg. I wasn't brought up to be part of the common herd. I wasn't brought up in Fartlebury Magna either. My adopted home town isn't just a place in Corsetshire, it's a state of mind: a way of life that we all hope will soon be lost forever in the long grass like a dog poo. It is hopefully forgotten but not forgiven and will be ready to splash up all over you if you disturb it with a strimmer.

CHAPTER ONE

"Our individual lives cannot generally be works of art unless the social order is also." Charles Horton Cooley

CORSET DAILY POST April 6 2002
'Vigilantes' Attack Home and Car
By Trixie Mann

Police were called on Friday night to a house in Fartlebury Magna High Street where a terrified family was cowering behind the sofa as a group of men armed with baseball bats besieged their house.

David and Lorraine Tripswitch and their son Rudy moved to Fartlebury Magna only three months ago. Forty year-old Mrs Tripswitch works as a receptionist at Bigg, Swindell and Company, Solicitors. Forty-two year old David Tripswitch is recovering from surgery but has been volunteering with Fartlebury Magna Scout Group as an assistant leader. Rudy Tripswitch, aged 13, attends Muddleton Malreward Comprehensive School.

Mr Tripswitch told the Post that he had been shocked by the violence of the men's attack. "They've completely trashed my car," he said. "I didn't know any of the men. I think it was a case of mistaken identity."

A police spokesperson said, "We have been made aware of a group of men in Fartlebury Magna who are self-styled vigilantes. They caused extensive damage to Mr Tripswitch's car and scared his family. We would never advise people to take the law into their own hands and would suggest that these men share their concerns with the police."

"Fat chance of that," says my husband, Windy, when he finishes reading the article to me. "Still, fancy that – vigilantes in Fartlebury

Magna!" He goes on (and on and on), "My snooker pal Mike Cannon is a copper and ..."

I stop listening at this point. I've heard quite enough about Windy's friend Mike Cannon (the big shot) and his proper copper's take on life and crime.

Windy is a good husband (not that I've got anyone to compare him with) and if it wasn't for his name he would be nearly perfect. His mother named her children after where they were conceived – she thought of it before the Beckhams did it in Brooklyn. My in-laws were in the Lake District when Windy became more than a twinkle in his father's eye and they later named their firstborn son Windermere. It could have been worse I suppose; he just wouldn't suit being called Ambleside. With the Miller surname he couldn't avoid the nickname Windy and late onset flatulence just adds to the appropriateness of his name. He did a lot better than his sister; she is called Lyme Bay.

Windy is continuing, "I'm going to the Men's Breakfast in the morning. I'm going to see if anyone knows what it's all about." The Men's Breakfast is held every Friday morning in Fartlebury Magna Free Church. It's the centre of village gossip. I'm sure there will be plenty about the vigilantes. It's not quite cricket, going after someone with baseball bats.

I'm glad he's going out anyway because I've got a lot of work to do on my application to the lottery. The WI wants to make an embroidered map of the village as it used to be. They believe it will help integrate the new residents with the old ones. I think it might take a bit more than a few afternoons of communal sewing to do that. Some of the old so-and-so's are handy with a needle but are more likely to want to give any brave immigrant to Fartlebury Magna a lethal injection with it. I'm dressing the project up to make it look as if the village still has a heart, but in all honesty my guess is that it had cardiac arrest some years ago and has stopped ticking. I offered to help the WI because I used to work in the National Lottery office in

London before we moved here so I have some idea of how to tick their boxes. I've been thinking about how to present this village, how to play up its individuality, its idiosyncracies, its idiocies. In marketing terms it must have a *Unique Selling Proposition.* I'm going to start writing the bid as soon as Windy goes out.

"What do you think is Fartlebury Magna's USP?" I ask Windy's back while he is putting his shoes on.

"USB? That's something to do with computers, isn't it?" he asks back. It's one of his more annoying habits, answering questions with questions. I don't know whether it's meant to be a joke or not.

"Go and have a good breakfast," I sigh. I can't be bothered to pursue it with him. Sure as eggs he would miss his bacon. I will have to work it out for myself and throw in a nice lot of well-known and well-loved rural stereotypes to make the funders bite.

'Fartlebury Magna is a large village in South Corsetshire that used to be agricultural.' (Now it's not cultural of any sort at all.)

'It's on the Corset Levels' (and its name says it all. There are no hills around here - thank you very much. The locals like it the way it is – or at least the way they think it is. A good many of them haven't ventured out past their privet hedges much for the past 40 years. They like being on their home ground where it's nice and safe – well, it is safe anyway.)

'The County Council ran a campaign a few years ago to raise awareness of its special landscape character. They called it 'Don't Forget Your Corset' because the Somerset Levels are famous but Corset's don't have a high profile. They can easily be overlooked' (especially by anyone standing more than ten metres above sea level).

'Fartlebury Magna has suffered repeated inundations of silt, mud and ...' If I could I would finish this sentence with *'bad humour'*. That is definitely the picture for the past few hundred years. Fartlebury Magna people are obsessed with mud, crud and flood. It could be why

they've been bogged down in an everlasting bad mood and so few inmates have had either the balls or the ambition to leave.

I've been staring out of the window quite a lot. Windy's back from his breakfast at the Free Church and I really haven't got much of the application form completed. I don't know why they call it a 'Free' Church. Everyone knows there is no such thing as a free lunch, and there are no grounds for thinking the church is any different. Windy sounds excited, his voice as urgent as the milkman's knock when I owe him two weeks' money.

"Katie, Katie! This vigilante group – Jim reckons it's been set up by Johnny Henchman. He's got a bit of a thing about paedophiles. Apparently he told Jim he was going to sort a few out."

We've known Jim a long time. Too long, I sometimes uncharitably think. He's about eighty now but he doesn't seem to have aged a day in the thirty years we've lived in close proximity to his bullocks. Jim rents a piece of ground at the bottom of our garden. He calls it 'a piece of ground' but it's an ocean of mud and muck in which a few Herefordshire steers paddle around up to their hocks in squelch. We feel sorry for these poor animals, who have to subsist on a mouldy bale of hay and the odd clout with a stick. I used to go up the garden and throw them my vegetable peelings and apple cores over the fence, but they're a bit slow, like Jim himself, and they couldn't wade to it before it sank under the substrate which Windy has dubbed 'quickshit'. I've given up trying to supplement their feed now. I just avoid looking their way.

Jim's a 'true local' as he puts it. His surname is Fardle so his ancestors probably evolved here, or if you don't believe in Evolution they were miraculously fashioned from the dirt of Fartlebury. Jim quite often looks as if he is made of dirt. When we first came to Fartlebury Magna, he tried hard to answer our questions and make conversation, so he seemed like a friend in a hostile land. He told us about his upbringing: “I didn’ do school much, did I? I did ‘elp on the farm. You’m all clever, you be, eh? Eh?”

It’s a surprise to me that Jim goes to the Men’s Breakfasts, because the clientele is largely middle class, but Jim’s got friends in high places – or what passes for high places in Fartlebury Magna. (No place is very high round here.) He’s going to join them soon; he’s been co-opted onto the parish council. I can’t begin to imagine the contribution he will make to debates.

I’m even more surprised that Johnny Henchman goes to the Men’s Breakfasts. He’s such a nasty piece of work for the Free Church to welcome through their doors, even though they claim to be there for sinners. “That’s awful,” I say, but I can’t stop myself adding, “And what does Mike Cannon, the big shot, think?”

“Well, actually he was very quiet on the subject.”

My sarcasm rises like bitter bile in my throat. “My God!” I exclaim, a little too loudly. “How unusual!”

Windy shoots me a look. It’s not withering me but only because I’m not a tender plant. We understand each other after forty years together so he’s used to what I call my ‘witty ripostes’ (what he calls my ‘shitty retorts’). I’m retorting right now:

“But do they think there’s any truth in the rumour that the victim was a paedophile?”

Windy has wandered back into the hall, taking off his coat. I follow him and straighten it on the peg.

“Mike Cannon says there are 17 people in Fartlebury Magna on the Sexual Offences Register, so maybe he is one. He could be. Mike said he might have moved here to get away from his past.”

“But it could have caught up with him.”

“Yes,” says Windy, “something like that. Or maybe it really was a case of mistaken identity like the bloke said.”

“But what do the men at the Breakfast think? What do you think?”

"I really don't have enough information to go on, Katie. I can't have an opinion without more information." He pauses while he puts his slippers on. "But some people reckon Johnny Henchman was on the right track."

I'm interested in what goes on in Fartlebury Magna. I'm especially interested in a bit of scandal and gossip. I've been feeling that I need to get more involved in the community. That's a bit of a tale in itself so, as Jim would say, I'll just put you in the background.

The parish council is run by an old retired tax man (Fishface I call him) and his vice chair, Johnny Henchman, (the very same man who Windy just accused of beating up paedophiles). Fishface works hard but his outlook is sour. His councillors accept him because none of them have the energy or interest to do the job themselves. They don't make it easy for him: they have enough energy and interest for that. There is no social cohesion on Fartlebury Magna Parish Council. Dry old bones. They rattle like a medical student's practice skeleton.

Fishface runs the meetings on wrath and sarcasm and spends his days trying to get an hour's work out of the sullen scruff they have as their clerk. She wears baggy old tracksuit bottoms and a dirty tee shirt as her clerking clothes. He doesn't like the way the tee shirt isn't baggy to match her bottom and, anathema to him, it shows off her figure. Windy says Fishface told Johnny Henchman that she was immodest and indecently 'big up top'. One day he even went so far as to tell her so.

"Your attire is not very business-like," he apparently said. "I'd like you to wear something more suitable for an office." The clerk had complained to Johnny Henchman about it and he passed on the complaint at the Men's Breakfast. Men like women to be appropriately dressed. Fishface allegedly even told the poor woman not to flaunt her chest size.

"If you want me to wear decent clothes you lot had better start paying me a decent wage," she said, or so Windy says Johnny Henchman says she said.

Apparently Fishface would have sacked her as soon as look at her miserable face but she knows all the council rules. She knows she is the employee of the whole corporate bunch of bananas. The other councillors don't know what she's like. They never go near her office so there is no way they would ever agree to sacking her, not all of them at once – least of all if that's the proposal of their Chairman. She seems a nice enough girl to them I suppose. They never speak to her. They know she isn't very efficient, and Johnny Henchman says she's not very obliging either, nor even very ornamental – but who is in Fartlebury Magna?

Johnny Henchman is Fishface's sidekick as well as his vice-chair. I'm not particularly clear about which vice it is, but I do notice that they aren't natural allies or friends because it is obvious that Fishface looks down on Henchman because he is a retired dustman. What they do have in common is that they both enjoy the i-dotting and the t-crossing of parish council life. They like bringing to the meetings their daft schemes, backed only by their own bigoted, half-baked opinions and foisting them on other councillors.

I'm going along to the council meeting to ask if they will support the WI embroidery project. I know better than to ask for money. All I want is a letter of support. I ask if I can tell them about the project and they must have misunderstood me, or misheard me, because they immediately think they can tell me about the project instead. One granite-faced greybeard points his filthy finger at me and growls, "What do we want a 'broidered picture for? Who's going to want to look at that? Waste of time." (This is in the category of a fully-baked opinion.)

I smile sweetly through the perma-frost and say, "The WI feels that it could help with social cohesion in Fartlebury Magna." Fifteen pairs of eyes swivel towards me, well, not Henchman's pair – one of his eyes looks resolutely at the opposite wall.

"We don't want anything to do with that," says Johnny Henchman. "Too many people on the social as it is."

"It's about getting the different strands of society together," I say.

"I don't know anything about embroidery," says another, "but I don't see how you can get the different strands together. Only one person can sew at a time, and anyway, where are you planning to hang this picture when it's finished? There isn't any room for any more so-called projects on the walls in here."

I look round at the drawing competition entries from 1926.

"All those against supporting the embroidery project," barks Fishface.

Hands shoot up like Nazi salutes. I am outraged. "You can't do that," I say. "I'm not even asking for money."

"You've had your turn to speak," says Fishface. "Next!"

I watch the rest of the performance with growing disgust. I see that the parish councillors en bloc enjoy the bullying arising from their real or imagined status, throwing their weight about like wellies at the Summer Fair. They enjoy putting down any innocent member of the public who attends a meeting with hopes of getting parish council support. "We're not here to do anything for you!" Fishface shouts at the young woman who wants to set up a hockey club. "We're not made of money!" he shouts at the scout master who asks the council to pay for black bags for a national litter-picking day. "We're not here to listen to your complaints! We're only volunteers!" he scowls at an old woman whose grand-daughter has fallen off a swing onto a bit of sharp metal. "She wasn't skewered by it, was she? She's lucky we've got a swing. They're very expensive."

"Who inspects the play equipment?" asks one of the younger councillors. Emily is about 60 with a face that looks as if she is sucking a lemon. Fishface looks at the clerk. The clerk looks at the floor. The floor looks back at Fishface. They are all wondering whether anyone does inspect the play equipment.

"Dunno," says the clerk.

"The groundsman," says Fishface.

"Can I ask him to deal with the spike then?" Emily asks.

Henchman pounces. Hah! Someone on the edge of his web at last. "No member of the council may give instructions to the employees of the council. Standing Order 36."

"Well, can the Chairman ask him then?"

"Certainly not. No member of the council, not even the Chairman."

"No wonder nothing gets done around here," I think. In Fartlebury Magna it's not so much life in the slow lane as life on the hard shoulder.

At the end of the meeting I put my hand up and catch Fishface's eye (which is very clever of me because he didn't throw it very well). "Is the council doing anything about the vigilante group that targeted a house in Robin Road?" I ask before he has time to take his eye back.

"Where's Robin Road when it's at 'ome?" asks one of the councillors whose blinkers extend to a blotting out of the 550 new homes at Pratts Dell.

"I thought it was in the High Street," says another, "but Robin Road is off Starling Drive, which is off Blackbird Avenue."

I know it isn't but I don't like to argue. No, really. I don't. He's confusing it with Wren Rise.

Henchman is talking to Fishface. He is multi-tasking, scowling at me at the same time.

Fishface says, "You can't speak now. You should have asked your question in Public Speaking Time. Come again next time if you've got another question."

I'm an innocent. "When will the next meeting be?"

Fishface looks at the clerk. She doesn't catch his eye either. Butterfingers.

"It will be on the notice-board. Look on the notice-board. We give three days' notice of meetings."

Johnny Henchman glowers more gloomily in my direction. "It's the law," he says. "There's only five minutes for the public to speak. You wasted all your time on that bloody stupid embroidery business. You should have asked about vigilantes then if you're so keen to know what's none of your business."

"I didn't know the procedure," I say in my defence, but they have stopped listening. Fishface is looking at his watch.

"If you want to come here and ask us questions, you'd better find out how parish councils work," says a particularly vicious old woman, whose broomstick must be the one I can see propped up by the door.

Yes, I think I will.

CHAPTER TWO

"There is in every village a torch – the teacher, and an extinguisher – the clergyman" Victor Hugo

Next thing I find myself out of work and at a bit of a loose end. It was just a casual job working in an architect's office, but he had designs on a younger woman and went back to the drawing board. I've never had a career. It just never seemed worth the hassle when there was so much to do at home. There were lots more under-employed women like me when we were young in the seventies – and back then men didn't need any help with paying the mortgage. It was a sacrifice we young wives made for our men, having no status, intellectual stimulus or money – there was no daytime television or home computing then either. I make cushions and jam. My friends who have careers never make jam and they buy their cushions from Jean Paul Gaultier.

Almost all my friends are graduates and they just assume I am the same but lazy. I can hold my own in conversation and they never guess I didn't go to university. No-one has ever commented on my lack of experience in drinking men under the table because maturity and motherhood has taken from them that important under-graduate skill and levelled the playing field. I like to know things so I used to do evening classes or distance learning courses, and to make a bit of pocket money I delivered catalogues or phone directories, worked in shops or offices, or cleaned other people's houses. (That's always seemed a lot more attractive than cleaning my own.) In any case it has always suited Windy to have a nearly full-time carer and it means I have time for the WI projects. But since the children left home I am a bit bored. There's only so much room in the house for cushions and jam.

My brush with the dustpan of parish life has swept a fluffy seed of an idea into my head. There's an election coming up for district and parish councils. If Jim can do it so can I, so I take myself down to the parish clerk's office and ask how to apply. I try to get her on my side; open her mind to new possibilities. It's a lost cause. Her mind is as tightly shut as a baby's fist around something lethal it found on the floor.

"There's always more going on in Bumford Sock," I say. Bumford Sock is our next door parish. "They seem to have a lot more facilities and more pride in the place too." She looks at me with total disinterest. "They've got a nice website as well. It's got mug-shots of the councillors. Some of them are even under 50." There isn't a flicker of interest, no change in her glass-eye gloominess at all. I don't know how she does it.

"I've come to get a form to apply to be a councillor at the next election," I say cheerily.

"We don't have elections in Fartlebury Magna." She barely looks up from her dot-to-dot puzzle. "That's not the way we do things. If you want to be co-opted best thing is to talk to the chairman."

That raises the stakes, and my hackles. In the interests of democracy I determine to make sure there's an election. I know there hasn't been one as long as we have lived here, so that must be at least 30 years. I trot off home and make a couple of posters on the computer. They say *Fartlebury Magna Needs You!* and more politely, *Please Consider Standing for Election as a Parish Councillor in May.*

The 21-seat council already has eight vacant seats. The thirteen councillors in office at the moment are definitely an unlucky number. I realise that I need to find at least ten new people and even then there wouldn't be much of an election as the empty seats would just suck up the new blood like super tampons. We need a whole gang of recruits to stage a coup. In Fartlebury Magna there are always plenty of people who think they could do as well as the current council. Consequently, the village is full of well-meaning, nice ex-councillors because anyone nice and normal soon gives up swimming against the tide (and against

Fishface and his shoal of piranhas). It's just too difficult on your own to resist the rush of effluent when the sewer gates open at the monthly meetings. I have to find enough revolutionaries and I know the revolting people I find need to be willing to stand up and be counted and then sit down and work as a team.

Windy has seen my posters. I know he is not very impressed with my computer skills. He says he doesn't particularly want to come on the council, but if I don't get ten new people he will relent and make up the numbers. He helps me put up the posters but in deference to his shyness we go after dark.

A few days later the phone rings and a male voice I don't recognise says, "Are you behind the fly-posting asking people to consider becoming a councillor?"

"Yes. Why do you ask?"

"You want to watch out. It's illegal to put up election posters without putting your name on them."

"They're not election posters."

"Yes they are. They're promoting an election. They're asking people to stand for the council."

"That's not like asking people to vote for someone, is it." I say it as a statement, not a question.

"I'm just telling you the law. It will cost thousands to hold an election. People don't like the council wasting money unnecessarily. Watch out or the Fartlebury bods will bury you."

"Who am I speaking to?" Click. Thoughts tear through my mind slamming little brain doors behind them. One thought is about the self-styled vigilantes and their baseball bats.

I ring the Electoral Services Officer at County Hall: "What if I want to draw attention to the fact that there hasn't been an election here for more than 30 years? Can I put up posters?"

"You can put up election posters on private land. If you put them on lamp-posts or anywhere else without permission of the landowner that would be fly-posting."

"They aren't election posters. They are just to try to get people to stand as councillors so we can have an election here. The parish council should be trying to get new recruits themselves, but they don't. They never do."

"You would need to put your name and address on the bottom, and '*published and printed by...*' otherwise you could be breaking the law. Election regulations are very strong. It isn't a civil matter. It's a police matter."

I quake in my Crocs.

"Thanks," I say. I will have to face up. I will have to go public and come out as a campaigner. In the meantime I need a flying start to whip round and take the posters down before I get into trouble. I get my bike out of the shed.

Of course I should have realised that there was really no rush to comply. The tribal elders aren't likely to do anything. Half of them are on their last legs, or not even on their legs at all – two of them ride right into the village hall on their mobility scooters scattering the other councillors with cries of *"Mind your backs!"* One or two of them leave their zimmer frames behind their chairs. Their dander isn't yet up because they haven't even noticed the posters, but it's going to be. Oh yes. It really is. I'm going to have to watch my back.

My next set of posters comes clean. I write them in blood. Well, I pretend to. I find a cool, in fact chilling, font and my posters with blood-red dripping text look like adverts for a Halloween party. *Fartlebury Magna Needs New Blood. Let's Give the Council a Transfusion.* At the bottom in a minuscule font size for legal reasons I have added: *Katie Miller, Fartlebury Usurpers Committee, 20 Church Street, Fartlebury Magna.*

Because I am going to have to watch my back more closely – and every other part of my anatomy, I put them up in even darker, but cheekier places, like the parish council noticeboards. They change the posters advertising last year's car boot sale so rarely that I think it might be weeks before they notice. I hope people will like the acronym. I like it a lot. Everything needs an acronym these days.

I ask Jim if he would mind if we put a poster up in his front garden. Jim lives in one of the very few remaining unaltered cottages on the High Street. It's a bit ramshackle but it has its original woodwork (in original natural wood now that the paint has completely flaked off). It has a typical Corsetshire steep roof with terracotta tiles and no gutters. It is fancifully named Greenhill Cottage. As there are no hills round here, green or otherwise, I ask Jim how his house got its name. "Ooh ah," he ponders. "Mebbe there was an 'ill once. My cottage is as old as the 'ills, my gramfer told me." Jim was born in the little cottage, as were most of his bullocks. No wonder he seems as old as the hills too. But he is generous enough not to mind my request, or not to understand, and we put up a prominent sign right on the High Street. Now all I need to do is pray for success.

There are half a dozen churches in Fartlebury Magna but 'the church' tends to mean the parish church, high in every sense, and mighty. It's dedicated to St John the Evangelist, but everyone just calls it St John's. I assume that's because half of them can't spell it even if they can get their speech impediments round it.

The parish council has a historic tie to the parish church, not just all over the country, but even here in Fartlebury Magna. A hundred and twenty years ago Fartlebury Magna Parish Council was formed from the 'Vestry' - a group of the great and good men of the parish - and, of course, they actually, literally, were all men in those days. There tend to be no councillors in Fartlebury Magna who are 'great' or 'good' now. But back in the day, councillors were, in the main, farmers - so-called ‘gentlemen farmers’ - plus the Vicar and schoolmaster. There are no gentlemen farmers left in Fartlebury Magna. Only far-from-gentlemen farmers. Like the ones that PC Bigg-Toze told me about. Like me, our beat officer just loves a bit of gossip.

The story goes that when Foot and Mouth disease was ravaging the country’s livestock in 2001, farmers up and down the country (and side to side) were keeping warm by rubbing their hands in glee as they anticipated the compensation payouts. (Not all of them, of course; some were keeping warm by standing within five miles of the DEFRA infernos for sanitary disposal of livestock, or to be totally accurate, deadstock.) Anyway, at that time Fartlebury Magna Parish Council, fearing economic collapse, or bubonic plague, or thinking it was the same as BSE and they might stagger on their way to milk the cows, decided to blockade the village and not allow vehicles to travel along the High Street. One of the four farmers still on the council, Phil Jenkins, following in his father’s and grandfather’s perishing wellies, said it was a risk to his stock having vehicles drive into Fartlebury Magna, spreading disease, so he and his mates took some bales of straw and blocked the road. I can imagine Phil’s excitement. On the rare occasions that he gets animated, one of his eyebrows twitches wildly and threatens to fly right off his face, instead of clinging on like a hairy caterpillar as it usually does. I expect old Jim helped them out. He gets the odd idea hopping from neuron to neuron through his cider-pickled grey matter. There’s not much to get in its way in there, under the rural thatch.

PC Bigg-Toze told me it was like a re-enactment of the Three Little Pigs with farmers huffing and puffing to get huge bales of straw into place to create a road-block at each end of the High Street. He said to Phil Jenkins, “What’s up, Phil? You can’t block off the road, you know.” And Phil told him they were worried about Foot an’ Mouth. Bigg-Toze was obviously very proud of his reply, and grinned from sticky-out ear to sticky-out ear when he told me that he said: “You’ve put your foot in your mouth, Phil.” He could have had them for breach of the peace as well as obstructing the highway, but it’s too much paperwork.

“Anyway,” he tells me later, “you have to make allowance. They’re a different breed – farmers.”

‘Yes, a rare breed,’ I think to myself, ‘sadly, not yet endangered.’

***

The early parish councillors were self-elected from the few who had the time and self-assurance to want to boss other parishioners about. We might say those with a sense of leadership. (Or, in these more cynical times, we might say ‘leader shit’.) Anyway, you get my drift – the Vicar was historically a key player in the game, providing the premises for the meeting and the education necessary to drag the local old nags to the local government water. It’s not the same Vicar these days of course - even though he does look as if he’s been here a hundred years and he talks like it too - but other public school educated, plum-in-mouth incomers have taken up the challenge to try to cure the souls in Fartlebury Magna. (I think quite a few are incurable.) Fartlebury Magna’s vicars have, without exception, come from elsewhere in the country but they have some kind of holy dispensation and are immune to the prejudice I know as ‘Fartlebury Fascism’. It is historically accurate to say that they have been men. I doubt that Fartlebury Magna will be having a woman in a dog collar anytime soon – unless the men regard it as ‘suitable attire for the occasion’, of course. They might like a bit of dressing-up for all I know about such things.

I’m constantly racking my brains now, trying to think of people I can ask to join me in a revolution to over-throw the parish council. I remember a very nice woman I used to know called Maggie. I liked Maggie. Our children went to school together. She is bright but not showy; she always seemed to have high standards and low heels - my sort of woman. So I track her down and I ask Maggie if she will consider standing for election to the parish council. However, when I share my plan with her she doesn't seem to think it is anything to do with democracy, even though I explain that she will have to fill in forms and persuade people they should vote for her and only if she is the one with the most votes will she win. She says she will pray about it and if it is God's will she will do it.

Maggie is the wife of the newly self-appointed pastor of the community church. She's the best kind of twenty-first century do-gooder, genuinely doing good around Fartlebury Magna, giving away Easter eggs outside the convenience store in April, handing out mince pies in December. The community church calls this 'outreach'. They mean to entice more people to their church on a Sunday in the hope of getting more free food. Quite a few of them have had too many mince pies already.

I've got a few reservations about churches. I've tried all the different brands in Fartlebury Magna over the years – except the RCs. You know where you are with Catholics. They go to Mass on Sunday (or Saturday if they are too busy) and avoid hell. Anyway my sensitive throat can't stand all that incense and I have heard it's possible to strangle yourself with a rosary. With most of the other churches it is a bit less dangerous, but a bit less clear-cut and a bit less tangible. Maggie and I both had a dalliance with the Wesleyans when their minister was young and good looking. That was when Maggie left her husband Charles and found John. She found Jesus and John at the same time and left me behind. I wasn't in the market for a new life of either sort. I quite liked the one I'd got. After a while she and John decided the Wesleyans were a bit reserved for them. They thought they could do a better job of being holy so they designed a logo and a website and John became the pastor of the church that meets in the Village Hall on Sundays. They live by faith, Maggie tells me. I think it sounds pretty much like sponging off your friends, but what would I know? They are obviously holier than me (and thou). I gave up on churches years ago when I got to know the congregations better.

Anyway, a few days later God says *Yes,* I guess, because Maggie joins FUC – although she always says it in full. She doesn't like the four letter word that I like to use when discussing our campaign. She is also going to help me find some more FUC-kers (but she doesn't put it quite like that). She has been putting pressure on me for some days and now the boil is ripe for a squeeze. I'm slightly scared that the poison will erupt with filthy consequences but I can only go with it now. She really thinks Pastor John will be able to help. He will know people, she says, who would like to be involved. "In any case, it's time you met him anyway."

I find almost at once that I'm not so keen on Maggie's husband John as I am on Maggie. He wears a *Jesus Loves You* badge and has a symbolic fish on his car. Their infant church operates a kind of cartel, presumably inspired by the success of the Mafia, who run something similar, looking after their own. (The Devil does that too.) The church has hairdressers, builders, an insurance broker, an upholsterer and probably others I don't know about. By displaying the little fish they hope to get a business advantage over their rivals. The godless hairdressers, like the one I use, don't get a look in. The church money is thus cycled in a closed circle - apart from the stuff Maggie and John spend in Waitrose getting mince pies and Easter eggs.

John has shown me to a cosy little room and I retreat into the depths of a large old horsehair-stuffed armchair. Maggie is banging about in the kitchen. I think I had better start by explaining that I'm not a church-goer of any sort but I have a lot of sympathy for Wesley. I have even read his Journal. I tell John that I like to do things properly, that I like things to be right, that I want to get rid of the current parish councillors and get some new blood in there so we can improve things in the village. He nods. I get the impression he thinks I am bonkers. Actually I'm coming to that conclusion myself, listening to myself talk. I say to him that lots of us are motivated to do good things in society. I know that the Methodists have a good youth club and send money to Africa and stuff like that but I would like us all to work together. In Muddleton Malreward, I say, the churches all work together and put on stuff for the community as a united front. They work with the Town Council and the do-gooding groups. That makes him a bit defensive.

"There is a meeting of church leaders here every year or so," he says, "but it's hard to get the congregations to work together. Old prejudices die hard."

"If they die at all," I murmur. I think I should just make conversation for a while. It's all part of my charm offensive. Or offensive charm. "What do you think about Fartlebury Magna having its own vigilante group?"

"Well, I don't think anyone should go round threatening violence," he says. I'm nodding sagely with a non-committal look right up until he finishes his sentence, "… but we are called upon to fight evil."

"How do you know the guy was evil?" I ask. I think that is a very reasonable question but perhaps my voice was tinged with indignation. I personally think there is no smoke without fire, but I don't like the idea of the man being judged guilty without a trial.

John sighs as if I am very stupid. "We're all evil, Katie."

"Yes, but not all of us have people coming after us with baseball bats."

I think he is going a bit far. I'm not evil. Not very often, anyway. John then suggests I join him and Maggie in prayer. I shake my head vigorously. I'm terrified. It's private and personal, your communion with God. You shouldn't let other people in on your private thoughts.

Best keep it to yourself, in your head. Save praying out loud for when you're drowning in the sea off Margate.

"I understand what you want to do," he says. "Why not join us, Katie? Why not throw yourself into working with us at the community church? We could let you have your head. Lots of people would be glad to help you and support you in your projects to improve Fartlebury Magna. At the end of the day if you don't have God's blessing what you are doing will fail. Do your good works through our church instead. Otherwise you are banging your own gong, taking the law into your own hands and essentially no different from that vigilante group some idiot has set up."

I'm a bit taken aback. "I'm not going to advocate violence. It's not the same thing at all."

"No, but if you are not for us Katie, you are against us. I think you should think about your own spiritual needs and come and join us at the community church."

"Thanks," I say, standing up. I don't think I'll wait for coffee after all.

"By the way," says John, getting to his feet too, "have you looked at our website? We are doing a bit of a survey."

"As a matter of fact, I have," I say, glad to be back on familiar, secular territory.

"Good," he says. "What did you think of it? We have just completely re-vamped it. The guy who was attacked by vigilantes, he's a nice chap, Scout leader and all that, he did it. He's a computer professional and he just offered to do it for nothing. He's made a lovely job of it."

I'm not sure if he's kidding me, after our earlier conversation about evil.

"He's not all bad then," I say, heading for the door. The irony is lost on John. They take themselves a bit too seriously at the community church.

"No-one is all bad, Katie. You might need to remember that." I think that is some kind of a hint of chastisement because I implied the present parish councillors are rubbish.

Maggie seems unsurprised that I'm leaving. "See you soon, Katie," she calls from the kitchen. "Come on Sunday. We start at 10.30."

John follows me closely to the door. Before he opens it, he gives me a hug. I can't quite be sure whether it was a Christian hug or an unchristian one but I can't wait to get out of there. I'll stick to Maggie in future. I just want to get back to my campaign and FUC the lot of them.

***

At the WI I have met a woman called Hilary. She works for the County Council in a 'community development' role. I think Fartlebury Magna needs some 'community development'. I give her a call that evening in the lull between doing very little and doing nothing at all. This used to be my busiest time of day when I had a job and children at home. It's good to use the time productively. Hilary tells me that parish councils can do a lot of good in the community supporting and encouraging people. When I tell her my idea to stage a coup she is immediately enthusiastic, plunging in up to her waist. At that depth you have to use both feet. The mud is smelly but she's dauntless.

"I'm in! Count me in, Katie. I'll ask around for some other people too. We'll need a few other people to join us. I'll ask around."

I'm happy about that. She probably knows quite a few Guardian readers. I would like to raise the tone. I'm definitely going to up the anti - I'm anti most of it. Hilary makes me feel positive. Maybe I'm not mad after all. I can't wait to tell Windy how well it is going.

"Well done, old gal," he says. Clashing our coffee cups we look each other in the eyes and say, "Fartlebury Magna!" It is a beautiful moment only slightly rushed by Windy's need to warm up the TV for the UEFA Cup match in which some unknown Baltic state will humiliate a slightly better known one.

I have done quite well whether he will listen to me or not. Maggie and Hilary are definite, Penny and Jenny probable, Bill and Gordon are our token males (although Windy might be one as well) and there are another four who are willing to be councillors but haven't time to campaign.

Those of us with the time do a bit of door-to-door canvassing in the weeks leading up to the election. It's a bit of fun for most of us, but some take it seriously. Hilary has made some rosettes for us to wear. They say NEW CANDIDATE on them. We chose pink as our campaign colour, which is a bit annoying for the male candidates, but to be fair, most of the colours have already been taken by other political parties. Gordon has turned his rosette brown with a bit of boot polish (he says it was boot polish anyway). He browned it to overcome his embarrassment at being associated with a lot of feminists. Those were his exact words. I told him that feminists don't like pink either but then he said he didn't want to look like a Gay Pride activist. There's no pleasing some people.

I am finding out which residents vote, and it's not as many as I had hoped. The voters fall into two camps. The village is full of vigilante talk. People either don't like Fartlebury Magna becoming the kind of place that has a vigilante group, or they do like Fartlebury Magna being the kind of place that has a vigilante group. Sometimes I throw into the conversation, especially if I can see a booster seat in the car in the drive, that there are seventeen people in Fartlebury Magna who like having sex with children – and they are just the ones that have been caught. That seems to shake them up a bit. I tell them what a good relationship I have with PC Bigg-Toze and how we aim to tackle crime together if I am elected. I think I'm gaining ground … until one night I wake up in a sweat thinking that I might have been talking to one of the seventeen. He has dark sunken eyes in the midst of grey and black shadows reminiscent of a Goth's eye make-up the morning after it has been slept in. He shows no expression at all and says only two words: "Fuck off."

"Well, that's an interesting term to use because our campaign …" but he shuts the door, if not quite in my face at least very, very close to it. It's a good job my nose is quite snub and petite. (My mother liked to call it retroussé.)

I arrive at one door just as a boy about twelve is dashing out of it in his Scout uniform. "Sorry, I'm late!" he says to me, then turns and shouts, "Mum! Someone to see you."

His mother arrives smiling in spite of it only being me in my FUC-king pink rosette, and we have a pleasant chat about local politics. It turns out she is Johnny Henchman's daughter-in-law so she has a bit more knowledge of local politics than most. I could see the genes of Johnny Henchman in the boy's body shape now she mentions it. The torso is too long for the limbs and the shoulders too narrow for the head size. This gives the small adult Johnny Henchman a swaggering gait, and his growing grandson a school shirt that won't tuck in.

"I don't always agree with my father-in-law," she explains. "He's inclined to see bogeymen everywhere. Says Mark shouldn't be allowed to go to Scouts – he doesn't like that bloke they've got helping down there: Mr Dipstick. He takes a bit too much interest in the boys, he says. That was because Mark did tell him that some of the boys say Dipstick's a paedo, but it's just kids' talk. He was joking. He's a nice man, that Dipstick. He's helping the boys to keep safe on the internet, so Mark says. He's a whizz on computers. The kids like that, don't they? Anyway, I can't stop him going to Scouts just because of gossip and rumour, can I?"

"Of course not," I say, fingering my rosette to remind her of the purpose of my visit, "but if elected I would work closely with the police to monitor the local people who are on the Sexual Offences Register."

"Police? I've got no time for them. When we were burgled they did bugger all. It was the copper's own son doing the burglaries at the time for his drug habit. They didn't even investigate it. They're all in it together. No, my father-in-law says if something wants doing, do it yourself. I thought you believed in that too. That's what you said in your leaflet."

It's not quite true. I wrote about the community getting involved in making the place better – I meant litter picking and helping at the youth club. Not hunting down paedophiles while carrying dangerous sports equipment.

CHAPTER THREE

"They always say time changes things, but you actually have to change them yourself." Andy Warhol

I never thought I would wake up on an election day and feel too excited to eat my breakfast, but the great day is here and my stomach is clouded with butterflies. There might even be a few hoverflies in there hanging about in mid-air. I can't wait to get going. I have pinned on my lovely pink rosette and added matching pink ear-rings.

Windy won't let me pin his rosette on his new jacket and I am finding him a bit slow to get going this morning. "There's no rush," he says, "nothing's on fire."

"My innards are," I gripe. "I need to get out." The adrenalin is building up and I feel like a pressure cooker. The steam will seep out through my ears and embarrass me if he doesn't get a move on. I start to pace up and down the kitchen swinging my arms like a gibbon.

Fartlebury Magna is not just flat, it's linear, stretching along a ridge of solid ground like a piece of knicker elastic. The village developed in this long and drawn-out way back before the Middle Ages because the old High Street was the only bit of terra firma then. Soggy marsh surrounded it for miles. One false step and your shoes were soaked and your socks rotting. Old Jim remembers in the 1950s punting from here to Muddleton Malreward five miles away because the fields and roads were all flooded in the winters before the new river was cut. I try to imagine him as a boy with a long pole, but I can't.

At last we are on our way to the village hall. It is situated as if it was randomly thrown down at an angle to the road, which provides a useful triangular space for a bench for drunks to sit on and a bin into which they can bring up their beer. Someone missed it last night and the stomach contents of an avant-garde pavement artist (or just some other sort of artist beginning with P) decorate the pavement with glistening multi-coloured pointillism. Fortunately all I can smell is Windy's Brut – he has evidently splashed it on all over, an imperative he received deep in his sub-conscious back in 1966. I step over the used condoms.

Today we can vote for both parish and district councillors. Outside the hall, perched precariously on the steps, the usual bunch of political activists ask to see our polling cards. "No thanks," I say.

Windy hands his over. "Why not?" he asks in a low voice as we step together over the threshold. "I've read it up," I say. "You're under no obligation to respond to those people. Why should I make it easy for political parties?"

Windy shrugs. He thinks I'm being bolshy for the sake of it. He hasn't got a grasp of history. He doesn't know what those Bolsheviks were like. I'm more like Ghandi, or Martin Luther King, leading the populace to rebel through passive resistance, but when I say that to Windy he glances at me with incredulous pity before he says, "Like hell you are. That's such bollocks." Good job I know he's joking.

We go into the village hall and stumble through the darkness into the area where the polling station has been set up with its hardboard booths and the dominant Victorian black metal ballot box. The voting slips are enormous and after I have drawn my carefully placed crosses like someone who can't write their own name, I need all my origami skills to get the paper into the ballot box. Windy is struggling a bit with his but I dare not help. The assistants would probably call PC Bigg-Toze. You're not allowed to touch anyone else's voting paper and I really don't want his vote disqualified. I think I probably need all the votes I can get. That is really why I am here, to cast my vote for myself.

It is very exciting to see all the NEW CANDIDATES listed on the ballot paper. We all have the same description: WORKING FOR

FARTLEBURY MAGNA in the space under our names where you usually see the political party. Almost all of us anyway. There are twelve new candidates including Windy. We realised in the end that he had to decide one way or another and stand for election. I told him he couldn't wait to see how things were going or he might miss his chance, so he decided he didn't want to be left out, seeing as I was having so much fun. The one person who doesn't have WORKING FOR FARTLEBURY MAGNA under her name is Mavis Wilson. She lives in Fartlebury-under-Marsh, a tiny hamlet which is part of the Fartlebury parish. I think Mavis has delusions of grandeur and sees herself as Chairperson of a Fartlebury-under-Marsh parish council. She insisted on having WORKING FOR FARTLEBURY-UNDER-MARSH under her name. I did try to tell her that she will have to work for the whole parish but her logic was flawless: her voters would all be from Fartlebury-under-Marsh, so she needed them to know she was working for them. I can't argue with that.

Hardly anyone under the age of seventy goes to vote, especially not for a parish council, and even the old-timers don't really know the rules, so we have had to work quite hard to make sure people know who we are and that we want change. Fartlebury Magna is divided into four wards, just like the mental hospital down the road. The different wards have varying numbers of councillors depending on the number of electors living in that ward. We don't want votes wasted on the dross representing the status quo, so we have carefully schooled our electorate so they understand that *Waste Not Want Not* does not apply on polling day. Even though a voter might have six votes, they don't have to use them all up; if there are four NEW CANDIDATES standing in their ward, they can use just four of the six and vote only for our FUC-kers. Unfortunately, to some people this sounds like waste. The older generation doesn't like waste and it goes against the grain to use four votes when the authorities say that you are allowed to use six. The wheely bin generation won't have that problem. Just throw in what you like. Out of sight out of mind. No-one can see it anyway. And if they do, it's none of their business. I don't think like that at all. What I do is everyone's business and I expect them to hate me for it.

As well as the door-knocking, standing at front doors gossiping mainly about the shambles the council is in at the moment, we also have a leaflet with all our names on and some text blurb telling people what we are standing for (the parish council) and what we stand for (modernising it). I've learned such a lot about letter-boxes in the last few weeks. And people. And dogs - especially dogs. I didn't previously know that there are some that are so devious that they sit silently by the letter-box and let you approach. It's only when you have your hand right through the door, trying to get past the draught (and hand) excluders, that these cunning mongrels launch themselves with ferocity and velocity. I've grown very wary of those and once my delivery is made I withdraw my hand as if the letter box is red hot. On the whole, notwithstanding their pets, people have been very nice to us. I have learnt that Fishface has made a lot of enemies in the village who will not re-elect him. I bet he hasn't been out door-knocking. He didn't even bother with an election leaflet.

As we walk home from the polling station I notice the proud pink posters saying MILLER in several front windows. Windy is wittering on but I can't take in what he is saying. I'm just so hyper. I feel as if I've been shaken until my blood has turned to Coca-Cola. It's fizzing away from my feet to my freckles.

The hours pass really slowly and I can't settle to anything until it's time to return to the village hall in the evening. Almost all the FUC candidates and their supporters are here, dressed up to the nines (or at least to the eights). Mavis is in her only dress, last seen at her cousin's wedding in 1989. It's a shame she didn't have time to find any tights as the purple thread veins are very prominent against the thin, ivory, shin skin. The pink bedsocks don't really go – although I concede that they are bang-on campaign colour. Counting is already under way so I prod Windy and tell him we should have come earlier. He never takes any notice.

The polling staff have in front of them large A3 sheets of paper all printed up with the names of the candidates. Annoyingly they are going to count the votes for the district councillors first. The Labour candidate, a thoroughly nice chap, lifelong Trade Unionist, quiet, unassuming, knows his place, is sitting in the corner with a Thermos flask. He's got no-one with him and he doesn't really need to watch because he knows he will poll the least number of votes. This time there is a 'Save our Schools' candidate and a Christian Socialist candidate and even they are likely to beat him. The Christian Socialists wanted crosses on the ballot papers but as it's not a registered political symbol for a registered political party they weren't allowed. They couldn't even put it on their rosettes. There is quite an entourage with their would-be councillor. She's brought her parents and her boyfriend and his parents and they are all very boisterous. She is demonstrating her credentials by smiling and nodding to all her opponents in a social and Christian way. The 'Save our Schools' supporters are, on the other hand, nervous and intense. I recognise one of the teachers from the junior school and give her a friendly nod. She looks through me and carries on with her earnest tactical discussion with an old grey-beard who looks as if he might die while waiting for the results to be announced. Most of the FUC candidates are here: Hilary's work colleague Tracy with the cataclysmic cleavage has brought her mother; Jenny is holding hands with her quiet little husband and they are both wearing clean jeans pressed with a crease down the centre of the leg; Annie is with her loud and large partner, Tim; Hilary, in the biggest rosette of all, is accompanied by her girlfriend Jess; Gordon is with his thin little wife; Penny Finkless has dragged along her husband Martin, on whom no-one has ever clapped eyes before; and there is Maggie with John, whose huge silver cross would rival the Bishop's. (His isn't making a political statement so he's allowed to wear it.) We gather in a corner like a gang of woodlice behind the skirting boards.

Jenny's husband whispers to me, "I'm so glad you led this campaign. The village needs a better council. I'm sure you'll do well."

"We can hardly do worse than the jokers there at the moment," I say, catching sight of Penny Finkless breaking off a conversation with Mrs Daily, one of the existing councillors. "Were you having a Daily dose of vitriol?" I quip as she slinks up to our little group.

"She's quite nice underneath," says Penny.

"Really? She wasn't very nice about the WI embroidery project." I remember Mrs Daily's potent scowl, as if she was personally pained by the idea that anyone should want to represent Fartlebury Magna in silk. "Has she got a soft underbelly then? We'll have to stick something in it," I am laughing. I suppose it's my nerves. I'm not usually so aggressive.

Mrs Daily is standing right beside me: "I don't agree with what you've done. It's a disgrace. I hope you lose your deposits."

"We haven't paid any deposits," I say lightly. "It's all free, democracy at parish level."

Why doesn't she know that? Oh yes, of course. She's never stood for election before. None of the present councillors have. She is about the only one who has bothered to come along, too. "It'll be a late night," she says. I think she is blaming me for that as well.

"Better late than never," I say.

"What's 'usurpers' when they're at home anyway?" she asks.

"It's like when a person who's not the rightful king takes the throne."

"That's a daft name then," she says, and I think maybe it is but I couldn't think of anything else beginning with U.

She is going back to the counting table, duty done. The district councillor has been democratically elected: a Conservative Margaret-Thatcher look-alike, whose blue-rinse runs right through her like a place-name through rock. She doesn't live in Fartlebury Magna and rarely visits it because her electors here are so, well, common. She is standing up now, thanking her election agent, her party helpers and her dear little doggy, who is cocking his dear little leg against the curtains on the stage, and she promises to do her best. The affable Labour man in the corner congratulates her and goes home. It's the 26th election he's lost. "Good luck," he says brightly to me as he leaves.

We NEW CANDIDATES all move up to take our places by the table. Let battle commence.

The automaton tellers begin to tell. They take a folded ballot paper from the pile shaken out onto the middle of the table and draw a tiny little diagonal line in the next space across the sheet against our names in turn, one for each vote. The NEW CANDIDATES watch as the little lines creep across the columns. The nervous tension is palpable and I think if the others have any palps at all, they will be feeling it too.

Reginald Archibald Jackson Tulip is there, watching, scornful but anxious. I admire his long aristocratic name chosen for him by a farmer's wife with a great sense of style. His name has given him courage and clout. What a great gift. It's a pity his mother failed him in the matter of manners, character and broad-mindedness. He is indisputably narrow in the mind department, while absurdly broad in his speech and waist. I venture half a smile at him. I shouldn't have bothered. He's looking at Tracy's chest. I shouldn't mind really. My conscience is clear. My chest doesn't excite anyone. But I have exercised my democratic right. Like tens of thousands of election candidates before me I think I know best. I think I can turn the parish round. Reggie turns away, perhaps dazzled by my shiny self-assurance, or sated by the sheer size of Tracy's boobs. I turn away too, protecting my eyes from the glittering display of democracy being exhibited on the counting sheets. I feel elated and deflated in turns. As the count progresses it really does begin to look as if Fishface is losing his seat. Or is he? Yes, his little line of lines is shortening compared to ours. I think we're home and dry.

The atmosphere in the hall is euphoric. It's a quarter to two in the morning and the count has finished. We have already seen enough to know that we have done it. Just like on television we wait and wait for unreasonable lengths of time for the Presiding Officer to make the obligatory announcement. Eventually he thanks his staff and tells his audience the names of the chosen ones. We have done it. He confirms that a round dozen of us, every NEW CANDIDATE who tried, has succeeded in being elected. We will all become big fish in a small pond. Well, small fish anyway. I smile. We've beaten the buggers. We're going to show them what a parish council should look like. Maggie comes up to tell me she has been praying and fasting all day. It's a shame the fish and chip shop closed at midnight then.

Windy and I are the last of the NEW CANDIDATES to leave the Hall. I haven't been up so late since I had babies to tend to. Windy grabs my hand and propels me up the High Street against a cold wind. I am chattering as much as my teeth and he is putting up with it. This is how I know he is very pleased for me.

Windy and I married young. In those olden days it was known as 'having to' get married. Sure enough there didn't appear to be many other options if you had been unlucky enough to 'get caught' as people called it. That makes it sound like a game of chase. It wasn't much of a chase with us. Windy and I just fell in love. Nowadays they would say we were just kids ourselves and I would be a statistical disaster, a teenage mother. It wasn't all free love in the sixties. We met before the sexual freedom hype that came with the contraceptive pill. We just had boyfriends and girlfriends one at a time in our crowd. No real sleeping around. Not much sleeping anyway, not much sleeping at all. It wasn't comfortable enough to fall asleep in bus shelters and haystacks anyway.

At that time Durex reigned for what was discreetly called 'family planning': discreet nudges and winks from the barber, at least that's what Windy and other boys told me. "Something for the weekend, sir?" If it wasn't Durex it was chancy withdrawal if the bloke was up to it, or luck. Windy and I tried and relied on all three of these and in the end the latter option failed us.

I didn't try to be brave or shoulder responsibility on my own like the young women of today. "We'll have to get married," I said to Windy. He had been hoping for a few more years of carefree sex and irresponsible behaviour but he nodded his agreement. Always one to acquiesce, that's my man.

My father bore the disappointment well. Outwardly he and my mother accepted it as almost normal (which actually it was before legal abortions and women having enough confidence and social security payments to go it alone). They immediately plunged into the wedding invitation list, telling me which old relatives had to be invited and which could be left out because they hadn't sent a Christmas card last year. Windy and I didn't get much of a say. That's how it was done then, and after all, they were paying. We were just grateful for their help, did as we were told, and promptly cleared off to London as soon as the knot was tied and the apron strings loosened.

Anna was born six months after the wedding. Windy didn't take to the fluffy bits of parenthood. It was a job to get him to hold the baby. I was at home with the baby, he was the bread-winner. I kept the baby quiet, the house clean, the shirts ironed and I cooked the food that he put on the table. Not that he ever did put it on the table in any literal sense. That was women's work. Four children later he was proud to boast that he had never changed a nappy. "I couldn't," he said. "My stomach's not strong enough."

Windy and I had a party for our Wedding Anniversary last year. When I reviewed the guest list I was sad to realise how many friends had divorced or died. It seemed tactless, or heartless, to be flaunting our wedded longevity when others had lost someone along the way. Sometimes I feel a bit sorry for myself, missing out on the fun of new romances and the chance to have sex with someone else. I am not always sure that Windy appreciates how well I look after him. I sometimes think I am like his Gaviscon: he keeps me in his pocket in case he needs me to neutralize his stomach acid. On one level I'm not grateful for what I've got. This is probably because I watch too many romantic movies and make unfair comparisons. After all, Windy is no Hugh Grant. Films make it seem boring to be married to the same man for so long. Here we are, muddling along, devoted, happy enough, but in reality just busy with life until it ends; filling it up to make glue for our monogamy, mending our monotony with a sticky patch like mending a slow puncture. On the other level I'm very happy tonight to be walking along next to the kindest, most decent man in Fartlebury Magna.

Or, as I tell my friends, 'it could be worse'.

CHAPTER FOUR

"Life's hard. It's even harder when you're stupid." John Wayne

Ten days later the round dozen new councillors step up to the mark. Some of us are rounder than others but every one of us FUC-kers has been elected and that is the main thing. We troop down to the parish clerk's office en masse to sign the paperwork. Each of us must declare our willingness to serve the community and write down any interests we have. The clerk is unhelpful, making us write down our memberships of all local clubs and whether we like gardening. I don't mind declaring my membership of the WI. I can see that might be relevant, but I've never even been to the Flower Arranging Society meetings. "It is an interest though," the clerk says. "I saw you carrying a bunch of flowers once, and you're interested in local history so you should definitely put that down." We also note important things like whether we are directors of huge international corporations ('none of the above').

At last we begin to work together. We sign up for training; we think we know what we are doing. We help the clerk to decide to move on. We make up a Health and Safety policy. We begin to pull things together, like the edges of a corset, slowly but surely drawing in the corpulence, re-distributing, re-modelling, re-creating. It's all going very well. We are Fartlebury Magna's Blair's Babes, mainly women, mainly under fifty - which is outrageously young for a parish councillor. But under the surface, under the unity, lie tension and politics. The others vote me in as Chair. Strangely, some of them seem to think it is being kind – one says, "You deserve it." I don't see it as any kind of reward myself, but I might as well give it a go. No-one else seems keen and I think I will make quite a benign dictator.

Evelyn, one of the old counter-revolutionaries, staggers up to me in the street one day. I can smell something strong on his breath, but

I'm not sure whether it is alcohol or sheep dip. He is gurning like a gudgeon. "Anyway," he says, "now we've got a lot of incomers on the council..."

"Newcomers?" I see this as a gentle correction but he doesn't notice. I suspect he can't hear through the hair sprouting from his ears.

"Yes, incomers. What do you know about Fartlebury Magna and how we do things round here?"

I would like to say, 'What do you know about Fartlebury Magna yourself?' but I'm too polite. "It's good to have some new blood," I say. He probably thinks I mean the fresh ideas but, as I look at him, I'm also thinking of Fartlebury's gene pool.

"You're the Chairman now."

I venture another small correction. "Do you mean 'Chair'?"

"Chairwoman then," he says. "You'll have to keep them in order. They won't know how to behave in meetings, that new lot."

"We've all been on the training for new councillors run by the County Council so I think we do. We know about best practice, Evelyn."

"I don't think they know much about our ways here in Fartlebury Magna," he grumbles.

"No, but they know how a parish council should be run. We haven't always been doing things right here in Fartlebury Magna. We could do things much better." I take my hesitation in hand and accentuate the positive: "We ARE going to do things much better."

"You incomers want to change everything. We're all right as we were."

He sniffs and wipes his dripping nose on the left-hand sleeve of his jacket, adding another to the many shiny, slimy, silvery streaks. "Can't talk to you all day. I'm a working man. I've got things to do," he says, and heads off to the betting shop.

The betting shop is cunningly situated next to the post office so people like Evelyn can collect their benefits or pensions and reduce their income at a stroke without making the slightest effort whatsoever. I expect the Government gets it all back in betting tax so it's quite a good thing really. It's good for selling houses too. '*All the local facilities within easy reach,*' as Fartlebury Estate Agents say. Their shop-front is on the other side of the post office with fluorescent orange paintwork. In foot high letters it just says '*FART* a big gap and *GENTS*'. If a punter's horse comes in at 100-1 they might be able to afford a deposit on one of the ex-council flats in Fartlebury-under-Marsh so they can eye up the property market while they wait for their horse to come in. I have no idea what Evelyn might do with any winnings. Buy a new jacket I would hope.

***

We have to devise an advertisement, a job description and a process to interview candidates for the post of clerk. The job has never been advertised before – they always used to find a friend of a friend, or a friend of a relation, or a relation of a friend, who could type. In fact they often turned out to be the same person - friend or relative to the whole council. Some of the former councillors are trying hard not to be left out of the excitement. They muscle in, despite having to ask me what HR is and why we are doing it. We have a fairly democratic process with a number of FUC councillors involved in the recruitment process. Against my better judgement, but in the fast flowing stream of democracy, we employ Newman Bickerstaffe. He has no experience of parish councils and just the amount of self-confidence that is dangerous in a certain sort of man. I feel an instant dislike.

On his first morning he lets himself into the parish council office as the new clerk. I am waiting for his arrival so I can welcome him. He quickly closes the door behind him and adjusts his trousers. Apart from a brisk 'Good morning,' he treats me as if I am invisible. He ignores all the fine words that I have plucked from the air outside the office. He lays his briefcase down on the desk and opens it. He's still not made any eye contact with me. Taking out his Waterman fountain pen and silver propelling pencil, he closes the case carefully and stows it under the desk. He notices that I have prepared a list of outstanding work that needs his attention. I try to engage him in conversation about it but he dismisses me with an imperious look. I want him to work on the things on the list: the things we have employed him for, for example. He scans it impatiently. Nothing here to bother a man of his capabilities and experience. He will start right away by studying the council's budget figures. It's difficult to penetrate his aloofness and I soon withdraw into respectful silence.

After lunch Hilary, my Vice Chair and the Chair of the Finance Committee, bursts into the office. "How are you finding it, Newman?"

"Oh fine, thanks," he says, adjusting his trousers.

"Not too many irate calls from the public then?"

Newman smiles. "Actually I decided to unplug the telephone."

Hilary frowns. "I don't think we should unplug the phone Newman." She looks at me for support. I haven't even noticed that the phone hasn't been ringing. I thought it was just a quiet morning.

"Well," he says - rather too sharply to be polite, "I thought you wanted me to get on with the budget. I can't do figures with a lot of interruptions about potholes and street lights that are out of commission."

Hilary sighs. "Just this once Newman. Let's get the budget done."

I scoot off home at this point. I've promised to look in on the WI sewing bee.

By the time Hilary leaves, Newman is sure she understands how he intends to work. He has made it quite clear. Oh yes, no-one is going to mess him about like this council has messed his predecessor about!

When Hilary rings me later she is not happy. "Jumped-up little twit!" she exclaims. "You can't let him get away with that!"

"Good grief, Hilary," I say calmly, "it's his first day! He needs to find his feet. We need to make sure he knows what he is doing."

Hilary explodes. "I know Katie, but we need a clerk, we need him to take orders, we don't want the tail wagging the dog."

"It's his first day, Hilary. It's his first day, Hilary." I learned about the broken record technique on an assertiveness course some years ago. Fortunately I've got a good memory. "It's his first day, Hilary. We need to let him find his feet."

"I think he's found them," she says, "and he's put them under our table – with a firm hand."

***

Newman is a rather remarkable man. He is widely and often described as 'an awkward bugger' and I have to concur. He wouldn't agree to a handover period so he could learn the ropes. He said he couldn't stand anyone looking over his shoulder. He appears to be quite comfortable about lying to the council and I think I've caught him once or twice. But above all, his arrogance is his hallmark. He wanted £35,000 a year and he was going to New Zealand for two months in December and January because he needed a holiday. The council could take it or leave it. We took it because we couldn't function without a clerk.

He sits there at the meetings next to me, breathing heavily, legs splayed wide, jaws set, fists clenched. He is all psyched up and ready to tackle anyone who gets in the way of his bureaucratic processes. If it's not that, he's spoiling for a fight with me. He especially has it in for me because I keep finding his errors and omissions. In my dealings with him I am like a bumble bee at a window, beating on and on in error, trying to pass through a solid object.

"So, are you going to answer the phone tomorrow?" I ask.

"I suppose so," he says quietly. It isn't a very positive answer. It reminds me of myself as a sulky teenager, not willing to admit to anything, good or bad, wanting only to show contempt and rebellion. I plough on. Dealing with Newman feels like being stuck in heavy, wet clay. The plough is definitely losing momentum with each conversation I have with him.

"It's one of your core responsibilities, Newman, to deal with the public's enquiries."

He clears his throat. "My responsibility is to act on behalf of the council and carry out its wishes," he says with finality, then drawing himself up to his full five feet four, he asserts: "Councillor Miller, I have to remind you that the chairman of the council has no more authority than any other councillor when it comes to instructing staff."

Not that old chestnut. I thought we had put that one in the back of the cupboard after we had roasted it. I bat back, "We have decided it is a priority to answer enquiries from the public."

"I take orders from the council, acting on decisions made by resolution at council meetings," he vollies coolly. He is on a roll. (I, meanwhile, feel I am still on my dry crust.) "In law, Councillor Miller, the leader of a parish or town council is a Chairman. I have noticed that you like to call yourself a Chair. That just sounds ridiculous, don't you think? To be just a piece of furniture? In law you are a Chairman."

I pause, thrashing round in my mind for another riposte. A shitty retort would do. Whatever would Hilary think about it? She is much more of a feminist than me.

"It's rather antiquated," I say weakly.

"Perhaps so," he smirks, "but I think you will find that I am right."

***

Hilary is reputed by some to be a (hushed-tone) lesbian. This is no surprise to me, but it's not the kind of thing Fartlebury Magna has come across very often. Jim snarls the exciting news at me one evening as we leave the hall. "I don't believe in... what she is... homos," he says. "It's not right, not in Fartlebury Magna."

"What's not right?" I ask, my probe going further into his soft tissue, from the rear.

"You know, you must know, she's got children and brings them up with another woman. It's not natural." He pauses, "And she doesn't shave her legs or armpits."

"Well, neither do I, Jim," I say. That has discomfited him. He looks me up and down, almost with interest for once. "Does it really come down to that?" I ask with an exaggerated sadness in my voice.

"Some people don't think it's right, her being on the council. It's not Christian."

I shoot him a warning frown like a poisoned arrow from a bushman's bow. It's aimed right at his centre forehead. "That kind of talk could be illegal. Haven't you ever heard of Equal Opportunities?"

Jim grunts and scurries off to do whatever it is he does to relax between bouts of inactivity.

Hilary is intelligent, unconventional and fun. She's bright and takes a very balanced view of life. I don't care whether she shaves her legs or not, so long as she doesn't care whether I shave mine.

***

Newman comes to work on the train. He carries a leather briefcase and an umbrella and wears one of those gents' outfitters' beige gabardine macs that we all associate with flashers. I wonder why he has chosen that coat. I would never let Windy have one, even if he wanted one. I wouldn't even know where to buy such a thing. You never see them advertised. '*Ideal for flashing at kids in parks*', '*Keeps out rain and prying eyes until you are ready*', '*BUY ONE NOW – the must-have coat for indecent exposure - and its fleecy lining will save you from decent exposure as well'.*

Newman has settled into a routine. He arrives at the office at about 9.20am and leaves at precisely 14.55 in time to walk to the station for the 15.20 train home. He takes small steps so he looks as if he is in a perpetual hurry. His coat is always buttoned up and the belt fastened.

There has been yet another complaint about him from one of my active councillors. "I'll have a word," I say. It comes out as limp as Newman's handshake.

"Newman?" I say one morning as he enters the office pulling his coat up and tugging at his trousers. He says hastily, "The trains were running late because of the rain."

I ignore the explanation. "I'm here to talk about the Communication Strategy."

Newman sighs. "Councillors needn't worry about that. I am the focus for communication with the council."

"We feel the public needs access to their elected ..."

He interrupts me even though he has his back to me as he hangs up his coat with one hand. Where is his other one? The thought distracts me for a moment but I return to attention as he says, "However, I am the focus for contact with parishioners."

"Yes of course," I say lamely. In fact it's more than just one leg that has stopped working; I feel paralysed. I suppose I'm too late to flatter his ego now. I'll just have to press on, pressing his buttons. Ugh! I picture the buttons on his flashers' coat. Worse, I am now thinking about his flies! Does he have a zip like a normal man, or are his formal trousers from the same outmoded outfitter? Are they old enough for buttons? At length I get to the point: "The Communications Advisory Committee has come up with some recommendations, Newman."

His pain is so obvious that I nearly reach for the new first aid kit we have supplied in the office as part of our Health and Safety measures. "We would like it on the next agenda."

"The agenda's much too long already," he parries.

"Nonetheless Newman, we need to put it on the agenda." Before today I have often wondered what happens when both parties have been trained in assertiveness. Stalemate must eventually be reached, however skilfully words are deployed. I'm ever so slightly worried I might have met my match. I am unintentionally holding my breath, waiting for him to say, 'Check Mate.'

"Councillor Miller, the agenda is full."

"Well, perhaps we can defer some items till next month?" I feel like a fly in amber. I don't like it but I'm trying to compromise.

"Councillor Miller, the agenda is the clerk's. I am the clerk here, am I not?" He is not going to compromise.

"Of course Newman. I was ..."

"The clerk is the proper officer of the council and the clerk's role is to formulate the agenda."

"Please Newman, would you include an item on Communications so that the advisory committee can report back to the council and get a vote on their recommendations?" I am not exasperated. My tone is as level as the landscape outside.

"Bullying the clerk is a serious matter," Newman says, looking at me and holding my gaze. I mustn't waver. He isn't a wolf. I can look away. "The Local Government Association has a bit of a campaign going at the moment."

I consider backing off but, despite what he says, I feel as if I am the one being bullied.

"Newman, I am not bullying you. I am trying to discuss in a very reasonable way the need to put an item on the next agenda."

"And I'm telling you, Councillor, hmm, Chairman, that the agenda is my concern and not yours."

I let my eyes drop to the floor. I am distracted by the fact that Newman's shoes are very muddy. Has he been through the children's play area on his way here?

"OK Newman. We'll do it next time."

"Possibly," he says, gloating over his success, "if there's time."

***

Newman's second month is starting badly. He has been soaked by a lorry splashing through a puddle too close to the side of the road outside the High Street office, so when he arrives it is plain to see that his trousers are uncomfortably damp and his shoes squelchy. I hear his key in the office door – 'his' office door – and I suspect he has already noticed that the light is on. The door is unlocked and I am sitting at the desk – 'his' desk. Good grief! He must be wondering who on earth has been eating his porridge.

"Oh there you are, Newman."

"Good morning," he says coolly, taking off his coat. "Can I help you?"

"Agenda conference!"

'Oh no,' I can see him thinking, 'I'm not going to let her start interfering with my agendas now!' but he just says, "I'm rather wet."

"You'll soon dry out, it's warm in here. I thought we should formulate the council's housing strategy and make it fit with the district council one. I've got seven other items for the agenda."

Oh God, a chairman with ideas. I can see him recoiling.

"And we need to get it out by Friday. The last one was rather late."

He clears his throat. "Actually, in law, councillors only have to have three days' notice."

"Come on, Newman. People want a week's notice. That's what councillors have in Bumford Sock."

Newman smiles. “We agreed, I think, that I would be running the office.”

Hilary rings me. “It’s not on the agenda.”

“What’s not?” But I know what’s not. I know what’s what and I know what will not be. I am just playing for time.

“The Communication Strategy report.”

“No. I’m afraid Newman wouldn’t do it.”

“Fucking bastard!”

“Hilary!” I chide her, as if she was the naughty person, not him.

She laughs. “He knows how to get the upper hand.”

Now I feel a fool. I am weak. “He said I was bullying him.” I sound pathetic even to me.

Hilary laughs again. “That’s ironic.”

”I will make him do it next month,” I say, but I’m not convinced.

CHAPTER FIVE

"If you do not resist the apparently inevitable, you will never know how inevitable the inevitable was." Terry Eagleton

It's one Sunday lunchtime when I am enlightened as to how the delightfully bucolic scene at Fartlebury Magna has been improved by the carbolic- and community-minded rustics who have formerly fulfilled the role of parish councillor. There is a very loud knock at the front door.

"Ah," says Windy, pouring more gravy over his mashed potatoes, "the natives are getting restless."

Joe Jenkins, a distant cousin (like most people within the Fartlebury farming community) of Councillor Phil Jenkins, one of the old codger councillors who led the Three Little Pigs escapade to blockade the High Street, is banging loudly because he is cross. I leap from my Sunday dinner as if I have been pricked with a pin. I don't know who I am expecting to be hammering at my door, but it certainly isn't Joe. He has never been to my door before (and he has never been to my door since). He is standing there, a bit like a scarecrow, but his arms are outstretched in front of him rather than to the sides. He is holding a bag. His size 12 feet are planted wide apart on the far edges of my doormat and his scowl is almost as broad. He is a bit of a West-country hill-billy (even though there are no hills round here, thank you very much). He is a country-and-western fan and wears high-heeled brown cowboy boots and a proper broad-brimmed Jesse James hat. Where the brim meets the upright part of the hat it is stained with grease from his hair. (I can't be sure whether it is Brylcreem or his own home-grown sort.)

I don't actually speak to him when I answer the door. I am too surprised to see him. He's not one to waste his breath on social graces anyway. He is angry and I am hungry so when he grunts and hands me the bag I just take it with a quick, ‘Thanks, Joe.’ He splutters a bit because he is hoping for a bit more conversation, or confrontation.

“That’s your job now, that is.”

I look disinterested. I’ve been practising that look in front of the mirror for when I meet former inmates of the council chamber.

“You’ll have to climb up and deal with that.”

I’m not going to let my curiosity show. I just repeat, ‘Thanks Joe,’ and close the door so I don’t have to look at his scary face any longer.

I dump the bag in the hallway and go back to my roast beef.

“Was that Joe Jenkins?” asks Windy. He has almost finished his dinner.

“Yes, he’s brought me a bag. I don’t know what’s in it but he says it’s my job now.”

“Haven’t you looked in it?”

“No. I want to eat my dinner!” I snap like a clothes peg. “You open it if you like.”

Windy does like. He lays down his knife and fork and gets the bag from the hall. Inside the bag is an enormous Union flag. What is up to me?

Dawn is coming. The light is rising from the horizon. I now realise what Joe means. He has climbed up on the churchyard wall, secured the flag and got it flying from the flagpole every Queen’s birthday for as long as he can remember. Bless him! He thinks that’s going to be my job now. He hasn’t heard of Health and Safety, being a Fartlebury farmer, but there is no way councillors should be clambering about balancing on walls to put up a flag. I am going to ask Newman to do it.

Newman and I aren’t really getting on. I feel that we are in a subtle war that hasn’t been declared. A Somewhat Cool War. He calls a Staffing Sub-Committee meeting but I chair the Staffing Sub-

Committee meetings and I know nothing about this one until the agenda plonks onto my doormat. It's been hand-delivered. If I had known he was coming I could have pretended to be a wily dog and silently thrown myself at the door and sunk my teeth into his soft white hand. I tear open the familiar envelope. The meeting is next Tuesday. That's the day I definitely told Newman I was going to visit my aunt in London. I open my laptop and send him an email.

From: Katie Miller
To: clerk@fartleburymagna.net
Sent: 10 July 2003 10.32
Subject: Staffing Sub-Committee

Hi Newman
Thanks for the agenda for a Staffing Sub-Committee meeting. I cannot attend on Tuesday. Please would you re-arrange?
Katie.

From: clerk@fartleburymagna.net
To: Katie Miller
Sent: 10 July 2003 11.43
Subject: RE: Staffing Sub-Committee
As you should be aware, the Staffing Sub-Committee is the province of the clerk, as I am line-manager for the council's other employees. I shall tender your apologies.

Newman Bickerstaffe, Clerk to Fartlebury Magna Parish Council

Steam is burning my ear-drums from the inside. The bloody man's hand is so upper it's way over my head, waving two fat fingers in the air.

Shortly after half past two I present myself at the parish council office. It's a small room packed with filing cabinets and desks. Newman likes to look busy so there are always files and piles on his desk. They don't relate to any current workload but only I would notice that. I smile sweetly, "A word, if I may, Newman."

"I'll shortly be leaving," he says. He says it very shortly.

"It needn't take a minute, but I believe you are contractually obliged to give us 37 hours a week." I smile again. I'm glad I cleaned my teeth before coming out.

Newman's hand slips to his trousers and he makes the adjustments necessary for his comfort. Poor man. I've been thinking about his problem. I conclude that his manhood is either so small it gets lost in his baggy pants, or it's so big he can hardly contain it. That thought gives my spirits a bit of a lift. Maybe he's always touching himself up in front of me because he finds me sexy. I suppose he might take me for some kind of dominatrix. I smile again. I'm going to be full of artificial sweetener now.

"Newman, on the way here I noticed the hedge is overhanging the pavement outside number 21 High Street."

He reaches for a pencil and writes something on a long list.

"Thanks," I say, smiling more broadly. "And..."

"I need to leave in a minute," he says, looking at his watch.

"I won't detain you," I say, my mind only full of how to detain him. '*If I was your teacher, I would give you a detention,*' I think. How else can I hold him back?

"The railings at the War Memorial are in a terrible state. Have you seen them?" I slip easily and fluently into the female fluttering mode, my speech quickening in pace and full of questions that don't need to be asked and cannot be answered. I don't give him time to answer. I just move swiftly on.

Newman reaches again for the pencil and makes some notes on a messy piece of paper. He doesn't look up when he says, "I shall miss my train..."

"Did you see how pale Penny Finkless is looking? She isn't at all well, is she? Do you think we should send flowers while she is in hospital? Or do they let people have flowers nowadays? Do you think I should go and visit her? You know, on behalf of the council?"

Newman shrugs and looks at his watch again. "It's a matter for the council, or for the chairman, not for the clerk." I've got him now. He looks quite agitated.

"Do you know how much money we've got in the budget for computers, Newman? I would like to consider buying some new software so that we can get a better website going."

Newman grunts. "About £200, or £250."

"Well, that won't get us far, will it? The cost of software these days… We need to raise that on the agenda, don't we, Newman? Then there's hosting and serving and all that."

Newman sighs like a tired gas boiler. He reaches for his pad and sits down wearily, resigned to catching a later train. "We would have to move the money from somewhere else. Would you like me to put it on the next agenda? I do know someone locally who might help us with selecting the right software and setting up a new website."

I am so effusive in my thanks I think I'm in danger of appearing sarcastic but I still have one item to discuss with Newman, one instruction to give Newman, or, as I am thinking of it - one aggravation to give Newman.

"I've got the council flag here. Would you be so good as to arrange for it to be put on the flagpole next week for the Queen's birthday, Newman?"

"I don't like heights," he says. I raise my eyebrows to new heights. "It isn't the clerk's job. It isn't in my job description. I haven't got the right shoes for it. I might need protective clothing. I don't like heights."

I am sitting very still, letting him deflate like a hot air balloon full of local councillors. It's my new tactic: watching him dig himself in. I silently hand him the flag.

"Perhaps I could get someone to do it by next week," he says.

"That's right, Newman, you do that."

I leave, walking on air. I've never been so delighted to celebrate the Queen's birthday.

***

As the weeks roll on we are settling into an uneasy truce, Newman and I. He thinks he is getting to grips with most aspects of the job. The office is in a mess but he says he doesn't have time to look at the old systems. He clears drawers of filing cabinets by throwing out the old files and he opens brand new ones, nice new shiny ones, on every topic as it comes to his attention. For the most part this system is working well. When he needs advice he rings another parish clerk. When he needs truly local advice he rings John Shelton, Chair of Fartlebury Magna United. He rings the district council about roads and drains. He feels on top of the job and on top of Fartlebury Magna's councillors who are now properly in their place (under his thumb). He knows best. He is their adviser. They don't read their agendas or minutes most of the time so he always comes out on top. He undoubtedly has a low opinion of them - bone idle bumpkins, the lot of them – but he never says anything incriminating – at least not to me.

He can't call Hilary and me idle of course, so he complains instead that we do too much. We are always giving him work to do with our ideas for change and improvement. He says plenty about that, incriminating or not. I suspect that the only change he wants is a change of Chairman and Vice-Chairman. He would like someone in the Chair who is too busy with other commitments to bother with parish council affairs; someone too stupid to understand how things could be done differently; someone who wouldn't be onto him.

I am reading some correspondence in the office, and reading Newman's mind, when Phil Jenkins blunders into the office, right on cue. He is an oaf of a man, every unrefined movement of his large frame shouting out his peasant ancestry – not that I believe it to be entirely human. Half man, half scarecrow, half-witted, that's Phil. His clumsy movements put me in mind of a scarecrow whose mother mated with a robot but I know something of his ancestry. There were Jenkinses on the parish council when it was formed in 1897 and both his father and grandfather, and a smattering of uncles, have been Chairmen. His mother was said to be a gypsy, but she stopped telling fortunes and threw away her crystal ball soon after Phil was born, probably in disappointment that she hadn't predicted the disaster. (Hilary said she probably couldn't see any future in it. I think maybe she could.)

Phil Jenkins has a vision for the council. It is to do nothing for as long as possible about everything possible. In addition he likes to stop anyone in the village doing anything either. In that respect he would have made a creditable successor for Fishface and maybe he resents me for preventing that. Mind you, in one way Worzel is very different from Fishface. As a local landowner he won't stand in the way of progress if it means development on farm land, especially if the farmer is a parish councillor, and/or related to him, but otherwise he thinks we should keep our green and pleasant land. This approach has served Fartlebury Magna well for a hundred years. He likes the village the way it is. It's homely like his farm – a bit run-down, a bit untidy. The rubbish spills out of his barns in haphazard heaps, just like the new housing spilling outside the virtual building line known as 'the village fence'. No point tidying up for incomers: they don't appreciate the countryside. They don't understand how it all works. If they want litter-bins and zebra crossings they should go back and live in the towns.

The Jenkinses benefited a lot from a vicious local developer known as the Butcher of Fartlebury. The population of the parish grew in less than a hundred years from 900 to 9000. That means an awful lot of new houses have been thrown up, or a lot of awful new houses, on new estates, some awful, some not. Some of the houses are built on piles. (That could explain the pained expressions of their inhabitants.) So much of the land is unsuitable for development that they've had to squeeze in new housing wherever they could, particularly on land owned by the Jenkinses, when Phil's father was Chairman of the Council. I've heard that in the 1960s the Butcher of Fartlebury stalked around the village making offers, taking offers, buying up and knocking down the old houses. Beautiful old houses too – the reprinted black and white photos knock your socks off. Their only crime was to occupy a useful plot of land. There used to be a Tithe Barn, a Georgian Rectory and 16th century thatched farmhouses all along the High Street. It was a beautiful place back then, what the locals might have called 'pictureskew'. Except they didn't. They mostly called it 'a useful bit o'cash'.

The Butcher of Fartlebury had neither a scruple nor a care and the council hadn't even thought of preserving anything then, so they let him eviscerate the High Street – they wanted to widen it anyway – and he tore out Fartlebury's heart. He quartered the gardens, jointed the paddocks and his deep cuts and chops savaged the village green. Fartlebury's now got lots of utilitarian little housing estates off the High Street, and jolly good for commuters they are too. We've got Peewit Avenue where the peewits used to display in the spring, Mallard Close where the duckpond was filled in and the oxymoronic Meadow Drive where the tiny houses are packed so close together that you can barely see a blade of grass. Lots of them are what is now called social housing, although paradoxically the behaviour around them is often distinctly anti-social.

Some of the Corsetshire villages are really pretty. They have kept their old heart and old architecture. Their vernacular buildings are mainly of limestone mined from local hills. There aren't many hills but the few we do have, including Bumcrack Hill at Bumford, have chunks bitten out of them by dragons or local small-scale quarrying, depending on who you believe. Fartlebury Magna has some walls made of this local stone. The Butcher of Fartlebury couldn't be bothered to re-build stone walls so he left the old ones as the property boundaries, a hideous mis-match with his cheaply-built bland and angular rendered breeze block boxes.

Of course the farming fathers and grandfathers had it made. The Butcher had a field day. Literally. The Jenkinses sold him their fields and their shelter belts, their orchards and their cowsheds and he made a killing. They turned Fartlebury Magna from a village into a town and lived well off it. Now their children and grandchildren want to stop progress. "We don't want Fartlebury Magna to turn into a town," they say. (They mean they don't want to have to do any work for incomers and townies.) Councillors, I've got news for you. To the rest of us Fartlebury Magna is a town: a dormitory town, where everyone is chronically sleepy, but a town nonetheless and developing a town's problems, with unseemly modern trends like vigilante groups going after so-called perverts. If that's modern life, you can keep it, according to the locals. Give us Cranford any day.

There is a new word in Phil's vocabulary. It is one of the best words he has ever known. It has FOUR syllables. Apathetic. His daughter told him what it means. It gives him a ready-made answer whenever some incomer wants to show interest in new facilities for the parish. The residents are apathetic. They won't support it, they won't pay for it, they won't use it, they won't reply to questionnaire surveys, they are just apathetic. And he has a great fall-back position if some cocky middle-class newbie in some ugly five-bedroomed house over-rides apathy and suggests an improvement in community infrastructure: it isn't in the budget.

Not that Phil Jenkins is quite sure what a budget is, or what it looks like, or how things get into it (or out of it), but he knows this is the way to neatly see off any project that needs council support. It was something he picked up from Fishface. The council does a good job keeping Fartlebury Magna just as it has always been. I know he thinks it's a shame there are all these women on the council now, and a worse shame that they weren't even born here, but on the whole the diminished Old Guard are managing to keep the council as they like it: run by the clerk and requiring from them neither decision nor thought. I am beginning to realise that twelve new councillors wasn't enough. We should have ousted all the old trouble, usurped the lot of them.

Phil has come to deliver a letter to the clerk from his neighbour, complaining about the noise of rooks cawing in the mornings. Phil then takes off on a protracted whinge. He says he doesn't like coming in to the centre of the village because of all the people around in the High Street, 'like a lot of sheep – stoopid things, sheep'. These flocks of parishioners get in his way when he is trying to walk from his tractor or landrover to the parish council office, or more often to the pub. He has to take silly little footsteps so people might think there's 'something wrong with him'. I don't smile. I don't want to encourage him, but I can't help wondering if he means that he fears people might think he's got a cork up his backside. Newman gives him a bit of a stare at this point. I think he is unsure whether this is a dig at his own short strides. I have always put Newman's mincing gait down to his problems with his under-carriage.

Phil, meanwhile, has got into his own manly stride. There are too many people crowding out the doctors so he can't get an appointment. Too many children filling the schools. Too many toddlers wanting to have a swing. Too many teenagers boozing on the playing field. In his day it was just four of them down there with their cider. Now it's dozens, shouting and swearing. He never shouted when he was young, and if his Dad heard him swear he took a horse whip to him or chased him with a pitchfork. There was proper discipline in those days. Some people even say there are drugs being used down there on the playing field now. That can't be right. Where would anyone in Fartlebury Magna get drugs from? Bloody incomers, saying things like that. Phil pauses momentarily having come to a natural hiatus.

I clear my throat, "Excuse me, Phil, Newman and I have work to do."

Phil shuffles off, leaving a little pile of straw on the floor and the lingering odour of the cowshed, and Newman and I resume our planning. It's not exactly planning as I know it. I suggest improvements to the way things are done; Newman suggests I mind my own business. After we've had about a twenty-minute tussle, Tracy breezes in, followed by a flurry of thistle seeds because she has been in the countryside. I can hear her Jack Russell terriers whining their protests in tuneless yaps outside.

"Ah, Katie!" she says, "You're here! I've got something to tell you - and Newman."

Newman makes it clear he does not want to be told anything and turns to his computer screen. "Go on, Tracy," I say, indicating that she has permission to speak to me.

"You know I walk my dogs up Bumcrack Hill," she begins.

"Yes," I reply, but then so does half the dog-walking population of Fartlebury Magna and Bumford Sock, so that's not news. I wait for the punch-line.

Tracy's neck has blotched red and her face is pinker than usual. "I think something ought to be done about the unsavoury types up there in the car park after dark."

"Oh yes?" I show a little interest but she was probably going to tell me anyway. "Drug dealers?" I suggest. They are the most unsavoury types I can think of at the moment.

"I called in there with my friend Eric last night. We had been out for the day and the dogs had been shut up at home, so I said to Eric, 'Let's just bundle them into the car and take them for a quick walk up the hill.'"

I wonder where this is going. Bumcrack Hill I suppose, since that is the object of her concern.

"We parked in that little lay-by just before you get to the car park, you know? We thought it was a bit unusual that there were a few cars in the car park itself. Some had their interior lights on." She cleared her throat. "We let the dogs out and sat in the car, just chatting, you know - we were deciding whether to get out because we weren't sure what was going on - and a car came up behind us and flashed its lights." She pauses and looks at me. "It was quite scary, actually."

"Why? What did the other person want? The flasher, as we might say." My light-hearted remark makes Tracy frown.

"You know, Katie, there were several cars in the car park. People were having sex. I couldn't see them but that's what they were doing and there were people out of the cars too, with torches. One or two of them had dogs with them. My little ones got in a tangle with a Labrador."

"Oh dear!" I can't quite believe my ears. I haven't a clue what she is talking about. Dog-fights on Bumcrack Hill? People having sex in cars, simultaneously, like a party? In my day at least couples had the decency to go somewhere quiet and secluded. I don't want to say that in front of Newman though. He thinks I am respectable. I find myself wondering if he has ever had sex in a car. Newman is looking very interested in what Tracy has to say. I hope I don't look too interested.

She adds, "And there was a tractor."

"A tractor?" I say, wondering who would park a tractor in a car park at night. How would you have sex in a tractor? Uncomfortably, I should think.

"Why do you think a tractor was there?" I ask. "Do you think he was going to help someone who got stuck in the mud?"

"These people were not stuck in the mud, Katie. I think the farmer was dogging too."

"What? Taking his dog for a walk, you mean?"

I catch Newman smiling. He looks like a gargoyle on St John's tower. Tracy glances at him too; I interpret it as a knowing look which is mocking me. Newman's eyes gleam as much as his teeth as he says, "Fartlebury Magna – a hotbed, so to speak – pardon the pun – of adventurous sex." Now they both snigger.

"Oh!" I gasp. I am now so embarrassed I could curl up and die on the spot if there was room in the office to lie down. I'm not sure if my embarrassment is more to do with them discovering my naïve ignorance, or the realisation that this conversation is about sex. (My mother thought it was very common to talk about sex. She probably thought it was common to do it as well.)

I try to steer the conversation into channels I am more comfortable with: "When they did the archaeological dig years ago, they found the car park was where the post-Roman community used to lay their dead," I offer hopefully as an alternative topic, which still relates to the place in question.

Newman grins at Tracy. "Nice to know people are still getting laid there then!"

I'm surprised at Newman. His upper lip is usually much stiffer. Now it is positively curling with the salaciousness of it all. "I've never heard of dogging," I say. It feels like a confession.

Tracy says, "Haven't you? It's all over the TV at the moment. It's quite a craze."

I don't watch much TV," I admit, and that seems another shameful thing to confess to.

"Well," says Tracy, "people are driving to Bumcrack Hill to have sex with strangers, in our car park, so what are we going to do about it?"

I think how outraged Jim will be to hear this. More people coming into the village who weren't even born here.

"It's not illegal," says Newman confidently.

"Isn't it an offence to public decency?" asks Tracy.

"No," says Newman, "you wouldn't see anything to offend you unless you joined in. Anyway no-one gets hurt. It's a Free Country."

"Can I speak to PC Bigg-Toze about it?" asks Tracy.

"Of course," I reply, "if you want to."

"Oh yes, he might like to know," Newman smirks. "He might like to make a special patrol up there."

"He could take the police dog team with him," Tracy giggles as she turns to the door. She closes the door behind her and the barking stops. Newman seems to find it hard to concentrate now and I've lost my focus too. I wonder if Windy knows about dogging.

I'm not sure if it's a coincidence - it probably is - but I can't help wondering if there's a connection between Tracy's discovery and the unprecedented vandalism of cars in Bumcrack Hill car park the next weekend. Apparently four of them got their windscreens broken. PC Bigg-Toze said they had probably been hit by a piece of wood falling from a tree. Or a baseball bat.

CHAPTER SIX

"It's better to be hated for what you are than to be loved for what you are not."   Andre Gide

I can't wait to have a new website. With a halfway decent website we can contact people who wouldn't come to meetings, we can reach younger people and ask them what they want in the village. It's a step towards better democracy. The twelve new councillors manage to win the vote. I framed the proposal very carefully and now the council has finally decided to make a tentative appeal in the local paper. The re-energised community is sending forth volunteers to help. There's quite a buzz around, and it's not just coming from Jim's cows, either.

"What are they like, these new volunteers?" asks Maggie.

"Do you remember that guy who was new to Fartlebury Magna getting attacked by men with baseball bats?" I ask back.

"Vaguely," she says. "A computer wizard wasn't he? I think he might have done the church website for John."

"Yes, that's the one." I am glad to have her confirm that he is a computer wizard, although I think it is a funny term for Maggie to use. I shouldn't think she approves of wizards. I bet she even steers clear of Harry Potter when she's in Waterstones. I continue, "Newman knows him somehow. He's just volunteered to re-design a website for the council. He's a professional apparently. He's been making new websites for the local churches, the dentist, the pre-school. He's a real philanthropist. He's been ill and unemployed so he's keeping his hand in, I suppose, while he convalesces."

"Is his name Tripswitch? I think he was the assistant Scout leader. Is he a short man in his forties?"

"Yes, Dave Tripswitch. He will work with the clerk."

“He’s been seriously ill, I think. I’ve heard he was traumatized by the baseball bat incident. He gave up the Scouts. I feel sorry for him, poor man.” Maggie always supports the underdog.

Dave Tripswitch and Newman Bickerstaffe are total opposites as far as I can see, but something must unite them because they seem as thick as Grandma’s custard. Together they will stride forward and together they will make a website. Other councillors and lay people have formed a committee to guide its development. Different people will take responsibility for certain ‘pages’ on the website but the clerk and Dave will apparently do most of the work.

I see our heroic volunteer limping along in the High Street one day and we exchange warm greetings, almost as if we know each other. He is an ordinary looking man, ordinary by Fartlebury Magna standards anyway, but I could recognise him anywhere. He is about 5 feet 5 inches tall (I can tell because he keeps staring me in the eyes and his are level with mine). He has mouse brown hair (I can tell that too because I have recently been watching the mice, (and rats), that live in Jim’s barn near our house). Dave is in his forties but has a young spiky haircut, one little ear-ring and jeans loose round the crutch like a teenager.

“When do you want me to start working on the website?” he says.

“Whenever you have the time. We’re just so pleased you can help us. It’s good of you to use your skills for the community.” I’m getting good at all this diplomacy.

He fixes me with his ugly green-eyed stare. “Just like you do,” he says with a sickly smile. It is so effective that I feel totally nauseated. “I was inspired by you,” he smirks without any hint of sincerity.

“We’ve set up a sub-committee to sort out what we want on a website. Do you think you could meet up with them soon?”

“I’d love to,” he says, “but it depends on my hospital appointments.”

“Naturally, you’re in charge. You set the dates to suit you.”

“Next Monday would be fine. I’ll do it after your full council meeting. I’ll speak to Newman and get him to get in touch with them all.”

That’s kind of him but maybe I should be doing that. I’m not sure I trust him and I definitely don’t trust Newman.

“I can do that for you,” I say.

“No, don’t worry. I’d like to talk to everyone and introduce myself.”

I should have phrased it differently. I should have said ‘I WILL let people know.’ But if he wants to do it I should be reasonable. I find my words drying up in my throat, stuck like a cabbage in a pea-shooter. “Must dash,” I say. I can’t think of a reason why I must. I’m in no hurry to cook the dinner.

“Me too,” he says, “I’ve got fifteen tablets to take at 5 o’clock. I have to take them regular.”

I give what I hope is a sincere, pained, sympathetic smile and add it to a little wave as I walk off.

On Monday at the end of the meeting I look around at the unlikely group of people with whom I spend most of my evenings out. “Now some of you are going to meet with Dave Tripswitch to discuss the council’s needs regarding the new website. Who has Dave been in touch with?”

I can’t read a single face. There’s nothing written there, they are all blank canvas like a railway bridge used to be before spray cans were invented.

Dave the professional computer hero strolls in tapping his walking stick alongside him like a blind man. “Right,” he says. “Now the boring bit's over, who's coming with me to the Fartlebury Magna Inn?"

No-one moves a muscle except to put on their coats and leave. Dave looks at me, "Isn't anyone joining us?" he says.

"Us? I wasn't actually planning on coming," I say. I was hoping not to get too involved.

"I know, but you said you would contact the other people on your sub-committee and give them notice," he says. "Where are they?"

"No, I didn't." It sounds childish the way I say it. "Penny!" I call out, "Can you join us to talk about the website?" Newman has broken the land speed record shooting out of the door. It's fair enough. He's got to get a train home.

Penny slinks over, flashing Dave a gummy smile like a chimpanzee on heat. "I can't stay too late," she says.

"That's OK." Dave oozes charm like a weeping sore. "I'm not fully recovered yet. I need lots of early nights." He winks at me, "My wife likes it that way."

"Oh, I'm sorry!" says Penny. "Have you been ill?"

"Have I been ill? I've had major surgery. I was in intensive care. I died. They had to revive me three times. I had my liver out, then my bowel and most of my lungs."

Penny looks at me. I look at the floor. I don't want to look up ever again, and I study the pavement all the way to the pub.

Dave finds us a cosy corner in an alcove near the fire. I get the drinks in because I think I have a duty as Chair of the council: the small-scale political version of *noblesse oblige* and all that. I am not comfortable standing at the bar and I don't think Penny is comfortable even 15 feet from it. It's not the bar's fault. The bar is the usual mock mahogany structure, puddled with beer and punctuated with tatty little cardboard beer-mats. It's the clientele whose shoulders you might have to rub that give me the willies. These are, frankly, just not my type, being excessively broad and exclusively male, grossly tattooed and shiny with sweat. Their raucous voices remind me of a rugby team. In fact they are the Fartlebury Magna Rugby team, but I don't know that until Penny tells me. (She tells me by drooling over the youngest and sweetest looking one, who has, I acknowledge, by far the most artistic tattoo on the back of his thick neck.) We have this conversation while Dave is in the Gents' toilet. He has had to barge his way through the rugby players to reach the Gents. There are tables on that side of the room but Penny wisely, using experience as her guide, refuses to sit there because of the proximity to the toilet door.

Fartlebury Magna Inn dates from the 17th century, one of the few old buildings to survive the Butcher. It has some amazing tooled oak beams. I know that because I admired them once when we first moved into Fartlebury Magna. They've gone now. I think the landlord has covered them up with hardboard because he didn't want the place to look too old-fashioned and attract customers like me. I don't exactly blame him. I can sit for hours over one white wine and lemonade. He's got it all hard lines and Scandinavian now. No curtains or carpet, no colour except 50 shades of white. It's nice and clean, which is more than can be said for his customers, but at least from his point of view they don't know when to stop drinking. Maybe that is why he sold off the old grandfather clock which had stood in the hallway for 150 years.

Dave returns from the Gents and makes a bit of a fuss about sitting down, as if his back is bad. Penny watches him intently and when he finally stops fidgeting she tells him she wants us to set up a forum so the website is interactive. "So people can tell us what they want doing – how Fartlebury Magna can be improved," she says.

Dave smiles. "Oh yes, we can do that."

Penny explains, "It would be a virtual parish pump, like the one at Muddleton Malreward. People would go there to chew the fat, like the washer-women of old."

Yuck. Chewing the fat. Dave is chomping on his pork scratchings. For someone with no bowel and a delicate stomach he's doing very well. He's on his second pint of lager and third bag of pigskin snacks. "What about the other content?"

"Mainly we want minutes, agendas, council news, planning recommendations, that kind of thing." Penny nods excitedly and adds: "Can we have a *What's On* page for the local organisations to publicise their events?"

"Of course, anything you say darling." Dave is opening his mouth as wide as a wicker basket to show off all the little bits of crackling stuck in his teeth. "It's getting late for me," he says, looking at a very flashy watch. "I need my sleep since the chemo."

Penny gulps. I know he's a sick man so I can conceal my shock and horror, but Penny doesn't seem to have realised how sick he is.

A podgy man with two ear-rings in his left ear and three in his right, who has a poorly executed tattoo of a wolf's head on his beefy arm, comes up to Dave and stands over us all, towering and glowering. "That watch you sold me, remember? It's crap. It doesn't work anymore." He's waggling a finger at Dave.

"You must've mistaken me for someone else," says Dave, but I know a squirm when I see one. "I've never sold you a watch," he says.

"Oh yes you 'ave, matey, and it's crap. Stopped working within a week. I replaced the battery but it doesn't work."

"Not me," says Dave, standing up to leave. He looks like a rat in a trap, his whiskers all a-twitch. I help him out by standing up too, and Penny follows my lead.

"Look mate," says Dave, "this is the Chairman of the Parish Council. Don't go making any trouble. You've made a mistake. I didn't sell you a watch. I've never seen you before in my life."

We leave the pub together. I feel as if Dave is using me as cover: I'm the hostage in front of a mad and unpredictable gunman. And I'm wondering what on earth I am doing with a man who sells dodgy watches in pubs.

At the next council meeting we report back on the form the website will take. The sub-committee members prepare themselves to take charge of it - under Dave's guidance, of course.

"Community involvement – super," I say. "We're ticking all the boxes."

And, of course, www.fartleburymagna.net is fabulous. Our Dave really is a hero.

CORSET DAILY POST 10 August 2003
CHAT ON, FARTLEBURY MAGNA
Report by Trixie Mann

Residents in Fartlebury Magna can now raise issues with their parish councillors in a new way.

Fartlebury Magna Parish Council has opened an online forum on its new website. Views already put forward by local residents have included suggestions on how to solve traffic problems and whether the village needs new sports facilities. There are now photos of councillors and details of how to contact them.

Minutes of meetings can now be found online and a local business directory is also being developed. Fartlebury Magna Parish Councillor Penny Finkless, aged 47, who is a member of the parish website team, said, 'We hope more and more people will join us in the chat room on the local residents' forum at www.fartleburymagna.net.'

Actually there are a few things in the newspaper report that aren't quite right. There are photos of only some of the councillors on the website. Some of the old ones won't have their photos taken, although I have patiently explained that modern cameras don't break however ugly people are. The details of how to contact councillors are even scarcer. Some of them don't see why residents should ring them up: they pay a clerk for all that. Penny Finkless isn't quite sure that she does want more people in the chat room. She still thinks of it as the parish pump – that idealised, black-painted, cast-iron piece of hardware with a little stone trough, around which the idealized plump housewives of yesteryear stand gossiping. The users of the forum don't quite get her vision. None of them are housewives, even if they are plump. They are inclined to moan and grumble about Fartlebury Magna in a very unflattering way. They are making demands. They want the grass cut more often, or their neighbours' hedges cut back. They want zumba classes in the village hall. For goodness sake, however much she likes composing tactful and clever political replies it does wear a bit thin.

Newman isn't keen on the council having a website. He likes his dusty leather-bound ledgers and the smell of sealing wax. His office is the next best thing to Dickens' Circumlocution Office. I nearly offered him a high stool and desk last week when he complained about his office chair. Apparently he doesn't like it being on wheels. It swivels unexpectedly and unnerves him, he says. I tell him he needs to sit still. I am telling him repeatedly that he has to deal with the website.

"I thought Dave Tripswitch was a personal friend of yours?" I ask innocently enough.

Newman seems defensive: "I only said I knew him. He isn't a friend. I've got enough to do as a clerk without all this. I don't want to learn Information Technology. There's nothing about a website in my job description."

"If everything we need you to do was in a job description it would be hundreds of pages long," I laugh. I think this is funny.

"Quite." He isn't smiling. In all probability he doesn't think it is funny.

I loudly and longly tell him the virtues of modern computer technology, and the benefits of interaction with the community. Newman's face crumples as his self-control crumbles.

"Councillor Miller," he says with a note of the pompous and an undertone of vinegar, "I am not wishing to interact with anyone, let alone members of the public." He says it as if they are still the Great Unwashed. One or two of the councillors might smell bad but most of the villagers themselves seem fine to me.

"Well, sorry Newman," I say. "At least the website will keep them at arm's length."

He has to agree with this. He can't really refuse now we have let him lock the office door every day except Tuesdays and turn off the phone when he is what he calls 'busy'. (I must take a look at his computer one day when he is out and find out what he is doing when he says he is 'busy'.) Newman is the embodiment of the Peter Principle. In fact Peter is his middle name. He has risen to his level of his incompetence, but it has to be said, we have no-one to blame but ourselves.

We agree that Newman will update the minutes and agendas page. Penny will do anything else required by the council. I will keep a watching brief. Too right I will.

The minutes haven't been added for three months!" says Hilary during one of her regular calls. It's too late for a phone call. I wish I hadn't answered it. I've been on the go all day and I promised myself I would sit down at 9 o'clock tonight and watch a couple of episodes of *Yes Minister*. Since I met Newman I find it hilarious.

"It's hard to tell," I say in the tone of someone being philosophical, "whether he is just incompetent or whether he knows what he is doing and is outrageously artful."

"I don't care which it is. You've got to regain some control."

I think Newman probably feels the same way about us. I wonder if he is watching *Yes Minister*.

"Good morning Newman," I say cheerfully. I try to get in an early jolly word before his mist droplets of doom and despondency condense around me and make me chilly. This morning his office is in thick fog. My fog lamps aren't working and my windscreen wipers don't go fast enough to deal with him. He is completely impenetrable. All I can do is slow down until visibility improves.

"About the website," I say hesitantly.

"David Tripswitch is coming in this afternoon to give me a short tutorial." He clears his throat. "More of a refresher course perhaps."

"That's good news, Newman, because we really need to get on top of this."

"He has been ill again but he is coming in especially to help me."

Good-ee. I breast the tape, the victor. "Would you mind asking him to update the other pages at the same time, Newman?"

"I can ask, Councillor Miller."

From: Dave Tripswitch
To: Katie Miller
Sent: 24 September2003 11.18
Subject: www.fartleburymagna.net

Dear Katie
Thank you for your 'interest' in my website. However I have a team of volunteers helping me. The clerk is now confident about adding the agenda and minutes as necessary so there is 'NO NEED' for you to get involved.
Yours sincerely
Dave Tripswitch, Web technologist. Computer specialist.

From: Katie Miller
To: Dave Tripswitch
Sent: 24 September 14.33
Subject: website

Thanks for all your help Dave. I'm glad to hear everything is going well. If we can just keep it all up-to-date that will be great! I know you must be very busy but I would be very grateful if you would just put on this year's financial information before you go away. We only seem to have the figures for last year on there. I do hope you have a lovely holiday in Thailand.
Katie

And a sigh of relief from me. He will be gone for three glorious weeks.

***

It's a good thing that Newman decided to take his holiday at the same time. He's been whingeing about his computer running slowly so I'm going to get it looked at while he's away. We can't keep asking Dave Tripswitch. It's not fair on him. I would like to stop Newman grumbling and make for better efficiency in the office. Simon (also known locally as Smart-Arse Simon because of his tendency to do well in the Fartlebury Magna Inn quiz nights) has booked us in for an hour 'at least'. I can do a few things in the office while he works so I meet him down there.

He switches on the machine and stands with his hands in his pockets while it boots up. It seems to me it needs re-soleing and heeling: the fan sounds like a double decker bus. Simon frowns. "It really is slow." I hope he's not charging us for that bit of computer diagnostic work. I wait. He waits.

I start on my list of phone calls and leave him to his work and his wait, occasionally looking up at him to make sure he's still awake. He's awake all right. He seems to be on high alert. His eyes have doubled in size since I last looked at him.

"Is something the matter, Simon?"

"God, yes. Look at this. No, I mean, don't look at this."

"What?" I get up and go to the computer. There on the screen Simon is displaying Newman's list of 'favourites'. There's *Beautiful Bonking* and *Sexy Ladies* at the top, then a few Government sites and other local councils, but half-way down we are back to other titles: *Pussy Galore, Puss-in-Boots, Crazy Teen Sex, Young Teen webcam*, and more. I look away. I'm feeling rather warm.

"Oh dear," I say. A pebble drops into the well of silence. It takes a long time before I hear the splash. Now it's Simon's turn.

"They've put loads of cookies in."

"Crumbs!" I want to crack a joke about biscuits but it seems inappropriate in the face of Simon's disgust.

"I'll wipe the pc history," says Simon. He's trying to think of something to say.

"Thanks." I'm trying to think of something to say.

"I could wipe the hard drive and re-install the software."

"Thanks." I remember Newman and his fiddling with his hands under the desk whenever I come into the office unannounced. Oh dear, this is unpleasant.

Of course the Old Boys don't believe me, or if they do believe me they can't see why it's a problem. They snigger behind their hands, nod and wink as if something funny is going on. They are remembering their experience of pornography in the 1950s – those enchanting black and white glamour photos they shared in the playground.

Hilary says, "That's it. Gross misconduct."

"Very gross," I smile.

"It's not funny, Katie."

No, she's right, it's not funny. It is completely gross.

So we sack Newman. I tell him he can go quietly with a reference, or he can wait to be sacked. He goes as he came. Clearing his throat and fiddling with his flies.

CHAPTER SEVEN

"A new broom sweeps clean, but the old one knows the corners."
Irish saying

Our new clerk is fortunately a workaholic like us. She has thrown away Newman's pile of quill pens and dusty leather ledgers and bought a new computer and software to handle the council's £250,000 annual budget. She puts in 80 hours a week with a smile and she has brought the financial records into the twenty-first century. She is also attractive – big baby-blue eyes, long red hair, long mascara'ed eyelashes, shaped eyebrows and heaps of charm. Unfortunately I am the opposite. I have none of those attributes. Maybe that is part of the problem. Still, I can think on my feet. The rest of them can't even think sitting down.

"Why do you stay on as a councillor?" I ask one of the Old School - actually 'school' isn't quite the right collective noun for Fartlebury Magna's old councillors, who, on the whole, seem to dislike education (mainly because they think they know it all already). They turn up for meetings without reading their papers at all, they sit there and ask questions they should know the answers to, and then they enter the debate with the greenness and intelligence of a Brussels sprout.

I've gone out of my way to ask several of them why they stay on. "Well, it gets me out on a Monday night," one says. The meetings are always on a Monday. It's like a religious festival for them. One evening to work, six evenings to sit and rest. Like everything else relating to the council, a kind of reversal of all that is normal in the world. One of the older councillors in terms of long service, if not experience, is Andrew Hall, who is continually hostile at the meetings declaring everything we do 'illegal'. He says he comes to the meetings '*to keep an eye on you lot*'. He speaks as if breaking one of the Standing Orders will result in summary execution, or at least a van full of riot police battering down the door to the village hall.

Andrew Hall isn't really a bright spark, even though he used to be an electrician. I engaged him once, before he retired, to put some new wall-lights up in our lounge. We hadn't had wall-lights before so I didn't really appreciate how long it would take and all the work involved. I was busy the morning he started on the job and Windy was at work. About four o'clock Andrew came looking for me. "All done!" he said, looking as satisfied as his face allowed. I walked past him to take a look at his handiwork and saw my new carefully chosen wall-lights mounted six inches above the skirting boards.

"Oh no!" I said. "I'm sorry you'll have to move them. They're no good to me at that level."

Andrew Hall looked hurt and dismayed. "You said they were low-level lights," he said. "Your very own words."

"Yes, but that refers to the level of light, like candle-power, not the height at which they are fixed to the wall."

"You said they were uplighters. They are designed to send the light upwards. You said so. You need them to be low or else there won't be enough space above them for the light to come out, will there, and it will just hit the ceiling."

"Well," I said, thinking about this and deciding not to argue, "you'll have to move them, I'm afraid."

"I've got to get home for tea," he said, "or my wife will give me hell."

Windy wasn't too impressed when he came home to find he couldn't have his armchair in its usual place to watch Football Focus. "You'll have to get him back," he said. This was as irritating as it was unnecessary. Of course I knew I would have to get him back.

We sat on our armchairs back to back in the middle of the room so as to avoid breaking the lights. Windy could squint over my shoulder to see the television so he was happy enough – especially when City scored. It was just a shame that when he leapt up in the semi-darkness, Andrew having disconnected the switch for the central light, he banged his shin on the coffee table.

I had been expecting Andrew to come back and right his wrongs but at about 10 o'clock I had waited long enough, so I rang his number.

"He's busy today on another job," said a grumpy female voice. "He told me you'd given him the wrong instructions. You'll have to wait till he can fit you in. He's very busy."

I told her it wasn't very convenient but she just snorted like one of Jim's cows, "I'll tell him you called."

Three days later, three nights later, Windy's shins by then being black and blue, Andrew Hall rang back. "I could fit you in tomorrow," he said and I jumped at the chance (carefully avoiding the coffee table). At that stage I didn't realise what would be involved in moving the lights up the wall to their intended positions.

He had to chase out a channel on each of the three walls. He didn't warn me, or use a dust sheet, so the lounge looked like Herculaneum when he had finished and I was sneezing and wheezing in the kitchen like a hedgehog with hayfever.

"Come and tell me exactly where to put them," he commanded. I resisted the obvious retort and obediently entered the lounge with a hankie over my mouth. "Little bit of dust," he observed helpfully by way of a warning.

I felt obliged to have the lights connected to the cables he had already put into the walls, so there actually wasn't much choice of position. I thought Windy would complain about two of the lights being on one wall and nothing on his side of the room, but I think he was just relieved to have his chair back in place by the time *Match of the Day* was on. He was slightly more annoyed when he got Andrew Hall's bill for nearly £400, and he never did come back to fill in the channels he made in the walls. I had to get a builder in to do that.

There's no sense of urgency in tradespeople, is there? It took seven months to get someone to look at it. We were very pleased to be thousands of pounds down in the end and at least have the lounge looking relatively reasonable again. Anyway you can see why I don't feel all warm towards Andrew Hall, and he doesn't like me much either.

My recruits, the 'Babes', the FUC Children of the Revolution, are doing well, of course. We are fairly intelligent, we want to improve local services, improve the way the council runs and by now a typical response from one of 'us' might be, '*We're having such fun*!'

We soon set our hearts on improving the place where we are now spending so much of our time. The parish council always meets in the village hall. It's a good old solid Edwardian edifice built by the Church just before the First World War. It has just the requisite amount of windows to ensure that it is always dark in the daytime, and ochre lights shaded by fifty years of dust keep light levels constant at night. It has attractively undulating parquet flooring with interesting pools of lighter oak where members of the Fartlebury Magna Mother and Toddler Group have wet themselves or spilt caustic citrus drinks. The old wooden tables used to be piled up at one end of the hall, offering splinters to anyone wanting to shift them. The village hall management committee hadn't thought about throwing them away, but I have laddered two pairs of tights on their rough undersides so I persuade them to purchase some clean new ones with formica coated tops and aluminium framed snap-dragon folding legs by giving them a grant from the parish council. The new tables have already been greatly abused by the village's other committees, who have parked their gum, prised the plastic strips off and spilt sticky drinks and permanent marker ink. So we still don't have anything smart, but at least they are light to get out and put away. Lisa usually puts the tables out on Monday mornings ready for her evening shift. She makes a special effort to ensure she and I get a clean chair each, and she does her best to find 20 others unsullied enough for the other councillors, not that hygiene matters too much for some of them. Some of the older ones come straight from the cowshed, as is their custom and practice.

The colour scheme in the village hall has seen better days. Better weeks, months, years, decades and aeons actually. The village hall management committee say we can paint the room if we organise and pay for it. Choosing paint by committee is a very hard job requiring ludicrously copious amounts of tact and diplomacy. I would like to blame the difficulties on the men, but I find some of my fellow female councillors have got strange taste too. The men think peach is a fruit, buttermilk something from the dairy, and have no idea at all what mauve is. Tracy is vociferous: "I once did a course in interior design." She favours jasmine and lime. Hilary says she's got some teabags like that at home and she thinks the hall would look splendid in heather and hyacinth. Evelyn huffs deeply and half the councillors blanch and put their hands over their mouths. "Hyacinth!" he exhales, giving his fellow councillors a good dose of his breath, "What sort of colour is that?"

"It's the next shade on the card to Halitosis," I whisper to Hilary, who manages a smile before resuming a defensive stance protecting herself from his breath with a large paisley handkerchief.

"We need something to liven us up," suggests Maggie. "I like Tracy's idea of lime, or even lemon, with a bit of tangerine as an accent."

"Ideal with our gin," I suggest with a grin.

"What do you want then?" she says, "Coffee and cream? Earth and peat, clay and cotton? We need to get a bit more adventurous and show people we are able to move into the twenty-first century and put some colour in their lives."

She's right of course. We do want to move Fartlebury Magna into the twenty-first century. It is our mission. We are the modernisers, the new brooms. We are getting things done and the community (at least the middle-class part of it) is whispering its approval. We've got a logo, headed paper, even a laptop so our lovely new clerk can take work home after her 10 hour day, or take it with her when she goes on holiday. Now Newman's gone, we need to re-decorate our meeting room and use our glorious new website to reach into No Mans Land from the trenches the council has dug itself into. Over the top, troops! We settle on mocha and marshmallow, with candy-floss pink doors and skirting boards.

All the talk of colour schemes has made me think about re-decorating at home, but nowadays I'm not home often enough to bother. I am wondering what mocha and marshmallow will do for us in the village hall and whether I would prefer to come home to coffee and cream in my own kitchen.

Our 1930s semi-detached house is in the old part of Fartlebury Magna high enough above sea level not to get flooded, unlike most of the housing estates. We've got a long garden full of wild flowers (and my fantasies). Jim's bullocks are usually part of the picture, straining over the back fence to grab a mouthful of daffodils or dahlias whenever they get the chance. I used to spend a lot of time out there because gardening is a form of therapy. They often use it to rehabilitate people in need of a bit of peace and quiet. I use it in just the same way. The phone rings and I run in from the garden where I was watching a white butterfly lay eggs on my cauliflowers.

"Katie?"

"Yes." I recognise Lisa's sweet voice. If voices were colours, hers would be candy-floss pink. Mine would be battle-ship grey.

"I thought I should let you know right away that Gordon has resigned."

"Oh dear. Do we know why?"

"His wife's not well. Something serious I think."

"OK," I say. "Please can you do what's necessary?" That's one of the many good things about Lisa. She knows what needs doing and she gets on with it. She doesn't need a lot of supervision. She is a self-starter and a finisher. I know I can have complete confidence in her and that she will advertise the vacancy, deal with the Town Hall, say all the right things to Gordon and his wife and deal with anything else that I don't know about but she does. After all, that is why she earns such a good salary and I do all this for nothing. I trust her so much that I don't need to listen too hard, and while she is talking I check my emails. I find one she has copied me into which sets my teeth on edge. I suspect her teeth are permanently on edge; they even look like it. I bet she gets dentists' bills to match. And I should think her jaw aches with the fixed all-day-long smiling too. I'm not going to strain myself with that.

From: Lisa@fartleburymagna.net
To: Dave Tripswitch
Cc: Katie Miller: Billy Shorthouse
Sent: 30 November 2003 16.43
Subject:

Hi Dave
Thank you for coming into the office to look at the computer. I enjoyed our drink last week. Must do some more website planning over a G&T sometime soon!
Lisa x

What is she doing copying me into correspondence with Dave Tripswitch which she signed with a kiss? I know people are quite free with their xs but surely not Lisa? She's too professional for that. It's a mystery I can't immediately solve and my brain feels like scrambled egg without the toast. She is continuing to talk and I can't get a word in, even with a long shoe horn. She is telling me all about Gordon.

"I'm really sorry he's going," I lie. I'm not really very sorry but in fairness Gordon has been a good member of the Fartlebury Magna Parish Council reform team - as he prefers to call our FUC people. He was a Buffalo, or a Lion, or a Moose or some other kind of animal philanthropist and he had to give it up to work with us because both organisations meet on a Monday. Neither side can budge. He can't be whatever kind of animal he should be unless he goes to their regular Monday meetings. He can't be a councillor unless he does too. He's a businessman - a self-made man, as he likes to put it. (I assume his '*Make Yourself a Man'* kit had some of the pieces missing.) Lots of self-made men go into local politics. I expect they're hoping to self-make a little more for themselves.

Gordon is short and fat, never dirtying his shiny black shoes by stepping on a pavement - he drives everywhere in his large leather-seated BMW. If the journey seems too short, for example if he is only going a hundred yards or so down the road, he sets off in the opposite direction and completes a long snakey route encircling the village in order to make his journey seem necessary – so he's not all bad: he must have a conscience about using the car to drive really short distances. Fartlebury Magna is like that – you can drive right round it several different ways because of all those bolted-on housing estates added to the High Street in the 1970s like chrome lamps on a rally car. They're frankly a bit outmoded now, and the chrome is flaking off.

"Don't you care about the environment Gordon?" I ask one day - but it's not that I have any antipathy towards Gordon - I quite like him really. I just find it fascinating how people can be so different from me.

"No, not really."

"Don't you worry about your health?"

"No, not really."

"Don't you worry about anything?"

"No, not really."

Now he's got something to worry about. Poor Gordon.

"…so I'll put up the statutory notices then?"

"Thanks Lisa, that would be great," I say and we both hang up simultaneously like synchronised swimmers. We're probably both holding our breath too.

The notices are soon up on the noticeboards informing Fartlebury Magna of the vacancy left by Gordon's resignation. Lisa rings me from the parish office. "Dave Tripswitch has asked me if he could be co-opted onto the council, but he says there is something he needs to talk to you about."

"OK," I say, "I'll give him a ring."

A surly teenager answers the Tripswitch phone with a grunt and is made more uncommunicative by the insult that the call is not even for him, but for his Dad. Dave comes to the phone and says 'Hello' in a sort of tone that fails to impress me but is obviously trying to sound sexy. I feel a bit uncomfortable even down the phone line. He tells me that he would like to join us on the council. He is not working at the moment because he is recovering from a serious illness, a very serious illness, a fatal illness, it's something terminal, "and you need to know that," he says. For good measure he adds, "And I've got a sore penis and fornication in my legs."

"Oh," I reply somewhat briefly.

I confess (but not to him) I am at a bit of a loss. I know about his poor health but if his illness is fatal, why is he recovering? On the other hand this is Fartlebury Magna, and miracles happen here (so Maggie's husband John says), so it seems rude to pass comment. As for the stuff about his privates, I would rather he kept it private. The clue is in the name. I don't need to know he's got a sore penis. Or why.

"Can you continue with the website?" I ask.

"Oh yes," he says with what I feel is undoubtedly a smirk, even though I can't see it. There is an indefinable smugness, a step up from the serious monotone he has been presenting to the council's website team. I suppress a little shudder. I think he is as creepy as Count Dracula's doorman, but I still want to believe he's harmless. Poor chap, he's clearly not well. And if he wants to spend his last months or weeks on the parish council that might be good for him; take his mind off things.

Gordon comes along to his last meeting and sits next to Tracy. Tracy isn't really well and she doesn't get to all the meetings either. She struggles with depression. I never know whether she is really ill, or if it is just her huge bosom weighing her down. I notice several of the old male councillors like to sit opposite her and watch her cleavage, perhaps hoping some white rabbit or other surprise will pop up out of it. Some of them ask her to pass them a pencil, or an agenda, so they can all see her stretch over. I idly wonder if they discuss their tactics and plan who will get her moving this time. School children would do that level of planning but perhaps planning is above and beyond our parish councillors, even with such a reward. There would probably be too much co-operation required. Anyway, Tracy seems to like the attention because she only ever wears scoop-neck, low-cut clinging tops. "If you've got it, flaunt it. That's what I believe," she says one day, eyeing my flat chest.

Dave, our would-be co-optee, comes along to take a look at the council's due process, starting as he means to go on, limping in after half an hour. "I can't sit down for long," he interrupts, and stands distractingly by the table. He shifts his position a few times with little grimaces.

While I am talking he starts bending over and whispering to Gordon behind his hand. Gordon tells me later that he asked what kind of cancer his wife had. "He must have misheard me," he says, "because he said he had had the same." Gordon's wife has ovarian cancer so I agree it does seem unlikely.

Dave duly becomes a councillor at our next meeting. Our modernising work continues over the next few months and he often puts his hand up (with suitably pained expression) to volunteer for various working parties. His ignorance is a liability and he is apt to show himself up whenever he opens his mouth, but he will learn, I am sure, and he is very keen. Lisa says he is always in the office, helping out with the computers. Anyway, he is our webmaster and without his help we wouldn't have a website, which is brilliant. We really need www.fartleburymagna.net. It's our greatest asset so I'm overlooking his faults for now. The publicity is good too. The parish council has always been very low-key in Fartlebury Magna and the local press loves it now we are generating some stories. We got a nice piece in the paper about the website this week, thanks to Trixie Mann.

CORSET DAILY POST   15 December 2003
PARISH COUNCIL WEBSITE WINS NATIONAL AWARD
By Trixie Mann

Fartlebury Magna Parish Council, whose councillors' average age makes them the youngest parish council in the country, has swept away the opposition to be awarded the Parish and Town Council Association's Award for Best New Website. One of the website's most popular features is its on-line forum, a kind of chat room for local issues.

Fartlebury Magna Parish Clerk, Lisa Purfitt, said, "We have a team of volunteers and they work with councillors and myself to provide an up-to-date service to parishioners which includes information on local events and activities as well as council minutes and agendas. We are very proud of the work done by our webmaster, Dave Tripswitch."

The parish council website can be found at www.fartleburymagna.net.

Before one meeting of the full council several of us are standing chatting while waiting for the door to be unlocked at the village hall. I am making small talk to pass the time. Hilary has been talking about her ambition to go on a hot air balloon ride. Why she would need any more hot air is beyond my imagination. I've certainly got quite enough of it in my life.

"It's on my bucket list," she says.

Jim looks at her wide-eyed: "What? You've got a list of buckets? I use buckets every day and I've never counted 'em let alone made a list."

"My bucket list is a list of the things I want to do before I kick the bucket – before I die," Hilary explains with only a few sideways glances at me to see if I am giggling. I'm not. Dying is a serious business.

"Like what?" asks Jim.

"Like climbing Everest, or llama trekking in Peru."

Jim still looks blank. He hasn't travelled far.

"Like showing the winning cow at the Corset Agricultural Show," I suggest, coming closer to home. Jim still looks blank. "Something you've always wanted to do, and want to do before you die – are there any things like that, Jim?"

"Mend my roof?" he suggests.

"Something a bit more exotic, something for yourself, an ambition you've had since you were a boy, perhaps?" Hilary tries.

"What, like winning the pools? Not swimming pools, is it? No, football pools, that's what it used to be. There's no football pools now, but there's the lottery. I likes that lottery. I likes they scratchcards, I do."

"Winning the lottery isn't quite the kind of thing for a bucket list because it's not something you can achieve by your own efforts. A bucket list is a list of things you will work for. A lottery win isn't something you can work for and achieve yourself, is it Jim?" Hilary says.

Jim is exhausted by such a long conversation with concepts of which he has no concept. "I'm knackered now," he says. "Feed my cows. That's my bucket list. Feed my cows before some busybody says they're too thin."

"They do look thin sometimes," I say hesitantly. "The ones at the back of our garden haven't got much grass, have they?"

Jim scratches his head. "They don't need much grass," he says. "They won't get fat on grass. Could you get fat on grass? My cows eat well. They'm a special breed – meant to be thin, they are. Posh people like some bones with their meat, don't they? Fetch a good price my beasts do. They don't have medicine, even when they're sick."

"Oh, are they organic?" Hilary asks.

Jim looks very alarmed. "There's no need for that kind of talk. It's not time for them to have the bull, and in any case, they're animals. They don't think of sex like we do."

Hilary and I both look uncertain now and I think it's time to move on. "It's not like Lisa to be late with the key," I say. Dave has just hobbled up.

"No. She's absolutely perfect, isn't she?" His eyes have switched from side lights to main beam. "She's a wonderful person. I wouldn't have come on the council unless she had been the clerk. I just wanted to work with her, get close to her." He goes on: she's this, she's that, she's like Superwoman, she's like the Virgin Mary (or perhaps it was Madonna), she's more beautiful than Cameron Diaz , she's.... His list of incomparable female superheroes gets longer and includes some names I don't know. His voice is getting higher and louder in excitement.

"Mmmm." I realise I am frowning and immediately hide it under a fixed smile. It is essential that I am friendly and smiling. I have to be professional; I am the Chair. Jim has gone over to speak to Phil Jenkins, Hilary has gone to check that she locked her bike.

I notice that when Lisa does arrive, her eyes meet Dave's and she gives me a sly glance then backs away like a ewe from a lurcher. Dave's eyes follow her as she bends down to undo the bolt at the bottom of the door. They are narrow now, boring through her clothes, through the tight pencil skirt, taut over her perfect derriere, through the navy blue jacket and the semi-transparent polyester blouse which shows off her perfect low-cut lacy Wonderbra. As she walks off into the meeting room his eyes remind me of taxidermy. They are the glassy eyes of a predator. I find it slightly unnerving but I push it to the back of my mind. I can keep it in proportion; I am the Chair.

The next month another councillor resigns. She is one of our modernisers and her intelligence will be sorely missed. The number of female councillors is falling, bringing an inevitable rise in testosterone to the council chamber. The new ones are drawn to the vibrancy and the action of the FUC-kers, but they don't really play by the rules. They sometimes even vote against me. That was never part of my plan.

Jeremy is our new candidate to fill the vacancy. It's known as a casual vacancy, and there is something appropriately casually vacant about Jeremy. He is a former Civil Servant - civil by name, civil by nature, but no-one's servant. He has taken early retirement and is looking for something to do locally that he might find interesting. He has come along to introduce himself and learn a bit about being a councillor.

"Choose your role models with care," I joke to him privately before the meeting. He looks puzzled. I am hoping none of the older councillors will open their mouths and put him off. It seems it wouldn't take much.

When it comes to Public Speaking Time he noisily clears his throat and stands up. I smile encouragingly and try to nod him on. He carries on revving up like a 1980s Honda 50cc motorbike. I am on the point of moving on when he blurts out, “I want to be a councillor because I want to do something good for people.”

“Aah,” sneers Dave. “How sweet.”

I thought Jeremy would be useful at the meetings but he’s actually not as bright as you might think a senior Civil Servant should be. He lacks a bit of credibility (and possibly masculinity too) because he wears a hand-knitted tank-top, reminding me of Frank Spencer in *Some Mothers Do ‘Ave ‘Em.* That was before the time of most of my reformers, but they still think Jeremy’s an anachronism. His mother knitted his tank top - how quaint is that? He is only in his fifties but he has the mindset of a woolly mammoth – a blue one. That’s all right. I can work with all sorts. He carries on with his introduction:

“I am the candidate for the Fartlebury-under-Marsh Ward.”

Jim growls under his breath, “You look more like a candidate for the Psychiatric Ward.”

Phil Jenkins thinks he will help Jeremy’s case by expanding on his credentials.

“He’s Cap’n o’ the Bowels,” he says, or that’s what it sounds like. That makes a few old-timers sit up and take notice. They would like to be captain of their bowels.

“Oh yes,” murmurs Jeremy, “I forgot to mention that. I’m a keen campanologist.”

Hilary looks at me and stifles a giggle. She leans over to whisper, “I suppose that’s why he’s so tentative.”

The only other thing I know about Jeremy is that he lives in a large detached house in Fartlebury Magna High Street. He has renamed the house Hartburn. I ask him why he chose that name and he tells me sanctimoniously that it means ‘deer by the stream’ and is a delightful place up north. I just can’t resist remarking on it being a form of indigestion too. Then he tells me it’s also his wife’s maiden name and the house is named in honour of his father-in-law who conveniently died and enabled them to buy it. I spend the next half-hour considering all the names his father-in-law might have bequeathed on the poor old house: Cockaday, Shufflebottom, Goodwilly, Badwilly, Spragg, Tinkler, Sprinkler, Haggard, or even Tripswitch.

Mavis pulls down her polka dot tee shirt, which is a size too small now that she is a size too big, and looks at me enquiringly. "Yes, Mavis," I say with a sigh.

"I think the residents of Fartlebury-under-Marsh would prefer to be represented by a councillor who lives there. Fartlebury-under-Marsh is really quite distinct."

Jim looks at me but he is not in the habit of waiting for permission to speak. He cups his hand to his ear and says, "Did she say Fartlebury-under-Marsh stinks? She's right there, missus. It's always been a stink-hole."

I decide to ignore this little misunderstanding. Mavis frowns and bites her lip: "The two communities are quite distinct. Fartlebury Magna is not like Fartlebury-under-Marsh."

I put on a look to convey the thought that I might be interested in what she has to say, so she goes on, "That's why we need a separate parish council. If we were a separate parish our councillors would come from within our own community, not from Fartlebury Magna."

"Well, maybe, Councillor Wilson." My wheedling words are worming their way out through my nose. "But councillors can be residents living within a mile or two, or people who just work in the parish, so in fact people from Fartlebury Magna could be on your hypothetical new council." I can't remember the exact rules but that is enough to make her scowl again. "Anyway," I add, "if people down your way are so keen on democracy, why didn't any of them stand for this vacancy in their ward?"

She's got the answer. "I will do a bit of a promotion, Chair. I'll find another person to stand for election against this candidate."

Jeremy looks uncomfortable. (I'm not surprised, considering the tightness of his tank top.) I point out with some satisfaction that it is too late for that. The agenda item is to consider co-opting Jeremy Rosewood and on that we must vote. "All in favour of co-opting Jeremy Rosewood?" and as they know no better, a majority vote him in. That is literally the last we will hear of him because it turns out he is a bit too shy to speak in public.

CHAPTER EIGHT

"Stupidity is the same as evil if you judge by the results."
Margaret Atwood

My friend Maggie is a useful ally on the council, although she's got a unique perspective on local issues as she sees any problems as the work of the Devil and the need to solve them as secondary to the need to pray about them. It's another way of being lazy really. She wants God to solve the problems without the need for human intervention. She doesn't interfere with the way council business is done though and doesn't embarrass me much. She pulls her weight (even though there is quite a bit more of it than there was when we were young). I really appreciate her until we have a meeting when the issue of council prayers comes up. Maggie is the only councillor who takes the prayers seriously. She keeps her eyes tightly shut and her hands open in front of her so she can catch any falling blessings, or spiders abseiling from the high ceiling.

One of the FUC councillors, Pam, moved here from a multi-cultural city. Fartlebury Magna has only one kind of culture, and that is in short supply. She was used to talking about multi-faith communities and knows the difference between a Sikh temple and a mosque. She even has a friend who is Jewish (and admits it, even in Corsetshire). Those are her qualifications.

Pam and Penny sit rigidly through the prayers at the start of the council meetings, eyes wide open. You might ask how I know that. It is because I am busy running with the hare as well as the hounds. (No wonder I am so tired sometimes.) Now and then I have to take a rest and sit on the fence - with my eyes open, of course, but I always say *Amen* out loud at the end. Sometimes I am the only one apart from Maggie. Phil Jenkins and the other farmers sometimes make a non-committal agricultural grunt but they generally leave matters of religion to their wives or mothers.

I admit I'm a bit concerned about all the talk regarding prayers and even more concerned about my lack of action on it. "Not making a decision is also a valid decision," I say to Hilary. I can't remember where I got that from. She raises an eyebrow in my direction. "Well, you understand," I persist, "you're religious, aren't you?"

Hilary starts in indignation. "I'm an Anglican, Katie! That means I like flower arranging and the hymns I learnt at school. I like the powerful notes of the organ and the pattern the stained glass windows make in the sunlight. I like the history and the ritual, the tradition. It definitely doesn't mean I'm having any kind of religious experience Katie. I don't PRAY, for God's sake!"

I laugh and blush. Clearly I've stepped on a weaver fish which has come in on the tide of controversy. "Sorry then," I say. "I'm just a bit worried about how Maggie might react." Hilary rolls her eyes. I know she thinks I'm weak. I change the subject.

"What do you think about council prayers, Lisa?" I ask the clerk when I get the chance. I don't get many chances because she is so busy.

"It's not a matter for the clerk," she says.

"But what do you think?"

Lisa frowns. "I don't know. It's very controversial. We should give councillors notice about the discussion."

"Should we even debate it? Is it for the council to decide, or the Chairman?"

Lisa thinks for a minute. "It's not really a matter for councillors. You should decide." She's just made her mind up. That very moment. It's not the response I wanted. I suppose I will plod on without a decision. I remember that Windy gave me some advice out of his great wisdom and experience when I became Chair. He said when in doubt you should always stick with the status quo. That's not hard when you're as paralysed with indecision as I am.

Men, on the whole, are not much like dogs: they are harder to train. But Windy is like a good dog. Sometimes he shows me spontaneous affection and licks my hand, but most of the time he just goes about his business doggedly ignoring me so long as I feed him on time. He likes to snooze in the sun and sometimes he likes to follow me around. Once or twice a week he gets under my feet. He's like an old dog: you can't teach him new tricks and he's not quite so eager to roll over and beg as he used to be. He tells me he wants to oppose me on the prayer issue. I metaphorically pat him on the head. "You can't oppose me, Windy," I say, "because I don't know what side I'm on."

At the end of the full council meeting there is a time we set aside for questions and for councillors to raise items that would be *Any Other Business* in any other committee. You can't have AOB at the end of a parish council meeting because the whole point of the agenda is to give the Great Unwashed notice of what is being discussed.

Maggie sticks her hand up as soon as I tentatively ask if anyone has any questions. "Is there any truth in the rumour that you are thinking of discontinuing having prayers at the start of our meetings?"

I hesitate and it turns into a long pause. It was cunning of her to raise this in public instead of asking me privately and she has caught me off-guard. My delay gives her time to find a holy tone of voice in which to continue: "Only you see, as a believer, as a born-again Christian, I think God is here in our meetings and when we pray at the start of the proceedings it gives him a chance to influence our minds so we make the right decisions."

All around her councillors are still, completely still, staring in an oppressive silence at the table tops. If anyone looked through the window now they would expect the tables to levitate, such is the power of their concentration. I clear my throat which suddenly seems as dry as a camel's toe-nails. "The thing is..." I begin.

Pam springs to life, “We say we want to attract new councillors. What if there’s a Muslim, or a Buddhist or even an atheist, who wants to be a councillor? What will we say to them? How will they feel if they come along and the Vicar stands up to lead us in prayers? He even makes us recite the Lord’s Prayer for God’s sake!”

I suppress a titter. Phil Jenkins shifts in his seat. I doubt that he knows the words to the Lord’s Prayer. His cognitive function is highly impaired by the clogging sawdust and straw in his cranial cavity. Without considering the risk of embarrassment to us all, I ask, “What do you think, Phil?”

“I can see what Pam’s saying, like,” he says to the table in a slightly audible mutter. Maggie, of course, can’t see what Pam is saying because she has a touch of selective blindness and deafness but Phil thinks he has said enough. It is more than he has said for a long time.

“We’re a Christian country.” Maggie’s off again: “We must be proud of our heritage. We ought to stand our ground.” Her voice has become strident. Some of the councillors are considering hiding under the table (so am I actually).

“I don’t think many of us really feel that the prayers make a lot of difference to the quality of our meetings,” I offer cautiously, ignoring her speech.

“Think how it could be without their moderating influence.”

God. I’ve got to lighten the mood. My mind is on the rack but I can’t think of anything.

“We need to debate this,” she says.

Perhaps I don’t need to lighten the mood. Perhaps I need to shut her up.

“I don’t think it‘s a matter for debate,” I say. “We don’t want it all in the press, upsetting people unnecessarily.”

That riles her. “If people are upset by the thought of their councillors praying, it’s a poor show, and we’ve let the Devil win.”

I try to muster up an intelligent thought but the only one that rises unhealthily to the surface like liquid fat on gravy is that the Devil usually does appear to win. I can't say that.

Pam comes to my rescue: "We don't all think in terms of God and the Devil, black and white. It's too simplistic. This isn't the Middle Ages." (Oh no? Phil Jenkins has perked up and I am not sure he agrees. I can see that he is reviewing his knowledge of history.) She goes on, "We live in a multi-cultural society." (What, in Fartlebury Magna?) Phil's eyebrows are dashing about in search of a smoothing iron. "This is the twenty-first century." She thinks this is indisputable but I know several of the old timers won't agree with that.

"We won't discuss this now," I say decisively. That is the one thing I'm sure of. I don't know whose side God is on but I think I've got a compromise to suggest. We can have a Quiet Time, a time for reflection that will suit people of any religion - even atheists. We can let the Vicar come now and again and tell him not to make us recite the Lord's Prayer, but we can also invite other ministers, maybe even a rabbi if we can get one, or a Muslim. I think there's a mosque somewhere in the county. Everyone will be happy and applaud my wisdom as they did Solomon's. And hopefully no babies will get hurt.

Windy wags his tail happily and later at home he tells me that he is proud of me.

And so starts the controversial modernisation of the prayer time at the beginning of the meetings. Maggie has taken it very well now she has realised her husband, John, can get a turn on the rota.

The Vicar has blotted his copy-book by not turning up twice when he was supposed to come. In any case I think he's poor value. He just dashes in, sometimes with trainers showing under his cassock, reads a few prayers stiffly out of an old book, and leaves immediately. When the Wesleyan minister comes he beams at all the frozen faces, slaps Phil on the back (making several of us cough and splutter in the ensuing mite-ridden dust clouds) and patiently sits through the whole meeting as if he's interested – which is quite a feat for an intelligent man.

The evangelical pastor upstages him with extempore prayers off the top of his head. He makes them topical too, praying for peace in whatever part of the world is currently in turmoil and for the survivors of train crashes and earthquakes.

"O Lord, you know about the earthquake in China. We know you know how many people have died. You know how hard it is for the West to get access and help the people who have been left homeless. Please give succour to those in need and make the whole of China turn to you and stop worshipping their false gods."

Not asking for much then. I thought it was a rule of negotiation that you start with small achievable requests.

John arrives with Maggie when it's his turn to say prayers. He is determined to make the most of his opportunity. "I don't read prayers, or say prayers," he says with an air of patient condescension, like a primary school teacher, "I pray". He substitutes "Father" for all those "O Lords". This makes sure everyone understands that he is in a close relationship with God. He's not his servant. He's a son of God himself. "Abba, Father," he starts. He says that's Aramaic for Dad. Phil Jenkins starts humming '*Waterloo*'.

John's not fazed: "We are gathered here tonight because we care about our community and the people in it (oh yes? All of us?) But we know, Father, that you know each and every one of us and you care about us more than we care about ourselves. Come into our hearts and minds and help the councillors here tonight make the right decisions that are based on your principles of justice and mercy and based on a love for the people of Fartlebury Magna and wanting what you want for them." (Crumbs, do we want what God wants for people? Does he want more dog bins?) I sigh, a bit too audibly, and John looks at me. "We pray especially, Father, for the Chairman, Councillor Katie

Miller." (Oh God, please no.) "May she speak with your wisdom and truth. We know your hand is on her. May she feel your guiding hand." (Oh God, please make him stop. This is something to live up to! If I don't speak with wisdom will it be my fault, or God's, or John's?) In my nervousness I jolt forward and knock my knee on the table leg which causes the water jug to slop a good helping of unholy water over the paperwork on the table. The ink begins to run on my agenda and pretty soon I'm looking at a clean sheet. Is that a symbol, a sign? John backs away as if he thinks it is.

Lisa's in flapping mode, grabbing and dabbing. So is Hilary. She's always been a dab hand in a crisis. I'm not doing anything. I think God is restraining me with his hand on me. Too bad he didn't put it on my knee.

Eventually the meeting starts and John goes to sit in the seats reserved for the public with a fixed grin beaming my way and a little wave for Maggie. I have to concede that the meeting might be a little less acrimonious than it has been lately, but that's probably due more to embarrassment than to the hand of God.

When Hilary rings me later (she and I always post mortem the meetings), she laughs about the spilt water. "Your agenda just ran away from you!" she giggles. "You looked so funny. You hadn't got anything to look at! You should have seen your face! Even Worzel Jenkins saw the funny side. You talking from a blank piece of paper!"

Thanks Hilary. That makes me feel a whole lot better. I go to put my wine down and miss the coffee table, dropping it onto the parquet floor. It has not just stained the oak but it has gently stroked the skirting board and wall too, leaving blood-red drip marks.

"What was that?" she asks.

"What?"

"I heard something - like something dropping."

"Yes, I think it was my heart sinking."

"Very funny, Katie."

"Or maybe it was my jaw dropping. I spilt my wine, that's all. I can spend the next hour cleaning up the mess. It's not as if I have anything to do. I was considering re-decorating anyway. Perhaps burgundy and crystal chips would be the flavour to go for."

"Oh dear," she has the decency to mutter.

I suppose it's not her fault. I'm not one to harbour a grudge and I don't want to fall out with Hilary, however annoying she is. "What about the meeting?" I ask. "Was it OK?"

"I'm not sure about John's prayers."

"The only good religion is a dead religion," I say, catching sight of my dark reflection in the window. I pull the curtains. I don't like passers-by to see me fully illuminated and at the moment I don't like being reminded of my dark side either.

She sounds a teeny bit cross. "Fine. I'll let you clear up your wine then. Goodnight Katie."

Next day I am peaceably sitting with a cup of tea reading the local paper when I reach the letters page and my peace leaves me for another woman. The Corset Daily Post publishes a lot of letters. The Editor is a woman but she is so successful she is always addressed as *Dear Sir.*

I have lived in Fartlebury Magna all my life and consider myself a god-fearing man. I am shocked to hear that the parish council is considering abolishing Christian prayers at the start of their meetings. Fortunately we live in a corner of England that is not polluted by other religions so I see no need for the trendy newcomers to force their city ways on us. Give villagers a say, I say, and I and everyone I know will vote to keep Fartlebury Magna Christian – even my wife, who is a White Witch of the Wicca tradition and she agrees with me on this one.

Yours faithfully, Name and address withheld.

I don't know who wrote that. It seems unlikely that it would be any of the newer councillors I recruited myself, but it could be someone from the former incarnation of the council. Fishface could write a letter like that, although I didn't know his wife was a witch. Not an official one anyway. I would like to discuss it with Hilary but like British Gas she is always experiencing a high volume of calls when I ring her. I will try to collar her before the meeting. She usually wears a shirt.

Phil Jenkins doesn't often initiate conversation but he shuffles up to me in the foyer of the village hall and mumbles, "I think we should go back to having prayers with just the Vicar from St John Ambulance." I thank him for his views and smile. He should watch out for bright sparks with all that sawdust around.

Hilary is hanging back and hands me a paper cutting. It's from the other local paper, the Muddleton Malreward Messenger, a freebie which doesn't get delivered to my street. As I walk to my seat I read the paragraphs below the fold:

People do hold different views on Christian belief but we all still prefer the authoritarian figure of the established Church to lead us in prayer at our meetings, not the Johnny-come-lately ministers of break-away so-called churches who have caused local disputes and upset.

As a council we can still serve and include people from other religions, even Jehovah's Witnesses and Muslims, but that doesn't mean we have to join in their heresies. I hope the council Chairman, Katie Miller, herself a newcomer to the village, will soon come to her senses and put an end to this multi-faith nonsense which doesn't have any relevance to our lovely corner of Corsetshire.

Yours, Mavis Wilson (born in Fartlebury-under-Marsh)

I quickly fold the scrap of paper again and put it in my pocket to enjoy later.

Mavis has a pleasant farmer's wife sort of face: broad and amiable, weathered and wrinkled with an inherited smile. She always looks the same to me – it's as if her hair never grows, her eyebrows never need plucking and her nails are always short and filthy. She is about 55 with wispy, wavy salt-and-pepper hair and tomato ketchup lipstick. Somebody told me she was a teacher and I believed it for months because she has that kind of bossy bearing, but when she had to declare her occupation on the new council forms, it turned out that she's only a dinner lady. Mavis wears polyester skirts and cotton tee shirts, mainly check pleated skirts with floral pattern tee shirts in challenging combinations of colours. (She came up with some interesting paint suggestions.) In the winter she adds a grey or black cardigan and thick woolly tights.

Mavis is proud of her career with children and refers to her knowledge of young people at every opportunity. "After a lifetime working with children…" she frequently says before making some grossly misleading and stupid comment that even Jim can see right through. I feel that 'after a lifetime working with children' she has lost the ability to think like an adult. On the other hand I think it's a good job someone is thinking about the needs of the young so I am very patient, kind and tolerant. Naturally.

Mavis wants the parish council to 'engage with youth'. Several of my colleagues feel ready for a change of subject so when Mavis suggests a distraction from the prayer issue, everyone who can put their thoughts into words is enthusiastic.

"What we need is a Children's Champion!" she recommends with a table spoonful of enthusiasm. She has read about it in the Parish and Town Council Association magazine. "Someone to speak out in favour of children and young people whenever things come up at the council," she explains.

Guess who volunteers? Our Dave. Bless him.

'That's good,' I think. 'That will keep his mind off his troubles.'

It seems to work as it is only a day or two before he emails Lisa and me, his mind very much on his new role.

From: David Tripswitch
To: clerk@fartleburymagna.net; Katie Miller
Sent: 18 March 2004 11.14
Subject: Child Advocate

Dear Lisa and Katie
Looking forward to helping out a bit more, although I will need to pace it. Can we rename the 'TITLE' 'Children's Champion' to 'Youth Advocate'. Kids of 14 don't think they are children. I've done a similar role in the Scouts and with internet security, this is a very difficult role and can be "VERY" sensitive. I had a recent criminal record check for a passport application but if you insist on me having another one, I would be grateful if the council can do this. As I told Lisa, I can go on the next Safeguarding course.
Dave Tripswitch
Computer Technologist and Web Developer, Parish Councillor

Good old Dave.

It's a couple of months since we appointed him and Lisa tells me he is getting on with things as Children's Champion. A small working party is supposed to be drawing up a policy. As I am not on that working party I have to try to keep out of it. Lisa will get him some training in 'safeguarding'. He will report back to the council on what he is doing. So far we haven't had a report from him at all but I'm not worried. You have to make allowances for someone who is sick.

We do have a problem brewing though. I can just hear it bubbling, fermenting, and the sweet, sour smell is getting up my nose. The fartleburymagna.net open forum for people to discuss local issues is being abused by one or two anonymous people. Rude and potentially libellous messages are being posted, especially from residents of Fartlebury-under-Marsh, which has somehow become a hotbed of discontent. Mavis Wilson is suggesting we hold a meeting there. I don't know what to think about that.

"What do you think Windy?" I ask.

"Can't do any harm, can it?" he says. "It could even shut old Mavis up. She's a moaner, isn't she? Making out that the Marsh-uns are hard done by all the time."

"OK." I'm relieved that another decision has been made. "Thanks, Windy. I'll do it."

I don't do it, of course. I ask Lisa to do it and two months later we find ourselves in Fartlebury-under-Marsh school hall for a one-off council meeting. The Marsh-uns have turned out in force - about seven of them. They all nod and prod their neighbours when Mavis opens her mouth, even if it is only to yawn. She glares at me like an alligator thrashing about in the muddy waters then goes in for the kill. It's Public Speaking Time and she jumps out of her council seat and runs round to the public seats, saying that she is not speaking as a councillor but as a resident: a Marsh-un born and bred.

"Fartlebury-under-Marsh is a different place to Fartlebury Magna," she says. We nod. We know. We are indeed holding our monthly meeting here because it is a different place. "We want our own democracy," she says. "We want the right to spend our own money on what we want. We are fed up with Fartlebury Magna getting all the money. We want equal rights. We are only a little place but we have a big heart and a big need. We want our own parish council."

She runs round to take up her place on the council benches (actually, infant size chairs) again. I nod to the next person in line to speak publicly. I don't trust myself to say much in reply to Mavis. Their own parish council! Whatever next? She really is from another planet.

From: Katie Miller
To: David Tripswitch
Sent: 25 March 2004 10.59
Subject: website

Hi Dave
Website is really great. Lots of nice comments from people. Thanks for all your work on that. The Forum is a bit controversial though – can we discuss?
Sorry you missed last week's full council meeting. Hope to see you soon.
Katie

From: David Tripswitch
To: Katie Miller
Sent: 25 March 2004 11.15
Subject: re website

I was late back from a hospital appointment so had to miss the council meeting. The Forum has 250 members and is very popular. If anyone is causing trouble just tell me and I'll sort it.
Regards,
Dave Tripswitch
Parish councillor, Web developer and Computer technologist. Youth Advocate.

From: Katie Miller
To: David Tripswitch
Sent: 25 March 2004 19.25
Subject: RE: website

Hi Dave
I know it's not always possible but it is very helpful if you can ring someone to give your apologies when you can't get to a meeting. I need to talk to you. Please could you give me a ring? Your phone was busy last night. We really need to talk about the Forum. Some councillors are getting complaints and giving me a hard time!
Thanks, Katie

From: David Tripswitch
To: Katie Miller
Sent: 25 March 2004 23.35
Subject: my website

Dear Katie
I have been ill and in hospital. I have sorted out the problems with the Forum now.
Regards
David D Tripswitch
Parish councillor, Web scientist, web developer and Computer technologist. Youth Advocate.

From: Katie Miller
To: clerk@fartleburymagna.net
Sent: 26 March 2004 08.37
Subject: council website

Hi Lisa
Please would you get David Tripswitch to take the Forum off-line? When you click the subject line for some entries you get a link to a pornographic site. It needs sorting ASAP.
Thanks, Katie

From: clerk@fartleburymagna.net
To: Katie Miller
Sent: 26 March 2004 10.27
Subject: RE: council website

Hi Katie
I have spoken to Dave Tripswitch and he says he has solved the problem.
Lisa
Clerk, Fartlebury Magna Parish Council

From: Katie Miller
To: clerk@fartleburymagna.net
Sent: 28 March 2004 12.14
Subject: bad links on website

Hi Lisa
The Forum still has these links. Please ask Dave Tripswitch to remove it or close it down. We really can't have the parish council brought into disrepute in this way.
Thanks, Katie.

Just before the next meeting I am surprised to find a handwritten note in my place at the table. It is marked CONFIDENTIAL.

Dear Katie
I am concerned that people might be upsetting you. "HOW DARE THEY". You have my personal guarantee that no-one will ever put you down, undermine you or talk behind your back in front of me without a serious tongue-lashing.
Please don't take it too seriously as I am sure you still have the support of most of council.

Regards,
David Tripswitch
Fartlebury Magna Parish Councillor, Webmaster, Web scientist, Website developer, Computer Architect, Computer Technologist and Young People's Advocate.

What does he mean – 'most' of the council?

CHAPTER NINE

"It's hard to fight when the fight ain't fair." Taylor Swift

Dave walks into the meeting late, as is usual when he comes at all. He is walking slowly and with a walking stick. I find these late arrivals distracting but how can I challenge someone who is struggling with such very poor health?

The meeting runs its course, with swift business reports from FUC councillors and the Old Guard every so often chipping in with their inane comments. Jim even has a chip he has been keeping behind his ear for just such an occasion. We are getting very used to this pattern. I find it disturbing that whenever I look up Dave seems to be staring at me, but I suppose he is probably actually staring at Lisa. She seems to be trying very hard not to look at him. Mavis asks a question: "Why wasn't it minuted that I asked about Fartlebury-under-Marsh having its own parish council?" I don't have to reply, thank goodness. We don't minute matters raised in Public Speaking Time and Lisa politely confirms the rule, letting me off the hook.

At the end of the meeting, just before I declare it closed, I think I will ask Dave to explain what has happened about the Forum. He theatrically struggles to his feet, leaning heavily on the table, and says that it is very exciting, that there are 250 members, that the website receives 250,000 hits a week. We are deafened and dumbed by the big numbers. Mavis looks star-struck. Dave then explains that it is not a member of the Forum causing 'the trouble' (he lifts his hands and makes little speech mark signs in the air) but a little robot somewhere in the Philippines who has randomly accessed our website and added the link from the Forum to an adult website. He says that it has been hard to solve, and to prevent it happening again he will need to buy a piece of software.

"Put it on the next agenda," says Tracy, staggering to her feet.

"No," he says, "we can't wait that long. Someone else will hack in while we're faffing about."

Tracy sits back down, her bottom wobbling like a walrus.

Disorderly discussion breaks out and echoes around the room as the hot air rises upwards into the big space between the warm pates of the councillors and the burnt umber ceiling twenty feet above. Those who are more used to chewing their lead pencils than clicking their mice cannot grasp the issue, while the more savvy FUC-kers realise that the Forum has to be made secure against further cyber attack. In the end Lisa comes to the rescue. It's as if she has pressed Ctrl Alt Delete – she is an instant remedy for a frozen council and starts Task Manager without delay.

"Why don't we call it essential Health and Safety work, then I can authorise it without a decision of council?"

What a treasure she is. It's a done deal.

I realise that it is quite a late finish tonight but we have covered a lot of business. We hold our meetings in a particularly dark little corner of Fartlebury Magna. Most of Fartlebury Magna's corners are dark because the last parish council to consider providing street lights met in 1952 and the lights are a bit past their best – in fact I've seen brighter glow-worms. I am always concerned for Lisa's safety leaving our meetings. I am bombproof myself: young people don't scare me, but some women are afraid of the dark and the people who might be hanging around in the dark, and I don't want Lisa to have any cause for complaint. Fartlebury Magna isn't exactly a hotbed of violence and crime but you never know who might have a grievance against the council. She and Dave are talking quietly in the corner and everyone else is leaving.

"Dave," I call out, "would you mind waiting while Lisa locks up and would you mind seeing her to her car?"

He pulls a most oily and cringe-making grin across his face, "Of course. Good night Katie."

"Good night." He makes me feel very uncomfortable, like having a stone in my shoe, but I haven't got time to stop and shake it out.

When I get home I make my cocoa and take it into the dining room. I decide to take a look at www.fartleburymagna.net and see how many members we actually have on the Forum. I sometimes respond to enquiries from the virtual parish pump and I've always had the impression that there are not many local residents using it. I am surprised to find my way to a hidden part of the site where it is possible to look at members' profiles. There are a dozen or so people I know and can recognise, even with their pseudonyms: Puffing Billy, George the Third; Dan the Man; Barmy Betty. I am surprised to see others whose names I do not know. I need to understand what is going on.

From: Katie Miller
To: Dave Tripswitch
Sent: 5 April 2004 07.15
Subject: Website Forum

Hi Dave
I noticed while checking out the issues being discussed on the Forum that I was able to look at the members' profiles. There are a dozen or so local people that I can recognise but I am puzzled to see members from Russia and China. Why and how are they interested in Fartlebury Magna's affairs?
Katie

I won't ask where the other 200 members are, but the question has crossed my mind.

Lisa rings me later in the morning and asks me to pop down to the office and see her. It isn't something she does often. These days she is usually too busy preparing her own agenda. When I get there she is sitting on the edge of her desk rather nervously and tells me Dave is stressed because I keep 'harassing him' over the problems with the Forum. I feel as if she has caught me out in a misdemeanour. The stone in my shoe feels like a boulder.

"He doesn't need that," she says pointedly. I notice her eyes being drawn to my very dirty shoes. My wide, big, unfashionable and dirty shoes - the ones with the stones in.

"And he told me something in confidence. He doesn't want anyone to know except you and me – but he's got another cancer. He told me he wants you to know because he might have to miss a lot of meetings but he doesn't want other councillors to be told."

"Oh dear. I'm sorry to hear that," says the automatic pilot. "Still, he misses a lot of meetings as it is."

"He's a bastion of the community, Katie," Lisa says with a hint of irritation in her voice.

"Mmm," I nod. I can agree with her assessment. He's a right little bastion.

When Bill Shorthouse rings me at lunchtime to talk about the budget for new play equipment he makes a remark about Dave's non-attendance at meetings.

"He's not been well," I say in Dave's defence.

"Huh."

In my book Bill is a miserable old bugger, the original grumpy old man, although in real life I don't think he's got much to complain about. He used to work for a bank and now has a big fat pension for his lack of trouble. He came on the council at the time of the coup to do 'something interesting' and fight off his midlife crisis. I thought he would prove useful with that kind of background, but I now know that what the council desperately needs is fewer bureaucrats and pedants and more people who can think laterally and work around the red tape, preferably sharp people who can cut through it and shred it - in triplicate. I don't believe Bill is having a midlife crisis anyway. I can't believe he ever left his adolescence. However, Bill is computer literate and has even looked at the website once or twice. He says, "Well, while he is at home convalescing perhaps he can update the website."

I could do without this, but I had better take a look at it again. A proper look. Not just looking for trouble, but imagining I am a parishioner looking for information. I haven't done that before because I don't have much time. We have a very busy schedule. We have eight committees and seven sub-committees, not to mention fifteen working parties. The idea of those was to cut the red tape, because the meetings wouldn't need a clerk, nor a published agenda and minutes. As most of the Old Guard don't want to go out more than once a week to meetings, it also means they are mainly composed of the more interested and intelligent councillors. Unfortunately, with so many people meddling, the tape is still a dark shade of pink and very firmly tied at both ends. I try to get to most meetings – in my own head I believe this is because I need to have an overview and know what is going on. In some other heads it is interference and I should butt out. Anyway, it keeps me busy.

As I thought, Bill is right about the website. No minutes have been added for six months, the accounts are over a year old and the current financial information hasn't been added. It looks a shambles. I need to talk to someone so I ring Bill back.

"You're right, Bill."

"Of course I'm right. The website needs updating. If that Tripswitch isn't going to do it isn't there supposed to be a team of volunteers? Can't one of them do it?"

He's right. I've told him he's right. He is right. Perhaps he has the solution. In the morning I will ask the volunteers to update the pages.

"Poor Dave Tripswitch," I say to Hilary after an advisory committee about the Christmas lights later that evening, "he's not well.

That's why he's been missing meetings. He can't seem to keep up with the website updating either."

She smiles like the Mona Lisa.

"What?" I ask sharply.

"Nothing," she grins, handing me a letter that needs an answer. "What did you think about the new ideas for the Christmas lights?"

I daren't get involved in the Christmas lights. I will certainly make enemies if I do. It's the one committee which is dominated by the Old Guard. They are trying to recreate the West End of London by painting a few 40 watt lightbulbs. It's Andrew Hall's area of expertise, apparently, and he is leading the committee. I look at the letter she has handed me.

"Holy Baloney!" I shout. "It's our resident irate resident wanting us to scrap the website and go back to having a town crier to spread the council news." (Not that Fartlebury Magna ever had a town crier because it never wanted to be a town. It would only have had a village crier.)

Hilary leaves me to get on with it. It doesn't take me long to knock up a letter when I get home. I think I should take some of the pressure off the clerk. She seems to have a lot of trouble with the office computer and it makes it hard for her to get through all the work she creates for herself.

FARTLEBURY MAGNA PARISH COUNCIL

Dear Mrs Baloney

I understand your concern about the Forum but our webmaster tells me that he has now sorted out the problem. Apparently it was not a member of the Forum causing the trouble, but a robot somewhere in the Philippines who had randomly accessed our website and added these links. Our webmaster has worked hard to solve the problem and

a new piece of software has been purchased to 'screen' any offensive material that may crop up in the future.
Many thanks for bringing the issue to our attention.

Yours sincerely, Katie Miller,
Chair, Fartlebury Magna Parish Council.

Lisa is sitting on her desk showing a lot of leg when I arrive for the Staffing Sub-Committee meeting. She makes a great show of crossing and uncrossing them, her high heels catching the light and flashing their patent leather mirrors which appear to be dazzling the male contingent. All the men fancy her. I'm staring at the toes of her shoes. Her feet are tiny but I still can't understand where her toes go. Her shoes are so pointed you could knit a jumper with them. Men love all that, I know. I just wear my sensible flat shoes. I'm too clumsy to be trusted to balance on an area smaller than a 5 p piece.

Dave bursts in after me, limping and wincing and leaning heavily on a walking stick. Lisa gives him one of her shy smiles and he sits down next to her, next to her legs, that is.

"You're welcome, of course, Dave," I begin. Any councillor can attend any meeting as a right, although only committee members can vote. "But are you here for anything in particular?"

"Just to see fair play for the staff."

On the agenda we have an item about staff pay scales but he's thrown me right off balance, even in my sensible shoes. That's the trouble with democracy. I would have preferred him not to know what was on the agenda.

When we get to the item about staff pay, Dave delivers a touching little speech about how wonderful 'the office' is, while he drools over Lisa. Of course he wants her to have a big pay rise. Of course I want the money spent on the community. It is only a couple of months since the clerk had a huge pay rise.

"We all know how hard our clerk works," Jeremy says. "Even a newcomer to the council like myself can see that. But there are things she hasn't been keeping up with lately and we need to find out if she's got much on her plate at the moment."

"Some councillors expect her to do too much," says Dave.

"I agree," I say. I'm cock-a-hoop to find something I can agree with and turn to my advantage. "We need to keep councillors out of the office. Some people are always in here having a chat."

Not me, however. Lisa has made it clear that I should keep away and let her get on with her work. I can guess at the ones who hang around the office. People without enough to do. The ladies that lunch and the farmers that fart.

"How do you know what councillors expect, Dave?" I add pleasantly, but it seems to have come out wrong.

"Oh!" simpers Lisa, "He's been helping me with my computer."

"Oh! Jolly good," says Jeremy, encouraged by one of Lisa's smiles. I am not sure what that smile means but it seems like a partly frozen lake. You might think a thaw is taking place, but under an inch of water there is still six inches of ice. Treacherous - and slippery.

We finish the meeting and I feel things are slipping away from me. I won't say the meeting is a disaster but the frost is beginning to show on the hoary carpet even though it's midsummer in here. I get up to leave. Dave bolts out of the door in front of me and rushes off, finding his limp as he reaches the High Street. As I reach the door I turn to Lisa and ask:

"By the way, how is Dave's CRB check coming along? Any news?"

"The police returned it. Dave didn't send the right ID. We've got to re-send the form."

"Oh well," I shrug. "We'll get there in the end."

Someone always seems to be taunting me lately. If it's not Dave, it's Penny Finkless. She's a funny one. She used to be a lecturer twenty years ago so she knows how to make it look as if she knows something when she knows nothing. It's a useful skill. She says she can't read all the papers for meetings because she's got dyslexia. Maybe she means anorexia - she's looking very thin lately. She loves a gossip with her friend Mavis – especially during full council meetings when I am trying to chair a difficult debate. Tonight I am expecting several difficult debates, so there may be quite a bit of chatting going on in the Fartlebury-under-Marsh corner.

The trouble with the Forum has re-surfaced. Hilary and I agree: we can't go on like this. We are not convinced that Dave Tripswitch is such a computer expert as he makes out. Nerd? Yes. Expert? Probably not. He probably knows as much about computers as Andrew Hall knows about electrical work.

Our main problem is that none of us has enough knowledge to challenge either of them when they blind us with science and technology. Fortunately Dave doesn't seem up for a fight this time. Lisa hints that he is busy with other projects at the moment. She seems to know a lot about him and I am trying not to notice. I am just very relieved that the Forum is no longer on the council's website, and we all calm down again, although there remain quiet stirrings of discontent bubbling away in the cauldron. (They are barely audible to me, as I am slightly deaf.)

From my perspective things do seem to be settling down again. Councillors aren't quite so ratty with me and I am unanimously re-elected to the Chair at the annual meeting. A half-hearted nomination for Penny doesn't even get seconded. Evelyn comes alongside me on the way out. "Congratulations," he says. I smile. That's gracious of him, the first nice thing he's ever said to me. Then through the heat haze and comfort blanket I hear him say, "You're the best chairman we've had since the last one." I identify with those people who have been shot, or stabbed, and eye witnesses report that they carry on with what they are doing because they don't immediately notice the wound. I am still walking towards the door, I am still smiling. I think he intended to stop me in my tracks. He wasn't being nice, I now realise. He was being nasty. They're a funny lot, the old codgers of parish councils past. He's just voted for me to be Chair, so why be nasty? I don't get politics.

I get Penny though. Poor Penny. She's been away from council meetings for weeks. She told me she was missing the money she claims every month for all her travel out of the county to various meetings and forums. It is putting her under financial strain. She's always keen to put up her hand, is Penny. Probably the only exercise she gets, apart from getting in and out of her car and waddling up to the grey front door of the little house she shares with her sister on one of Fartlebury Magna's East End estates. Tonight is her first night back. I'm quite proud of some of the other councillors, the way they have deliberately gone up to her and spoken to her. It takes a deal of courage to withstand a known olfactory onslaught – although, to be fair, they are used to dealing with their farms and all their shit, so I suppose they can't smell as well as other people. It must dull your sense of smell when you have generations of dung on your dungarees. It doesn't come easy to them, not to any of them, normal social intercourse. Probably normal intercourse of any sort.

Dave makes a big show of his entrance as usual. He is limping like a burlesque version of Long John Silver and leaning on his walking stick. Whenever I see him I am trying to notice whether the limp is always in the same leg. It's an awful thing to be so suspicious, but Long John Silver's leg was made of wood so he had some excuse, and I'm pretty sure Dave wouldn't be seen dead with a parrot on his shoulder. There's an empty seat next to Penny and it gives him the chance for maximum disruption to the meeting, so he heads for it. He sits down heavily (for such a small man). I am introducing our second agenda item but Lisa has stopped listening to me and writing in her pad, so I stop too. Penny is saying, quite loudly, to Dave, "I don't THINK so!" which has brought us all to silence.

After the meeting I ask her about her health (not usually a recommended course of action). I want to ask her what Dave said to her but it's a bit unprofessional of me to show an interest in gossip so I'm skirting round it like a shy horse doing dressage. Dave is engrossed in conversation with Lisa and Hilary. Penny lowers her voice. "That man is seriously weird," she says. "He's got a real problem. He said, 'What's been the matter with you?' and when I said I had had a heart attack, he said, 'I've had the same.' She is really cross. "Of course he hasn't had a heart attack!" She sounds very indignant. And so she should. Her condition trumps his any day. No-one can beat a heart attack for sympathy, especially when you're under sixty.

***

Tom is one of our best volunteers. He won't come on the council but he likes practical tasks so he helps Lisa with all sorts of little jobs, mending this and that, delivering things, moving things. Tom was one of the first to respond to Lisa's posters asking for volunteers to join a community web team. He has just retired from a computer-related job. He is getting to know Dave Tripswitch and now he's got me cornered before the monthly meeting starts.

"Where did this Tripswitch bloke come from then? What are his credentials? Is he qualified? Should we have references?"

Tom is a great help to the council but I don't think I know, and I don't think I care, about where Dave has come from. The answer could be Heaven. I find Tom's rants a bit intimidating. I keep a safe distance once the blue touch-paper is smouldering. I can tell it's smouldering now by the way his head gives a little twitch now and again as if trying to shake off a fly. The veins are standing out in his neck like blue sausages. "I can't get him to update the website!" he goes on. (Now he is really going on.) "I keep asking him. I must have asked him a hundred times. I can only do the pages assigned to me. Jeremy does the pages he can do – the community pages. I do the business and voluntary listings. Penny does the others, but Dave does the council pages apart from the minutes and agendas which Lisa deals with. We haven't got his password. No-one else can get into the council pages."

"I'll have a word," I say. I don't know at this stage which word I will have, and I'm not even convinced I'll manage at all to summon one out from under my tongue, but he immediately turns his back and starts haranguing someone else.

I'm as numb as a noodle as I cross the hall after the meeting; I don't even notice the dust kicking up from my feet. Dave breaks off his grin and puts his hand casually on Lisa's arm. "We were just talking about you, weren't we, Lisa?" Lisa blushes and looks at the floor. Is it my dirty, clumpy, dumpy, frumpy, flat shoes she is looking at, contrasting with her tiny Cinderella feet, encased in her dainty red patent leather winkle-pickers?

"Oh yes?" I ask brightly. Lisa's stare intensifies. She might melt my shoes soon if she doesn't avert her microwave blue eyes. Dave smirks.

"I'd like a word, Dave." He sighs and winces, leaning against his walking stick in a theatrical way. He has definitely seen too much pantomime in his lifetime – especially hammed-up versions of *Treasure Island.* I decide to drag Lisa in. I don't like their closeness. It makes me uneasy. I ought to put a little wedge between them. I sharpen the end of it before placing it.

"As I keep saying to Lisa, and I asked her to pass on the message to you – we've just got to get the website updated." Dave's eyes are now penetrating steel, a gimlet poking through my eyeballs and going for the soft tissue behind my eyes. I think it's affecting my brain. It's getting harder to think straight but I have to carry on. “It’s hopelessly out of date, Dave. We’re getting complaints. The idea is to give people current information.”

Dave smirks. “Tom can’t keep up then, eh?”

“Is it down to Tom then?”

“Well, I do my best you know, between hospital and GP appointments and other treatments, and you know my boy’s been at the Children’s Hospital for weeks – he might have a brain tumour.” He fades to a whisper. “I’ll try to stay at home and work on the website tomorrow, if I’m not in too much pain. Sometimes the painkillers don’t work enough. My wife can visit the boy on her own. She’ll have to catch the bus because she’s lost her glasses and she can’t drive at the moment, but she can manage. The boy will be disappointed but he’ll get over it. I know the website’s more important.”

“Oh no!” I say, my conscience re-emerging from the polite darkness of my interior: “Of course you must visit your son!”

I slink away, shame heavy on my shoulders like Great Grandma’s worsted shawl.

CHAPTER TEN

"Not all forms of abuse leave bruises." Danielle Steele

Windy isn't an aggressive man. He isn't a big man either. Five feet seven and slightly built, he hasn't been anywhere near a fight since 1958. He's the sort of man who uses his brain rather than his fists, and who prefers to keep away from trouble. He doesn't even express anger very often (although living with me I admit he often has good reason).

"Just popping to the post office," shouts Windy as he slams the front door. I scowl, my face creasing like a fitted sheet that's too big for the mattress. Why can't he close the door normally? I suppose his masculinity will out sometime, somehow. Anyway, I would rather he slams the door than slams me as some of the village wives get slammed. I smooth my tense face with my fingers. I don't really want my once rosebud mouth to look like a cat's bottom. I should let the slammed door go and relax those facial muscles. I should also get on with the washing up.

When Windy returns, the door makes a quiet click. Windy is pensive and quiet. He usually breezes in and shouts '*Hello*' so the quietness is unusual and unsettling. "The funniest thing happened," he begins, creeping into the kitchen. "I bumped into that Dave outside the post office."

"What? Dave Tripswitch?"

"Yes. He called out '*Good morning*' as we were walking towards each other. I thought it was an opportunity to say something about his emails to Tom and the upset he's causing by not updating the website so I said, '*I want to have a word with you.*' By this time we were near each other and he came right up to me, squared up to me. Too close. Nose to nose. Nearly touching. And he said, '*Not now. I'm on my way to an appointment,*' but then he turned away and somehow, deliberately, he brushed right up against me, a kind of shoulder barge it really was – we were in a big area. He squared up to me. He didn't need to be near me. He just barged me. It was funny."

It doesn't sound funny and Windy is shaking like a dog after a bath. "That's odd," I say. "Do you think he did it on purpose then?"

"Oh yes, it was completely, absolutely, totally deliberate. He then shouted, '*You wanna watch that!*' as he walked on down the pavement, yelling back over his shoulder, '*That could be construed as common assault.*' He's bad news, Katie," my defender says. "I'm not having anything more to do with him. You shouldn't have anything to do with him either. He's dangerous."

I can't really take it in. This isn't like Windy at all. It usually takes me a lot of hard work to get him to say anything nasty about anyone. But it's indisputable: Windy's got the wind up. A storm is coming.

"It was a real threat. He's capable of anything," he says again in the face of my silence. I need to process the new information.

Later that day I sit down to look at my emails. One jumps out of the list like a hob-goblin and it's definitely waving a little trident. I can't resist it. It's drawing me like an electron magnet. In the subject line it says WINDY MILLER.

When I open it I see a little slogan at the top in bold italics:

'Dedicated to Fartlebury Magna, its Friends and Families'

Dear Windy
Sorry I couldn't stop and chat this morning. I was already late for an appointment. Please feel free to give me a call or arrange a visit. My door is always open.
Best regards, David Tripswitch
Parish councillor, Youth Advocate, Web development manager, Computer Technologist.

My distaste for the little creep is growing. I don't feel so neutral any more. I don't feel like being professional any more. I feel like giving vent to my anger. I feel like a fire the morning after. To all appearances I am quite dead, but if someone just blows on me sparks will fly and I could burst into flames. There is definitely some heat below. Now I notice that he has copied the email to Lisa.

I pick up the phone.

"Hi Lisa. How are things going?"

"I'm very busy at the moment."

"Would you like me to come down and help with anything?"

I imagine her tiny face puckering up with a frown, her pointed chin hardening. "No, I'll get it done," she says. Then she adds, "Don't worry about coming down for an agenda conference tomorrow either."

"Don't we need to get on with that?"

"I'm too busy Katie." She really didn't need the assertiveness course we sent her on. It's just made it easier for her to get the better of me. There isn't the slightest hint of friendliness in her voice.

"OK, don't work too hard."

She will, of course. She's always hard at it.

Later I think I catch a glimpse of Dave hurrying past my house. He looks fit, active - 'jaunty' is the word I would use. He certainly isn't using a walking stick. Perhaps it's not him at all but a lookalike. But it looks like his coat and scarf.

When I'm hanging out the washing I find myself feeling insecure. I've been watching too many crime films. I imagine Dave coming at me with an axe. Windy said he is capable of anything. I'm shaking now. What if he walks right into my garden? I would be cornered. What if he is capable of anything? Well, something, anyway.

I go inside and lock the door. My world is flawed with cracks the size of Cheddar Gorge. What is going on? I'll go and sit in my lovely leather chair and see what emails have come in. The leather chair is a present from Windy. He bought it because I am always complaining about my back-ache and asking him to give me a massage. I suppose it was easier to pop into the office warehouse when he was in town and pick one up for me. When I got home from the parish council office one day, there it was. Now when I open my Inbox another surprise greets me.

From: Dave Tripswitch
To: Katie Miller
Sent: 6 May 2004 9.22
Subject: Confidential

DEDICATED TO FARTLEBURY MAGNA
Dear Katie
Before I go away I need to tell you that Councillors are not satisfied with the way things are going and are talking behind your back. I can't defend you unless you stop bullying the staff.
*Just a friendly "**WARNING**".*
Regards, Dave Tripswitch
Parish councillor, Youth Advocate, Web developer and computer professional

Dave has been busy. He has also sent an email to Penny and the rest of the web team. I get copied in to these 'as a courtesy', as I am Chair of the council. I have to seize what courtesy I can.

From: Dave Tripswitch
To: Penny Finkless
Cc: undisclosed recipients
Sent: 6 May 2004 14.56
Subject: copyright

Just to make it 'CLEAR' before I go away for four weeks holiday, I own the copyright on the Fartleburymagna.net parish website. No-one else has the 'authority' to tamper with it. DO NOT TOUCH the website while I am away. If you do I will have no choice but to take 'LEGAL' action.
Kind regards, Dave

I am wondering what on earth this is all about. How dare he threaten our kind and lovely hard-working volunteers with legal action? It's ridiculous. The man is suffering from a huge dose of paranoia (and capitalisation and quote-markitis) as well as all his other ailments. Thank goodness he is going away on holiday again. I suppose you need a lot of holidays if you are as sick as he is.

***

"I'm off to the post office, Windy!" I shout up the stairs. With Dave Tripswitch out of the way I don't need to feel anxious or agoraphobic. I can lick my own stamps. I head off to the High Street where the post office stands majestically between the betting shop and the bank. That's right, a bank. In a village. In Fartlebury Magna's rural backwater to be precise. Rumour has it that the bank manager lives somewhere nearby and somehow managed to arrange for the bank to stay open when other bank managers were being culled in the South West like badgers. Actually the bank doesn't stay open in any real sense of the word. It hasn't been closed and been turned into flats, it's true, but it is only open three days a week from late in the morning until early in the afternoon (apart from the two hours when it closes at lunchtime). It has an early half-day closing on Wednesday afternoons, just as it did in the 1950s. I've never worried about a bank robbery because I doubt if the robbers could find it open. I've never actually seen anyone go into the bank either, but that's fine because it's something useful for the estate agents to use to promote life in Fartlebury Magna. Every house they advertise is in easy reach of all the amenities – including a *bank.* Newcomers to the village all say, 'Wow.'

I'm always careful in the High Street. I know about keeping my wits about me in the heavy traffic. (I have been trying to keep my dimwits about me as well, but they seem to be breaking away from me like ice bergs in the face of climate change.) I never take the zebra crossing for granted. I know it's not a force field. I know drivers won't automatically stop for zebra crossings, especially if they're busy on their mobile phones, or reaching round to the back seat to slap their children, so I wait until I can see the whites of their eyes, and make sure they are looking straight at me before stepping off the pavement. I'm going to cross now. Or at least I am going to stand by the roadside under the Belisha beacon and stripey pole and prepare to cross as soon as a driver condescends to apply their brakes. Here I go: I look right and there is a surprise. It's Dave Tripswitch - behind the wheel of a car. I am very surprised to see him: a) because I thought he had gone on holiday, and b) because I have never seen him driving a car before. I didn't think he liked to drive. People can't see you're limping if you are limping on the accelerator.

Dave is slowing down, his eyes straight ahead on me and I am crossing the road. He must have had a spasm in his leg or something because suddenly the car shoots forward. He looks grim and determined. He must be trying to control his leg but it's not working because the car is accelerating wildly. If it had been a better car it might have hit me but fortunately I am quite nimble and can get out of the way of an old banger like his. I reckon it would take an hour or so to get from 0-60 mph. I am sure he will stop and apologise for scaring me, or explain what happened, but that's wishful thinking (and maybe not even that because it's probably not something I would wish for). He speeds off like Lewis Hamilton.

When I get to the post office counter a young woman in the queue must have seen what happened because she asks me if I am all right. "Wanker!" she says. "I see him doing that quite often. He's a moron."

"He's a parish councillor," I say by way of explanation since she doesn't know who I am.

"Yeah. Wankers the lot of them."

Johnny Henchman is in the post office, queuing behind me. If looks could kill I would be dead for the second time this afternoon. I decide to ignore the look and make conversation instead.

"How are you?" I ask politely. As I receive no reply I can move on to the next question. "How is your daughter? And how is your grandson getting on?"

"He could get on better if you lot would do something about the perverts round here. Now there's a dogging site on Bumcrack Hill and we are the laughing stock of Corsetshire."

"I heard the doggers had gone away now," I say. "PC Bigg-Toze told me there were a few smashed windscreens. I wondered if it was anything to do with the Fartlebury Magna vigilantes?"

"How would I know that?" he snaps.

It's my turn at the counter. Nosey Natalie is busy sending a text. "Is that right?" she asks without really looking up, "Did the vigilantes smash the windscreens of doggers up on the hill?"

I shrug. "Seems likely, doesn't it?"

"They never proved nothin' about that weirdo Tripswitch, did they?"

"No." I have to agree. "But if there's no evidence…."

"Evidence! What's that got to do with it? If he's a pervert he needs to be taught a lesson. Like those buggers up the hill car park." She turns to look at the rest of the queue. "Ah, Mr Henchman, can I help you?"

My mouth opens. Natalie looks at me with surprise. I am flapping about like a fish out of water, opening and closing my mouth, stranded on Dogger Bank. I finally manage, “Excuse me, I was next.”

Johnny Henchman glowers at me and pushes past me. I am suddenly invisible, my politeness taking the form of a shield which renders me of no account to the locals whatsoever. Conversely, their rudeness and lack of manners makes them seem very solid. I go to the back of the queue.

CHAPTER ELEVEN

"You should never wrestle with a pig. You both get dirty but the pig likes it." George Bernard Shaw

One of the big issues of the day is the closure of the public toilets, or 'Fartlebury Magna's bogs' as Jim likes to say for effect. Penny wrinkles up her bulbous red nose, as if she is smelling the pungency of them from her seat. We've been forced into a decision by the district council, which has provided the convenience of conveniences for our village for many years. As they are now broke (the impecunious council, not the ungrammatical past participle lavatories), the choice is not, I'm pleased to say, *Use Them or Lose Them,* but more a case of *No Fees, No Wees.* The parish council now has the chance to take over the toilets or let them close.

We've had the debate. I couldn't make enough of them see sense – or maybe they just want to vote contrarily to spite me. I dismiss that thought as being bad for my health. Phil Jenkins, however, agrees with me for once. "If my grandfather was still alive, he'd turn in his grave," he says. "Where's a man supposed to go? You know, older men can't hold on for hours."

Hilary is tuned in to sexist remarks and adjusts her antennae. He won't get that past her. "If people of any gender are incontinent they should wear appropriate medical aids, or they should stay at home," she says.

"If we close them we won't get all the ..er.. yobbos hanging around there," says Jeremy, which seems to exasperate Hilary and causes her to pucker up her moustaches and big black eyebrows.

"I think that's very unfair to our young people," she says.

"No it's not," says Nigel, "The police are always being called to deal with drug-taking going on in the bogs."

Jim smiles. It's not very often someone picks up his words and uses them.

"Well," says Mavis, "after a lifetime working with children I know how difficult it is for parents who are out shopping with their children and they need a toilet, but it's not really fair for the parish council to pay for toilets in Fartlebury Magna High Street when we haven't got any public toilets in Fartlebury-under-Marsh so I think the ones in Fartlebury Magna should be closed."

"That's a good reason," says Hilary. It's obviously sarcastic but some of the older councillors look aghast at the unlikely alliance between the Marsh-un and the clever lezzy. I've had enough of all this. None of it is helping. I've spelt out the issues and the ramifications and now I will have to hope for the best.

"We should take a vote now," I say. "The issue is: shall we save the community £3,000 a year but leave people without a toilet? Or shall we provide public conveniences as a facility and find the money from our budget?"

The clerk interjects to remind me that we asked for parishioners' views in our last newsletter.

"And?"

"Only eleven replies but they mostly want closure to save having to pay more on the council tax."

"How much would that be?" asks Hilary.

"Eighteen pence a year on average," says Lisa.

"Well, why should we pay for a toilet for people? They should go at home before they set out. That's what my mum always taught me," says Evelyn. "Look after the pennies and the pounds look after themselves."

"Yes, that's right," says Tracy. "We don't want to go spending pennies unnecessarily."

"Is there any way of calculating how many people use the toilets and whether they are really necessary?" Penny asks. The silence is deafening.

"We'll have the vote now," I say, "but remember our mission statement is to provide good services for Fartlebury Magna residents."

I catch sight of Mavis's hand rising slowly like the lady from the lake, (except it has no sword in it) so I add, "Fartlebury Magna parish includes Fartlebury-under-Marsh, as we will all remember." I'm pretty sure not all of us will remember anything at all but I like to flatter them. "We didn't add Fartlebury-under-Marsh onto our mission statement because the clerk said if we put it on our headed paper we wouldn't have room to write anything else. Our parish is called Fartlebury Magna, but what makes it Magna is that it includes the hamlet of Fartlebury-under-Marsh. Magna means great, or big." I hope Mavis is satisfied. She seems to have withdrawn her arm back into the lake anyway.

Jim snorts loudly. I'm not sure whether he disapproves or if he's just woken up with a start.

"The motion is: '*To close the public toilets in the High Street.*' All those in favour please raise your hands."

To my horror eight hands go up. "Against?" I say, with a lump in my throat.

Only five hands go up. The other councillors present sit on the fence between the toilets and the public purse. It's just not like it used to be. When we started off on the council I just had to say the word and my team all voted whichever way I said. Now some of them seem to want independence, like India, Rhodesia or Scotland.

The district council takes no time in nailing up the door. People are soon to be spotted peeing in the bushes at the back of the butcher's shop.

Mrs Baloney rings me to ask me what she is supposed to tell the lorry drivers who stop outside her house and ask her where they can go for a wee. "Some of them even want a cubicle," she says. "They've been in their cabs for hours. I tell them they will have to go up to Bumford Sock. At least their parish council kept the toilets open there."

"It's a mark of civilization," says Hilary, "to provide public toilets."

I'm not surprised Fartlebury Magna opted for closure then. Lots of our villagers aren't even civil, let alone civilised.

I was only thinking earlier how pleasant it is that Dave Tripswitch has been quiet for a little while. I expect he's been in hospital, or in Thailand. He always seems to be somewhere, and I am never sure whether he is at home or not because sometimes he sends emails even though he's the other side of the Atlantic, or from his hospital bed. ("If he really is in a hospital bed," says Hilary. "How do we know he isn't just in his room?") My peace has been broken again because his name has popped into my inbox.

From: Dave Tripswitch
To: Katie Miller
Cc: Hilary Entwhistle; theclerk@fartleburymagna.net
Sent: 23 June 2004 20.03
Subject: confidential

Dear Katie
It's got to the point where people are just unable to support you as your not allowing them to complete their roles. We all believe your taking on way too much.
Dave

Poor man. He is quite unhinged. And he doesn't know his yours from his you'res. Perhaps it's the drugs he's on for his ailments. I think he told me he takes a tablet for apostrophes. It's been beautifully quiet while he was on holiday. I'm disappointed to have him back, but perhaps we can get the website updated now. I think I will pop down the road and get some ham for tea, while he's still busy unpacking and catching up with his paranoia and emails.

The traffic seems particularly bad in the High Street this afternoon and my progress on foot is faster than the cars converging on the school. As I turn the corner a car mounts the pavement to avoid a woman with a placard who is leading a group of young parents with pushchairs and toddlers on foot. The placard reads: '*Slow down you bastard and keep Fartlebury Magna safe*'. It is on a long stalk and in the safe manicured hands of Tracy. It has to be carried at a strange angle to her body because of her top-heaviness, but it will be well cushioned in the event of a drop in altitude. I can only read it because I am three feet from it. There is no chance that drivers will be able to read it.

"What's this about, Tracy?" I ask. "You might have been better off with fewer words."

"Bloody drivers, speeding along the bloody High Street at sodding school coming-out time," she shouts above the traffic, which is crawling along in first gear. (She definitely would be better off using fewer words. Several parents clap their hands to the side of their toddlers' faces to cover their ears.) "And some of the worst culprits are parish councillors," she adds.

"Who?"

"That Tripswitch. He's always in a hurry, isn't he?"

"Not to update the website," I smile back through the exhaust clouds. "You've got a lot of support for the march."

Tracy scowls, which is her default expression. I remember too late that she doesn't like to think about support because her community-size chest is always leading to community-size jokes about her. “What are you going to do about road safety?” she asks, as if it is my responsibility alone.

“We’ll get a crossing put in.”

“How much longer will that take?”

“We shouldn’t have to wait much longer. It’s on the list. The County Council promised me.”

“Jim and Phil said they could paint white stripes on the road as good as anyone else. We could make our own zebra crossing.”

“Don’t be daft, Tracy. Of course we can’t paint our own zebra crossing! Just be patient for a little while longer. It will be coming, very soon, I hope.”

We reach the school gates and turn off the High Street. I am walking a bit strangely now because Tracy has put me on the back foot but I quicken my pace in gladness when I see that the press has turned out to cover a story from our rural backwater. The Corset Daily Post photographer and reporter are both here to meet Tracy and her cohort. Naturally I ought to be in the photo. I am the parish council chair and anyway I’m more photogenic than Tracy. It has to be said that she is no oil painting. So I say it. I think she’s got something in her eye now. I don’t think she can be crying because I am sure she must be used to people saying things like that. The photographer arranges me with some small children and snaps half a dozen shots. Tracy is hanging around at the back like a wasp around the jam jar.

“I’m glad you could come,” she says, but I find it hard to believe. She would love to get a bit of limelight. However, I am glad she hasn’t got it - I think lime might only accentuate the parts that would be better disguised or hidden. Anyway, as I tell Trixie Mann the reporter, I know much more about the dangers of the High Street than Tracy does. And I’m the parish council chair. Surely there are some perks. I’m sure my electors would like to see me in the paper now and again to remind them of what I am achieving for them.

From: Dave Tripswitch
To: Katie Miller
Sent: 29 June 2004 20.54
Subject: CONFIDENTIAL

Dearest Katie
I am sorry to say I have had another two "INFORMAL" complaints about the way you are working and your blatant disregard for other peoples views. Unlike other councillors talking behind your back, I considered it better to email you.
Councillors "are" becoming concerned about the change in your character and the way you are treating other councillors.
Under these circumstances I will be taking a summer sabbatical "suspending my role" during the summer holidays to spend more time with my family and look after my health.
You are not listening or acting on the advice of people who should be supporting you.
Dave

I'm not sure what's going on but I'm in the swimming pool without my armbands and the bottom is sliding away from under my feet. In the circumstances such communications are best left to drift into the filter and disappear. If he's an attention-seeker and I ignore him he will go away. That's what you do to petulant children. I read Dr Spock.

CHAPTER TWELVE

"What is right is not always popular and what is popular is not always right"   Albert Einstein

We have a great day when we open the new zebra crossing at the beginning of September. Lisa is teetering about in her four inch stilettos and Phil Jenkins is wearing a cleanish looking tweed jacket with leather elbows. I make the mistake of standing near him. I stop breathing for a while to avoid the fragrant inhalation of moth ball and cow-muck.

Most of Fartlebury Magna has turned out in the sunshine. Not most of the councillors of course. They probably don't realise it is happening, or that they voted for it many months ago. Some of them might not even realise that they can go out without a car and walk on pavements. One or two might boycott the opening, and even the zebra crossing itself. At one meeting Evelyn said, "We never had zebra crossings in Fartlebury Magna when I was a boy and we all managed to cross the road alright." Jim said, "Hear, hear." Mavis just said Fartlebury-under-Marsh needed a zebra crossing too. She hasn't come today. I suppose she might have got run over trying to cross the single track lane she lives in when the one tractor an hour went by.

Lisa has brought her daughter along to the shindig because it is the school holidays and she hasn't got anyone to look after her. I have heard her talking about Millie but I haven't ever seen her. My eyes almost pop out of their sockets when I'm introduced to her. Millie, who is eight, is the nearest thing to a perfect child I have ever seen. She has big blue eyes and the blondest of hair with skin like magnolia emulsion (perfectly applied with no brush strokes and no bobbly bits). She is clean, tidy, pretty and she is dressed like a doll.

Millie seems quite shy so I try not to embarrass her by carrying out the interrogation that adults feel compelled to give to those younger than themselves. I limit myself to the kind of conversation kids like. “Right then?”

She looks at the ground and grits her perfect white teeth, muttering, “Yes, thank you,” in reply.

Lisa strokes her arm affectionately and pushes a coin into her hand. “Why don’t you go and get a cake? I’ll come in a minute.”

Millie slopes off, eyes down on the grass.

“It’s gone well,” I say in a very neutral, level tone.

“Yes, very well.”

“All good publicity for the council,” I say to prolong this positive exchange.

“Yes, that’s the name of the game.”

I study her face. She is wearing a very good well-fitting mask which completely conceals whatever she likes it to. She is also wearing a bright red lipstick I haven’t seen her behind before. It matches the stripe in her little cotton socks (bless them) which can be seen between the end of her skin-tight, ankle-length stretch jeans and her shoes.

We are weighing each other up, circling each other like cats. I’m done with purring. Little cat calls are more fitting now. As yet no-one else is tuned in to our low yowling and growling but we both know that fur could fly between us if one of us let down our guard.

Dave limps up smirking. Lisa is so relieved she lets out a little mew of joy. I fully expect to see her arch her back and rub herself against his legs but fortunately I am spared that spectacle. Dave stares at me, putting on his pillow-soft voice to say ‘Hello’ and quickly turning his attention back to Lisa: “Where’s that gorgeous little girl of yours?”

“Gone to demolish the cake table.”

“Shall we go and get some too?” He didn’t quite take her arm and lead her off, but it was a close thing. I watch them walk off together, smiling and eyeing each other like a pair of lovers.

I am standing here watching. I don't like the clerk to be so friendly with a councillor and I'm trying to work out why. I've nothing to hold against him except his emails and his grammar. He's a fool and a nerd and quite possibly, as Windy would say, a tool and a turd, but I can't quite put my finger on it – which is something of a relief.

Millie is coming to life. I can see her from where I am standing, bursting out of her hard chrysalis membrane. She is excited by something Dave is doing. It is little magic tricks, sleight of hand, pretending to find coins behind Millie's ear. It's so light-hearted and wholesome, like a well loved uncle with his niece. Why should I mind? Then I see Dave reach out with his other hand and give her bottom a little squeeze. Millie doesn't look too sure of it; even from this distance I can see her recoil. Lisa is laughing, oblivious, lifting her little pinched pointed foot off the ground like Marilyn Monroe. She can't take her eyes off Dave. Millie now doesn't seem to be able to take hers off the ground.

***

The full council meeting in July is quite acrimonious. I've noticed that most of the meetings are like that these days, with little asides and snide remarks across the table becoming more and more resistant to my chairmanship.

Dave Tripswitch has a new tie. It has images of Bart Simpson on it and it complements his Tom and Jerry socks, which are visible when he comes to meetings late, sits in the spare chair next to Lisa and pulls up his trousers to avoid mis-shaping the knee.

After the meeting Penny goes up to him, "You like the Simpsons then Dave? Bart has a great philosophy of life, doesn't he? Do you remember that one where he wrote NO-ONE WANTS TO HEAR MY ARMPITS on the blackboard? Hilarious, wasn't it?"

Dave looks a bit blanker than usual. "Ah! The tie! It was a gift from someone very close, very close, to cheer me up after my latest operation. I've been in hospital. Did you know?"

Penny did know but she puts on her best empathetic face. "Oh dear, not again. I am sorry."

That's enough for Dave. He says, "You don't know the half of it. They had to re-start me on the paddles you know. I was dying on the table and they had to re-start me. I've got asthma. You know, my breathing is all out of breath, and I had a heart attack."

Penny is looking away now, embarrassed. She has heard it all before. She stifles a yawn, forcing her eyes not to close and her mouth not to open so her expression resembles that of a python swallowing a goat. By the time she turns back to Dave he's moved closer to Lisa and is helping her gather up the spare agenda papers from the tables. Most of the other councillors have gone. They roll in like snooker balls, bounce off each other a bit and then roll off again. Very few of them want to explore the depths of the pockets or make a difference to the score.

Those of us who are left start stacking the chairs. I catch a little nugget of Lisa's golden dialogue with Dave.

"...he's going to Manchester on a course ... have tea with us ... Millie will be in ..."

My stomach gives a little lurch. I'm old-fashioned I suppose. Anyway it's tea she's inviting him for, not an orgy. And Millie is going to be there as well. Must be harmless.

Lisa notices me lurking and gives me a sugary smile. "Dave's coming over to sort out my – the council's – laptop."

"Excellent. Thank you Dave."

Dave Tripswitch isn't at the next meeting but Nigel's giving a report on the council's work with youth instead. He's not a great public speaker. He can keep going on any given subject for many a minute, with plenty of repetition, hesitation and deviation, but deviation is the main thing and it usually involves an agricultural anecdote or two. Nigel used to have a dairy farm but he says the Milk Quotas put him out of business. Selling off two fields for The Barton and Winnowing Barn Close didn't seem to help much, even though they raised millions, as he has been driving his latest Mercedes for at least the last eighteen months. Luckily for him no-one's remotely interested in what he's saying. I look around the table. Phil Jenkins is picking his teeth with a bit of twig he just found in his pocket (he wiped it first just in case he had used it for something else); Jeremy is picking his nose then wiping it off his fingernail onto a paisley handkerchief he keeps for that purpose in his breast pocket; Hilary is writing in her diary; Penny is fiddling in her handbag; Tracy is on a beach in Trinidad – I think she goes there during most committee reports; Evelyn is imagining her there, in a teeny-weeny bikini. I drag myself and my harness of wild horses back to the council chamber.

"...and to conclude, Councillor Tripswitch, our Children's What-do-you-call-it – Champion, yes, thank you – has been getting to know young people in Fartlebury-under-Marsh. He's been meeting them off the school bus and talking to them about the council. He would like the council to consider putting on a pizza evening for young people."

"He can put it on the agenda then," says Tracy, prickly as a hawthorn bush.

"I'll do that for next month," says Lisa.

"And what about his CRB check?" I throw in.

Lisa blushes. "It's on its way."

***

Hilary's on the phone again. She's really wound up about our 'Children's Champion'.

"Tracy says we shouldn't be letting him meet young people at Fartlebury-under-Marsh. What's he meeting them for? What's he talking to them about?"

I take these questions as rhetorical. "Mmm."

"I thought the role of Children's Champion was a reactive one. You know, he would speak up for children and young people's rights if they needed an advocate with the council? I didn't see it as a pro-active role. Did you?"

I confess I did not. "Look Hilary, I just feel a bit under pressure really to let him get on with it."

"It's not safe Katie. We haven't had his CRB check back."

I feel a little jolt inside. A jolt out of my complacency. It is like being kicked by a donkey. A few what-ifs fly over, flapping madly. I can feel the air they're displacing. "I'll have another word with Lisa."

By the next morning I'm a coward again. I feel weak and shaky at the thought of seeing Lisa. Maybe I'll just send an email.

From: Katie Miller
To: clerk@fartleburymagna.net
Sent: 17 September 2004 09.08
Subject: Children's Champion – urgent

Hi Lisa
Please could we sort out Dave Tripswitch's CRB check? I think we could come under criticism for allowing him to work with children and young people without one. It's in our policy. In any case I thought we were going to come up with a briefing note to guide him - a job description for the Children's Champion. Did you ever do that? I don't remember seeing it.

(I stop typing at that point to check the website for the minutes and check what we actually did agree to. The minutes haven't been uploaded yet).

I would be very grateful for your urgent help in this matter.

Katie.

I have a really bad feeling about this. Of course I'm sure there's no problem with Dave's CRB. I might not like the way he behaves but that doesn't mean there's anything wrong. We just need to get it sorted. I don't really think there's a problem with him, do I? Do I?

Then Mavis puts her head above the water line. In Fartlebury-under-Marsh, the even wetter part of our wetland parish, where marsh has persisted to this day and floods block the roads with regularity (and sewage), she is stirring. I asked her once how long she had lived locally and she said 'about 400 years' - a clever put-down for incomers like me which never fails to put me in my place. Mavis and I have never exchanged emails before, but I was always dimly aware that she's part of the Dave Tripswitch fan club.

From: Mavis Wilson
To: Katie Miller
Cc: clerk@fartleburymagna.net
Sent: 18 September 2004 11.14
Subject:

Dear Katie

You have been putting the Clerk under undue stress, among other things by making her responsible for the CRB check of our Child and

Youth Advocate. I have been helping her in the office and she is finding your workload very hard. My son got appointed recently to a county council position as a school crossing attendant and they were happy to employ him while he waited for his CRB paperwork to come through. Surely it can't hurt for Dave Tripswitch to be treated the same?
Mavis Wilson

I'm getting just a little bit fed up with the Marsh-un Moaner. I don't stop to think, I just start click-clacking away on the keyboard. It all happens too fast nowadays. If I had to find a suitable feather to sharpen and a squid to kill for its ink before I could start writing, the world would be a better place.

From: Katie Miller
To: Mavis Wilson
Sent: 18 September 2004 11.22
Subject: Re:

Hi Mavis
I appreciate that the Clerk feels under stress and is not coping well with her workload at present. I therefore think it unwise to copy her in unnecessarily to emails. You can perhaps enlighten me about what Dave Tripswitch has been doing at Fartlebury-under-Marsh and why it is so urgent that we can't wait for an enhanced CRB check? As you know, I like the council to operate to principles of best practice.
Katie

As soon as I click on *Send* I feel uneasy. I shouldn't be making enemies of anyone on the council, let alone Mavis Wilson. I should have picked up the phone and talked to her. That way there's nothing in writing. But it's too late – I've done it now. I ring Hilary instead.

"I've asked Mavis Wilson what Dave is doing at Fartlebury-under-Marsh and I've emailed the clerk and asked her to let me know what she's doing about the CRB check and whether she's come up with a job description for our Children's Advocate."

"Good. We really can't let them get away with it."

"Come on, Hilary. You don't really think they're trying to get away with something, do you? They aren't in anything together, are they?" It's only bureaucratic process."

"Might not be Katie. We can't take chances."

From: clerk@fartleburymagna.net
To: Katie Miller
Sent: 18 September 2004 14.27
Subject: Training for Children's Champion

I have booked Dave on a Child Safe Day for Voluntary Organisations which is being run by the County Council. This meets the obligation for training as detailed in the council's Child Protection Policy and his appointment meets the need for a 'responsible officer' - a role that he is very happy to fulfill.
Lisa.

From: Dave Tripswitch
To: clerk@fartleburymagna.net
Cc: Katie Miller
Sent: 20 September 2004 19.16
Subject: Training

Dearest Lisa
Yes please book me on the course on 28th November.

I am sure you know by now that I am trustworthy but I am happy to comply with the council's requirements in order to carry out the role to which I have been appointed. Even though I have had a recent criminal record check for a passport application, I have also started the process for my council roles as we agreed.

Please would you change the title on my registration form from Children's Champion to Youth Advocate.

I have done the same work in the same kind of role for the Boy Scouts and recently with internet security. It is a very difficult job and can be "VERY" sensitive. I will need your support.

Dave xx

CHAPTER THIRTEEN

"Knowing what's right doesn't mean much unless you do what's right." Theodore Roosevelt

The monthly Finance Committee meeting comes round and Hilary is on top form in the chair. She's got an easier, smaller committee than most. It's mainly us FUC reformers who are interested in the council's money matters. We are motivated by all our good ideas to spend money so we need to know how much we've got in the kitty. I don't think it's ever been like this before in the history of Fartlebury Magna. The parish council always saw its role as guarding the money, spending as little as possible within the community. As individuals, the councillors hated spending any money: they believed in thrift. Fishface changed auditors when one commented that the money raised through council tax was supposed to be spent on doing things for residents. The Old Guard saw their role as care-taking (only the emphasis wasn't on the care). Hilary makes a good chair of Finance and she doesn't believe in thrift. She is good at counting beans. She had lots of practice as the Church play group leader.

The only challenges at the meeting come from Penny Finkless (I reflect that she should be re-named Neverfink) and from old-timer Evelyn Harse (Harse by name and Harse by nature). Evelyn is a man - like the writer Evelyn Waugh. He is always going on about waste – not in the sense of dustbins, but he always talks about 'prudence with the public purse'. He thinks he is cracking a fine joke because Prudence is his wife's name, but everyone has heard it 300 times. I think if we had an actual public purse we would all be dipping into it much more. Up until now it has pretty much been the council's private purse for them to grip tightly to their communal chest because they fear being mugged. I don't know where the money goes. I look at the figures but I don't understand how we can spend so much and achieve so little. I know one reason is that Fartlebury Magna Parish Council has not kept up with investment in infra-structure. We've got street lights dating from the 1950s, playgrounds where no child wants to play. All around us villages have got multi-games walls and zip wires; all Fartlebury Magna's got is a bouncy duck and two rusty old swings. What we have got is new brooms and plans to put in some safety surfacing to comply with legislation. It's been a hard fight but we've won it. Evelyn regards every penny spent as an outrage against common decency.

"You lot want to spend thousands of pounds on playgrounds!" He is exasperated. "Children don't even vote. They don't pay taxes, so if we've got any money we should be spending it on adults."

There are lots of grunts of approval from the porcine members around the table.

Hilary decides to let this go. "The cheapest quote is £40,000 for the kind of equipment that children use nowadays."

"Can't we have a roundabout?" says Tracy, "Children love a roundabout."

"We had a Witch's Hat once," Penny says. "It had to go – it rusted away." Evelyn smiles. I know what he is thinking - he can see her in a pointy hat. "But it's never been replaced. That's my whole point," says Penny.

"No point putting in anything new," says Evelyn, "It'll only get vandalised."

We jump on this, Hilary firmly from the chair, right into the shifting sands of the other councillors' hearts and minds. It's no ordinary sandpit round here - more like a patch of quicksand, and you just can't let them drag you under.

"Actually Evelyn, the more run-down everywhere gets the more it gets vandalised. You keep somewhere nice and it gets respect."

"Huh," says Evelyn.

"It's proven by Government research," I protest. Evelyn always thinks he knows best. After all he's been a parish councillor for 35 years and his family have been in Fartlebury Magna for generations, not vandalising anything.

"We never had a playing field when I was a boy. We used to amuse ourselves by going for a walk in the fields and catching sticklebacks in the ditches."

"You call that trespass if people do that now. There isn't anywhere for them to play or just hang out with their friends," Tracy says.

"We never hung out in my day," Evelyn retorts crossly. "We never smashed up the play equipment neither."

"You just said there wasn't any," Hilary says.

"Oh no, neither there was, that's why we didn't vandalize anything."

"Of course not," I say in my most soothing voice. "You were a pillar of the community, I'm sure."

"Who are you calling a pillock?" he shouts. He's angry now and his shiny puce cheeks are deepening to chestnut. His grey eyes stand out from his grainy grey eye sockets like ping pong balls balanced in egg-cups. His temperature is rising and I can catch a whiff of very stale human rising from his tweed jacket.

"Why are you a councillor?" I asked him once.

"Gives me something to do on a Monday night. Gets me out of the bloody house. Away from the nagging wife."

I don't like Evelyn. His body odour is only one of several smelly issues I have with him.

We appoint a small group of councillors to work up some plans for the play area and bring them back to the council. We are now on Item 5 of the agenda: *To engage a web service provider.*

"Do we have three quotes?" asks Evelyn. He's lively tonight. I might have said, 'on the ball' if he wasn't so vociferously hostile to any ball games anywhere in the parish.

"Yes, here they are." Lisa passes round the photocopies she has been holding.

I don't know what she's doing for a photocopier at the moment. The glass broke on the other one and it's waiting for a repair. She couldn't offer an explanation of why it broke. Hilary says it's obvious: "How else could you break that tough glass?"

"What do you mean?" I ask innocently. "It must have had a weakness."

"She's got a weakness. Come on Katie – how do you think it got broken?"

"I have no idea."

"She sat on it, didn't she? She must have sat on it – you know – with no pants on."

"My God! Not Lisa, surely!" The penny was beginning to drop. Hilary is a woman of the world, a woman of the office anyway. She knows about such things.

"That's what people do, isn't it? How else could you break a piece of flat glass like that?"

"She doesn't weigh much."

"More than a sheet of A4 though!"

We have three quotes before us. Evelyn asks, "What does our web expert say?"

"He recommends Cam-Cam Services."

"Has he got an interest?" asks Tracy. She has been on the Code of Conduct training with me so she knows that if he has shares in the company, or any other financial involvement, or is friends with the director, he will have to declare an interest. There are two types of interest as far as the council is concerned: personal or prejudicial. "Is it prejudicial?"

"If he's got to work with it and he knows what he needs..." begins Evelyn, but Hilary sweeps him under the carpet.

"He knows the market, I admit," she says, "but we have to..."

"Go with who he recommends," says Evelyn tetchily finishing her sentence. I think he is wondering what the market has to do with it. Pineapples and cheap socks. That's what they have at the market.

"The cheapest quote and the one recommended are one and the same. It is in fact Cam-Cam Services," says Hilary. "All in favour?"

We obediently raise our hands and eyebrows. Lisa smiles sweetly (two lumps of sugar).

"Unanimous," she says with deep satisfaction.

We move to Item 6: *to agree emergency payment of invoice for repair of gas pipe at Fartlebury-under-Marsh.*

This is a new one on me. "May I ask how this has come about?"

Hilary gives me a sweet smile too, like a baby filling its nappy.

"As you know, we normally allow six weeks for payment of invoices, but the contractor, GasCo, agreed to do the work only if we paid within fourteen days."

"Why?"

"A former delay in payment, apparently." Hilary is looking pointedly at Lisa.

"We're black-listed?" I ask. I can see Hilary is enjoying herself so I go on, "But anyway, why is the council paying for the repair of a gas pipe?"

Hilary grins widely this time. I don't quite get why she is enjoying this so much.

"Lisa engaged a contractor as usual to put up the Fartlebury-under-Marsh Christmas tree. You remember we agreed to change the position of it after a complaint last year. He used a large spike to make the hole and – guess what – he struck not oil but gas."

Hilary smiles wickedly at me and I rather think Lisa has turned a little pinker.

“It was very inconvenient for the old people in the flats too. They had the gas off just when they wanted to cook their dinners,” Hilary says gleefully.

“Oh dear.” I take the tone from Hilary. “So how much has this little escapade cost?”

“Seven hundred pounds.”

“Seven hundred pounds? We could have bought seven Christmas trees!”

“The contractor must be insured for such events,” chips in Evelyn.

“Apparently not,” says Hilary with another smile.

Lisa butts in, “May I explain, Chairman?” She continues without waiting for a reply, “I asked Mr Cook, who dug the hole, if he had public liability insurance because it’s in our Financial Regulations and that is the procedure I follow. He showed me a certificate. But now it turns out that he isn’t covered for digging holes and breaking gas pipes. It isn’t his normal line of work.”

“Which is....?”

“Hmm, he’s a lorry driver.”

“Lisa!” I can’t conceal my surprise and consternation.

“Well, he’ll just have to pay out of his own pocket then,” says Evelyn.

“I agree,” I say.

“We have to pay GasCo who repaired the damage though,” says Hilary. “We must do that.”

“No, he can pay.” Evelyn looks at me. He’s throwing down his gauntlet.

“I propose we pay the contractor and Lisa then tries to recover at least some of the money from Mr Cook.” That seems a good compromise to me.

“All in favour?” snaps Hilary, and the hands of everyone except Evelyn shoot up. It’s nearly 9 o’clock and tonight is the second episode of *Murder in the Malverns*.

The tip of my tongue is crowded with words like, *‘Get a move on Hilary.’*

***

“So why was it so funny about the gas pipe?” I ask. It’s the morning after the meeting and Hilary and I are on our way to a site meeting at the cemetery. Fartlebury Magna has its own little cemetery. It’s not neat and tidy like most cemeteries because Fartlebury Magna Parish Council doesn’t have any tradition of spending money on maintenance. From what I hear, many of the cemetery’s long-term residents are restlessly tossing and turning because the grass isn’t cut regularly and the hedges are unbearably ragged. We are meeting some other councillors there.

“It’s such a hoot, Katie! Didn’t you realise? It was all to do with Dave Tripswitch, the whole business with the tree. Mavis Wilson and he cooked it up. Cooked it up!” she shrieks.

I smile weakly. “More like ‘cocked it up.’”

“Yes, but it’s Mr Cook, see, cooked it up...”

“Oh!” That’s the best I can do in the circumstances.

“They decided Fartlebury-under-Marsh deserves to have the same wonderful Christmas display and as much money spent on it as in Fartlebury Magna itself. Dave said he’d find someone to put a big tree up. He found Mr Cook.”

“Who, it seems, wasn’t even insured.” I laugh, but I’m not sure that it’s funny.

We arrive at the six-foot, wrought-iron cemetery gates. These are now unlocked so people can visit the graves of their loved ones. Fishface and his crew used to keep them locked. They didn’t like young people using THEIR cemetery as a short-cut to school. They didn't like old people using it to get to the day centre either. In fact they didn't like people using it full stop, wearing out their tarmac (which cost them tuppence ha'penny in 1936.)

A recently bereaved old gentleman who wanted to put flowers on his wife's grave but was too frail to walk round the long way, got so desperate that he climbed up on the railings to jump over, but he caught the pocket of his jacket on the spear head of the iron railings. Clothes used to be much better made in the days when his tweed jacket had been put together, so it held him fast, suspended in time and place like fruit in jelly until his neighbour came along. She had the presence of mind to go home and fetch her camera before she helped him down, so the local papers made a good story of it and the majority of parish councillors suddenly decided to over-rule Fishface (which they enjoyed anyway) and allow local people free access to their dead without let or hindrance.

Tracy and Penny are already there at the cemetery gates. They have been nosing around. "Are we waiting for anyone else?" I ask.

"Evelyn said he'd come if he didn't have to go shopping with his wife."

"Well, we needn't wait," I say, because I think he is bound to be going shopping. Maybe not just bound but manacled.

I give the background to the meeting.

"We're here because something has happened to the gravel area of the Garden of Remembrance. Some of you will remember Mrs Baloney coming to the council meeting to complain."

We look at it. The gravel area is no longer a gravel area. The tide of grass has swept in and covered the stones with grass.

"What happened here is that Roger, our former hired hand, put a lot of grass seed down before he left our employment."

"Why would anyone do that?"

"It seems Dave Tripswitch had some kind of argument with him about the state of the cemetery and ordered him to get on his hands and knees and get the weeds out of this gravel."

"Really?" says Penny. "Surely councillors can't give instructions to staff?"

"No, Penny," I respond in my best ironically patient voice, "they can't, but Dave Tripswitch either didn't know or didn't care about that."

"What's to be done?"

What indeed? I have been considering the options for weeks. "We can let it go to grass and cut it. Or we can apply weedkiller."

"No you can't," says Andrew Hall. "You have to have a licence to do that on public land."

"We can get a contractor to apply weedkiller. One with a licence."

"Not Mr Cook," says Tracy with a grin.

"We could sue Roger," Penny says.

"That would cost more than it's worth," Tracy frowns.

"We could make Dave Tripswitch weed it! It's all his fault!"

There! We look at each other. We are getting it off our corporate chest. He annoyed our handyman and caused this trouble, and he recommended a cheapskate uninsured lorry driver who put a hole in a gas pipe. What can you do? He's just a volunteer giving his time for the community. Bless him.

We decide to get our new cemetery contractor to deal with it. Or rather, as nothing can be decided outside of committee, we decide to recommend that course of action to the next committee meeting. By the time the poor man gets to do the job, the grass will have grown under everyone's feet, including Mrs Baloney's. That's the price of democracy.

“’Bout bloody time you lot sorted this place out!” shouts an elderly man from the safety of his mobility scooter as he shoots past us, Union Jack waggling behind his back. “Bloody disgrace!”

“Well, we’re trying,” I shout after his shadow.

Shortly after the site meeting we have an item on the council agenda to discuss the problem of people creating a new path between the cemetery and the churchyard. The churchyard is consecrated ground and belongs to the church. The parish council bought the land next door to the churchyard when Phil Jenkins’ dad sold off bits of the farm. It’s not consecrated. In fact it’s in an unholy mess. God knows how I’ve tried to get it tidied up but it’s like pushing water uphill with a rake to get the groundsman to do anything. There’s no precedent for it either. All the water flows downhill in Fartlebury Magna, or else stagnates in unwholesome pools.

Like many old parish churches, St. John’s can be approached by parishioners from every side and public footpaths run through the graveyard in all directions. They are mainly used by the people living on the Jenkins Road housing estate off Vicarage Close. Not satisfied with the historic paths, children and their grandparents, since the gates were unlocked, have been making an unofficial pathway between the graves and have broken down the old rickety picket fence to cut off a corner.

“That’s why we kept the gate locked,” says Fishface smugly from the public gallery, where he sits to taunt us. There isn’t a gallery, of course. This is the village hall. There isn’t much public either, as most people have more sense and better things to do on a Monday night, like putting out their wheely bins or spitting in a ditch. “We didn’t have all that, letting people cut through, when I was chairman of the council.”

“They never walked through there when it was Frank Jenkins’ orchard, neither, did they?” says Evelyn. “He saw off the scrumpers with his shot gun. Shot one of his own sheep once. Thought it was a kid from the school taking his apples. He was upset, he was. Killing his own sheep. You get fond of your own sheep. Bloody kids."

Penny gasps. Phil gives a coy smile, thinking of the fine example his father set.

I need to get them back on track, but once they find a topic they like, they fly off in all directions as if they've hit the proverbial fan. "What can we do to deter people from walking across the graves? Has anyone got any positive ideas?"

"Put up a fence," says Tracy.

"We could put up a notice asking people to keep to the paths," says Hilary.

"Or make a big six foot hole, like a new grave, right in the way, so the buggers fall down it," says Nigel with a wicked grin. "We could pile it up with wreaths and bouquets of flowers to make it look right." (Nigel's sister is a florist.)

"I don't think we should do that," I say mildly.

"May I speak, Chairman?" says Lisa. "You can't make a decision tonight because it didn't say on the agenda that a decision was to be made. Why don't I get some quotes for a fence and we can put it back on the next agenda?"

She's brilliant, that Lisa.

Old Jim has his hand up. "A six foot fence?"

"It's not Colditz," says Hilary. "We don't want it to look like a prison camp."

"It's no bloody holiday camp neither," snarls Jim. "My mum and dad are in there and I don't want kids walking all over 'em."

"They're nowhere near the unofficial path that's being made," says Phil.

"Ooh, aren't they?" Jim sounds unsure. "My niece deals with all that, flowers and Christmas wreaths and all that." (Nigel's sister is Jim's second cousin.)

"I think a six foot fence is a bit over the top," I say, trying to bring them back to the point.

"They kids'll all be over the top if it's any lower," says Jim.

Lisa interrupts again, "Excuse me, Chairman, may I speak?"

I nod. "If we put up a higher fence than the existing one, Chairman, we'll have to get planning consent."

"Who would check up on us?" asks Phil Jenkins, his cheeks as ripe as the cider apples in his grandfather's barn.

"It's not a question of whether we get caught," I say, feeling only slightly that I'm coming across a bit high and mighty. "We have to do the right thing and be seen to do the right thing."

"We only need a four foot fence," someone says quietly while I'm not looking.

"Five."

"Four foot's plenty."

"Five."

"Enough," I say. "I'll go and measure it before the next meeting. We won't need planning permission to replace the existing like for like. Let's move to the next item."

"Would you ask the councillors to vote in favour of deferring the item to the next meeting?" asks Lisa politely. Of course I bloody would.

***

I'm in the churchyard with Evelyn. He's tidying up his wife's grave and his parents' graves and some graves of his old cousins and great uncles and great aunts and grandparents – in fact virtually the whole south-east corner is the Harse Kingdom of the Dead. I've gone to look at the fence. He follows me, weaving between the gravestones like the old wino he resembles, except he is sober.

"If the fence is only four foot tall, they'll just climb over it," he says.

"That's all the existing fence is," I say, producing my tape measure to give evidence.

"That's five foot," he says.

"No," I say, only mildly irritated. "It's just over 48 inches. It's 124 centimetres. That's four feet."

Evelyn considers this. "It's a five foot fence though."

Back in the village hall next month we have an item '*to repair or replace the fence at the cemetery at a cost not exceeding £1000.*' When we reach the item Evelyn jumps in with the speed and alacrity of an antelope, but less grace. "The fence can't be repaired. It's rotten and the posts have gone. We need a new one. Did the clerk get some quotes?"

With a nod to me, Lisa reads them out, not giving away any information about the contractors who have drawn up the quotes. That's important because if the councillors knew who was pitching for the job, the Old Guard would be related to them, or know them from their schooldays and hate them. The Old Boys Network thrives in the countryside, just as it does in the higher echelons of Government and Industry. It's just that the Fartlebury Magnatites haven't been further than the village school and the lack of choice in partners means they all tend to be inter-related as well as best friends. Best friends apart from the families that feud, that is.

Evelyn's family, for example, all have a bright, florid face and sticky-out ears. You can pick them out all through the ages, from babies wailing in their car seats outside the post office, uniformed school children darting across the High Street, monosyllabic teenagers drinking lager in the car park and so on right through the Seven Ages of Man up to the wizened old folks sitting on the lawn at Corset Court Residential Care Home, with their streams of look-alike visitor-relatives and their loudly reprimanded children all called names like

Brendan, Bradley, Frankie and Kayleigh. They look so alike that when Windy sees a young woman in the High Street, he says to me, "She's an 'arse."

I am quite shocked. Windy doesn't usually use such coarse terminology, and I can't think what she might have done to offend him. Once I have seen her bright facial colouring and her ears however, I know she is not necessarily an arse - although she could be - but a Harse.

"For goodness sake, Windy," I say, "watch your diction."

Evelyn's family don't like the Iley family. I'm not sure how this arose, and I don't know if Evelyn knows. It's good enough for him that his father had no truck (or horse and cart) with the Ileys and neither will he, in honour of his father. His grandson Ben had a soft spot for Kylie Iley but they put paid to that by tying him to the bed every night for a few months.

"Is that a way to honour the dead then?" I asked provocatively once, when Evelyn said he didn't speak to Ileys to honour his father.

"It's one way," he said and then looked at me piteously. "You wouldn't understand, would you?"

He has a point. Maybe it is a valid way to honour your dear, departed parents, to continue their prejudice and hostility to others whether there's a reason or not. But I couldn't do it. For one thing I would end up with no-one to talk to. My mother wasn't given to warmth of feeling and she had a long memory when it came to imagined slights she had received. It didn't take much to tip her nose to the sky. In consequence I am not aware of individuals she despised; in fact her scorn seemed rather universal.

I drag my wandering mind back to the council chamber. Lisa is still reading out the quotes in meticulous detail. No names are mentioned and I see Jim trying to look at the letters from which she is reading. Periodically she lifts up the corner to shield the identity of the local tradesmen who have returned quotes in order to protect them from prejudice or advantage. Evelyn looks straight at me and clears his throat. I consider moving on without letting him speak, but now he's swallowed the frog it seems unkind.

"The quotes are all for a four foot fence," he observes nonchalantly.

I look at him in wordless wonder. "Yes," I finally say, "It's a four foot fence we need to replace."

"It's five foot," he insists coolly.

"Evelyn," I say, with a warning spear thrust I hope has passed through his liver, "it's definitely four foot. I measured it myself – and you were there."

"With one of those new-fangled tape measures what measure in metres and cents and minills, " he says, "with tiny little numbers you can't read."

One of their little foibles, these old men, is that they don't like to give in to the optician and waste their money on glasses. It's a badge of pride that they don't wear reading glasses. I don't know why they feel so proud of not being able to see anything smaller than a cow's vagina.

"I can read the numbers, Evelyn. It's a four foot fence."

"Five. It comes right up to my shoulders."

Jim pipes up, "It's five foot. My uncle Fred put that fence up when I was a lad, and I helped him. It was five foot."

I'm getting hot now and a bit dizzy. I should have worn a cardigan I could take off but I opted for something more woolly, so now I'm wearing a thick jumper to combat the chill in the room. You just never know how much hot air there is going to be, or whether it will be neutralised by the icy stares.

Lisa turns to me and whispers, "Shall we defer, Chairman?"

"Not bloody likely," I whisper a bit too loudly and rather unprofessionally. I'm losing my grip. I want to wrap a tea-towel round the lot of them and twist them hard. It's all getting away from me; they are sliding back into those terrible habits of Fishface's council, using delaying tactics and deferrals to make sure no decisions are made.

"We've already deferred it from the last meeting," I say quietly. "We need to make a decision."

Penny puts her hand up. "I don't think we should be made to rush a decision. I say we should defer it until the next meeting."

"Can we vote or not?" says Jim.

"I think it would be wise, Chairman," says Lisa, "to defer a decision until all councillors are comfortable with the requirements." She's got such a sweet smile. I can smell her toothpaste from here.

From: Dave Tripswitch
To: Katie Miller
Sent: 02 October 2004 09.47
Subject: Cemetery Management Committee

Dear Katie

I was surprised to hear that you had held another "SECRET" meeting at the cemetery. I was under the impression I was on the Cemetary Committee. This is another example of you riding roughshod over other councillors. You know I am on the committee and "VERY" interested in the cemetery, but you arranged this meeting without inviting me. This is just a friendly "WARNING" that you need to stop trying to do everything yourself.

Dave Tripswitch

Fartlebury Magna Parish Councillor, Youth Advocate, Web scientist, Web Developer, Website Manager, Computer Technologist

From: Katie Miller
To: Dave Tripswitch
Sent: 02 October 2004 10.56
Subject: Cemetery Management Committee

Hi Dave
Thank you for your email. At the last meeting of the committee it was agreed that a small group of councillors would hold a site visit and report back to the main committee. Volunteers for that group were recruited by a show of hands. Unfortunately you had left the meeting early and did not therefore have the opportunity to put your hand up on this occasion. It was not a secret meeting and its date was given in the draft minutes which you received two weeks ago.
Thank you for your interest. The group will report back to the main committee at the next meeting.
Please could you manage to find time to update the website in the next couple of weeks?

Thanks, Katie.

Up your jumper, Tripswitch.

CHAPTER FOURTEEN

"Before you start pointing fingers make sure your hands are clean."
Bob Marley

Fartlebury Magna has a cluster of garden centres around its northern perimeter. They have developed on good, fertile soil in the river valley. They were small affairs, businesses that developed out of one-man, one-dog nurseries growing their own plants and selling to local gardeners. Now a large horticultural emporium has opened with fol-de-rol and fanfares.

Fartlebury Magna Garden Centre has paved over the fertile ground to put in a car park big enough to hold two football pitches and on the rest of the plot they have built a conservatory the size of the Crystal Palace (but without the old-fashioned charm). No growing goes on here. It's just a shop front for horticultural honchos. Anything can be bought here that is remotely to do with a garden: wellies, weather vanes and water butts along with solar lights, string and secateurs. It's what the tourist office calls a destination. Coaches come from the Midlands to visit what is actually a department store set in a glass house. It's where I go to buy clothes and shoes, toys and books, cards and gifts and the paper to wrap them in. The shop has fresh cakes, pies and bread, meat and veg. It's a useful place for Fartlebury Magna residents but resented by its small shopkeepers, whose stock and staff cannot compete with that kind of style.

I've had a personal invitation for coffee from the new Managing Director. They're going to put in a planning application to increase the car parking even further into the fields. They are planning to build a restaurant, ice-cream parlour, roller skating rink and indoor playground and extend their patio centre. She would like to show me round her empire and talk about how she could help the parish council as she is under the misapprehension that we might be able to support their application.

I announce my intention to accept the invitation at the Planning Committee. Mavis Wilson has given herself a make-over and raises her thin-line drawn-on eyebrows. Her face looks like an emoticon on its side. She says, "I don't think you should go alone."

"I'm not in any danger!" vollies off the top of my head.

"I think you should have a witness to any discussions," she says, looking sternly at the table.

I let it go. I don't want an argument but I'm not turning up for a coffee and chat with a minder in tow. I'm not having Mavis Wilson tell me what to do either. Anyway, I've accepted the invitation, but I won't mention that just now.

I wash my hair and cycle off to the plush office of the Managing Director where we've agreed to meet. I surreptitiously brush my hair outside the door, looking round for CCTV. For some reason it's a shameful thing to be caught brushing your hair, almost as bad as picking your nose. The eager beaver rushes up and opens the door wide and shakes my hand as if its constituent parts need homogenizing. It's all very amicable. I'm not interested in their expanding empire but she is offering to give us a Christmas tree, some old chairs and benches for the village hall and makes hints about other stuff. I know my place. I'm non-committal. I will just take the offers back to the table. Not my delicious cappuccino though. I down that with great enjoyment, slurping up the foam and leaving a milky moustache round my mouth. I help myself to a chocolate biscuit. Mavis would have enjoyed this.

As I'm leaving, mounting my trusty but rusty old bike, she extends her forefinger and points to the highest point of her territory. "We've got a webcam up there; it shows live pictures of what's going on. Fantastic views all over the garden centre and the village."

I nod, showing a minimum measure of faux interest.

"I see you're trying to modernise the council, Mrs Miller. Why don't we set up a link on our websites? You could link to our webcam and have live pictures on the parish website, and in turn we could put a link to yours. I was looking at it – it's at www.fartleburymagna.net, isn't it? It's a very attractive front page, but – a little tip from the world of business – it is important to keep websites up-to-date."

I smile. I don't understand what would be the point in a link (or even if there is a point) but it's probably a nice offer. "Good idea. You could go through our clerk if you want to get things started."

Back home briefly, stuffing my face with crisps and chocolate standing in the kitchen, I think I should let Dave Tripswitch know. He'd like to liaise with them. It'd make him feel important and he can look into it all. I haven't got time to contact him just now. I've got to go and meet Mr Jones who has complained about the siting of a litter bin in full view of his house. Meanwhile Mrs Efficiency in the Garden Centre is jumping in with two feet; she has copied me in to an email she has sent to Lisa. It's only later I realise that she is a busy person so she deals with things as soon as they appear. Either that or she's bored.

From: Mariondrinkwater@garden-centre.org.uk
To: Clerk@fartleburymagna.net
Cc Sarah Jones; Robin Knight
Sent: 13 October 2004 10.23
Subject: website links

Dear Madam
Following a meeting with Katie Miller, Council Chairperson, I would like to progress the link from our webcam and an advertisement on your website with a direct link to our website. Please would you let me know how to proceed.
Regards,
Marion Drinkwater, Chief Executive, The Garden Centre plc

I had better let Lisa know straight away. I'm a busy person too (either that or I'm bored).

From: Katie Miller
To: clerk@fartleburymagna.net
Sent: 13 October 2004 11.36
Subject: Marion Drinkwater, Fartlebury Magna Garden Centre

Hi Lisa
Had a nice meeting with Marion Drinkwater. She is waiting to hear from the football club refurbishment committee about a date for their next meeting so she can attend. I think she might help out with some of the costs! She had attempted to attend the planning committee meeting last night at the village hall but no-one had told her it had been changed to tonight. In future if we change meeting dates I think it would be wise to put up a notice on the door advising of the change. She felt the council should have known she was planning to attend. She stood outside in the rain for fifteen minutes.
She also said that she would be willing to host a council meeting in their conference room and give all council members complimentary drinks. It might be nice to take her up on this offer, although I don't know how we would stand with public attendance. What do you think?
Thanks, Katie.

From: Mariondrinkwater@garden-centre.org.uk
To: Katie Miller
Sent: 13 October 2004 10.27
Subject: Katie Miller

Great to meet you today. I have chased the webcam installation date. It could lead to something really interesting.I look forward to welcoming you all to Fartlebury Magna Garden Centre for a future meeting, when the conference room will be provided to you free of charge.

Regards, Marion

Unfortunately the clerk seems to have temporarily lost normal service. I hope it will be resumed as soon as possible. She sends my new mate Marion a rather unhelpful email.

From: clerk@fartleburymagna.net
To: Marion Drinkwater
Cc Katie Miller
Sent: 13 October 2004 11.02
Subject: re website links

Dear Ms Drinkwater

I have no knowledge of the arrangement you mention. Please contact our webmaster, Dave Tripswitch, direct on webmaster@fartleburymagna.net

Kind regards
Lisa Purfitt
Clerk to Fartlebury Magna Parish Council

From: Katie Miller
To: Mariondrinkwater@garden-centre.org.uk
Sent: 13 October 2004 11.04
Subject: RE Katie Miller

Hi Marion

It was good to meet you and have a look round. Many thanks for inviting me. I hope the rest of the project goes according to plan. I will let our webmaster know that you will be looking to put the Garden Centre webcam link on the www.fartleburymagna.net site.
Best wishes, Katie

Actually Lisa must have already let Dave know about this idea. Apparently, she says, he isn't very happy about it. He says it could damage the website, or involve us in extra costs. I don't understand the technical details but I can't see what all the fuss is about. I asked him to look into it. He just could have said no if he thought it was impossible. He has asked for a separate email to be sent to him about it. I think he's just chucking his weight about. (He's not so thin now. Must be all those pork scratchings.) Goodness knows what he's making all this fuss for.

From: Sarahjones@garden-centre.org.uk
To: Dave Tripswitch
Cc: Marion Drinkwater
Sent: 08 October 2007 09.25
Subject: Fartlebury Magna Webcam

Hi Dave
As discussed, below are the html details for the Fartlebury Magna Web Cam.
http.//www.gardencentre.org.uk/pages/thegardencentre.checkourview.
Any problems please let me know.
Thanks,
Sarah Jones

How to Embed Web Cam Viewer into your website.
Web Cam Viewer is designed to be embedded into your own website. It allows visitors to your site to view live images from your camera and browse snapshots from the previous 24 hours. To enable Web Cam Viewer on your site just copy the HTML tag below and paste it into your webpage.

<script language = "javascript" type= "text/javascript"

From: Dave Tripswitch
To: Katie Miller
Sent: 19 October 2004 09.27
Subject: Complaints

Dearest Katie

I am sorry but I have had another two 'informal' complaints about the way you are working. Rather than being dragged into the politics behind the scenes, I considered it better to email you once more. Other councillors "ARE" concerned about the way you are treating other councillors. I can't support you if you won't listen.
Under these circumstances I will be taking an autumn sabbatical "suspending my role" during the ten weeks up until Christmas to spend more time with my family and look after my health.

Dave Tripswitch,
Fartlebury Magna Parish councillor, Youth Advocate, Web master, Web designer, Computer technologist, IT architect.

Crumbs, he is over-sensitive. Rather than having a sabbatical, he should get down the library and brush up on his ignorance.

I need to go to the office. It's ridiculous that I should feel so reticent about it. I'm Chair of the bloody council for goodness' sake! Why shouldn't I go to the office? It's just childish for me to feel intimidated by the clerk. Off I go, these rehearsed arguments in hand-to-hand combat with all my apprehensiveness.

When I arrive at the door, I put my hand on the smooth stainless steel handle and somehow freeze, unable to force my way in against the clerk's strong will. My pause lengthens to five seconds and suddenly I am aware of strange noises inside the office - noises that don't belong in an office.

I can hear Lisa's girly giggles mingling with the scraping of furniture and the deeper tones of a man's voice. I can hardly burst in and ask what's going on, can I? I feel as if I'm an intruder, an interloper, as out of place as a pig at a cocktail party. After a few minutes bent double with my ear to the keyhole I feel I am doing my back no good.

On my way home I meet Hilary.

"Been to the office?" she asks cheerfully.

"Yes, well, no."

"Yes AND no?"

"I went down there but I couldn't bring myself to go in. It sounded as if Lisa was busy."

"Busy?"

"It sounded as if someone else was in the office with her."

"You're the Chair, Katie. Since when does she have the right to privacy in the office?"

"OK." I'm full of resignation."But I'm going home now." I'm doing nothing about the rising flood waters. The defences have always worked before and anyway I've got to find something to cook for tea.

On the pavement outside our house Windy is talking to his friend Mike Cannon who has drawn up in his car and has his head out of the driver's window. I hear him ask Windy, "That guy who does the council website – Dave Tripswitch, isn't it?"

"Yeah, that's right," says Windy. "Do you know him? He doesn't seem very well known in the village. No-one seems to know where he comes from."

"No, I don't know him, not really, but I know who you mean. He was the guy whose car got beaten up by Johnny Henchman and his mates a few years back. Sorry, I shouldn't have given the game away. Forget I said that." Mike winks, "But we've had to caution him too, for trying to sell wristwatches in the pub. We thought they were stolen goods but we couldn't prove anything. Couldn't pin a thing on him. He's a bit slippery."

"Slimy, I'd call it," I say, getting off my bike.

Windy's face clouds over. "He's a nasty piece of work, Mike."

"Yes," says Mike, "I can believe it. I don't think anyone went after him with a baseball bat because he's a nice guy."

"He's been very difficult about the council website," Windy says, and I join them and nod in agreement. They both nod back. We are all too engrossed with Tripswitch's character to stop for pleasantries.

"I stopped to have a word with him in the High Street and he threatened me," Windy says.

"He didn't exactly threaten you," I say. I'm only trying to be fair.

"No?" Windy snaps back angrily. "It felt like a threat to me." He then goes on to tell Mike about the incident when Dave squared up to him in the High Street and I throw in the possibility that Dave had seen me on the zebra crossing and tried to run me over.

Mike puts his hand on my arm. "If you have any more trouble with him, you let me know."

"It's too subtle," I protest. "He's too clever. He leaves you feeling it's all in your head. We can't prove anything."

“Sometimes justice can only be done if you take the law into your own hands. We can prove what we need to prove,” he says. I think his left eye is twitching.

Mike looks directly at Windy and repeats, “If there’s any hint of trouble from him, I want to know. You let me know Windy.”

I feel quite cheered up. We can have the left-over meat from Sunday with sautée potatoes and a can of baked beans.

CHAPTER FIFTEEN

"Betrayal is the only truth that sticks." Arthur Miller

I think things are going rather well this week. After the full council meeting, Scarecrow Jenkins himself shuffles up to me. He looks like a day-centre patient in check wool slippers but he seems to have found his tongue to ask me how things are going. This seems a bit out of character but I'm glad relations are thawing. I tell him I think people have got over their various problems and issues and if we can sort out the website most or all of the things that have been troubling me will be resolved.

Phil smiles. "I don't know why you can't just get him to do it. He's supposed to be the manager of the website after all."

"It's not quite as easy as that," I say, "but I will keep trying."

"It's a pity Lisa doesn't find it easy to work with you. She seems to get on well with Dave."

"Mmm." Doesn't she just?

***

Tom has re-surfaced after deep immersion in his seasonal hobbies. I've never found out what they are because I am too busy with my venture into local politics. He is a good man though, committed to more local causes than most people could even name. If he's not rattling a tin and selling you a poppy, he's helping out the Brownies or sweeping the pavement outside his house. Now he's active helping the council too (and not just by sweeping pavements).

From: Tom Waterman
To: Katie Miller
Sent: 10 November 2004 09.05
Subject: website

Hi Katie

As you know I am part of the team of people who volunteered to help with the parish council website. It was agreed in July that we should meet 'soon' and Dave Tripswitch would give us tuition in our specific roles. It is disappointing that no meeting has been called and no progress has been made. Is there anything that you can do to hasten things along?

Warm regards, Tom

From: Katie Miller
To: Tom Waterman
Cc: clerk@fartleburymagna.net
Sent: 10 November 2004 18.22
Subject: RE website

Hi Tom

I share your frustration at the situation and hope to be seeing Dave Tripswitch about it later this week. I am sure the clerk will be in touch soon when we have a date for the meeting.

Kind regards, Katie.

From: Katie Miller
To: Dave Tripswitch
Sent: 11 November 2004 19.45
Subject: website

Hi Dave

I hope you are well and have had a good and restful holiday. The newly recruited web team is raring to go and looking forward to a meeting. Please would you arrange one soon?
Hope to see you on Thursday at the Cemetery Committee.

Thanks, Katie.

***

At nine o'clock on the dot the phone rings. I am just settling down with a glass of wine to watch *Murder in the Malverns*. I answer it reluctantly, partly because I am always afraid it will be Dave. It is Jim.

"I wanna know about these new-fangled web things. You keep goin' on and you think Fartlebury Magna needs to 'ave one, but I don't understand why village folk would want worldwide webs. We'm just a little parish, eh? Why'd we need any links with the world, eh?"

I am very patient. I explain that people can sit at home and look up the minutes of the council meeting and then email the clerk. "They can see what decisions we're taking on their behalf."

"Why should we help 'em do that? They can come to the meetings if they want to know what's goin' on, and they can speak in Public Speaking Time if they've got something to say."

"Not everyone can come out in the evenings. What if they've been at work all day and can't get a babysitter?"

"They can ask their parents to babysit."

"Not everyone has their parents living locally, Jim."

"That right?" I am not at all sure whether he is being sarcastic, or has never thought about other people's lifestyles.

Windy comes in and sees that I am trapped on the phone explaining how the internet works and that lots of people now have computers in their homes, so he kindly sets my favourite programme to record.

Half an hour later, just as I sit down again to watch a nice relaxing murder, the phone rings again. I reach it just as it stops ringing. I look at the number as it fades away. It's Penny Finkless. I suppose I had better ring her back. I put my glass down, not wishing to create another burgundy patch on the parquet, nor to taint the wine with sourness.

"Oh Katie," she says, obviously surprised, "I thought you were out. Well, have you looked at your emails lately?"

"Not since this morning."

"Well, I suggest you do. I don't want to say more but I hate things going on behind people's backs and someone has sent an email to all the councillors about you, and you ought to know about it."

She won't be pressed, so I go to the computer and press the ON switch instead. I will leave my wine in the other room.

I click on Outlook Express and the emails fall in, like shit from a seagull. One email is particularly corrosive and begins to etch itself into my eyeballs.

From: Dave D Tripswitch
To: Katie Miller
Sent: 19 November 2007 20.12
Subject: Formal complaint

Dearest Katie
With the deepest regrets please find the attached letter outlining my formal complaint.
Best regards,
Dave Tripswitch (Councillor)
"Dedicated to the people of Fartlebury Magna"

His email to Lisa is attached.

From: Dave Tripswitch
To: clerk@fartleburymagna.net
Cc: Trixiemann@corsetdailypost.co.uk
Sent: 23 November 2004 18.16
Subject: Katie Miller – formal complaint

Dear Lisa
Please print off and send this letter to all councillors as hard copy and send to the Standards Board and retain on file as my complaint to the Standards Board about Katie Miller, who has brought this council into disrepute by giving an unfair commercial advantage to Fartlebury Magna Garden Centre. She has broken the "CODE" of Conduct and exceeded her "ROLE" as Chairman.
Yours kindly, Dave

The letter to the Standards Board for England is attached. My intestines are working like an electric screwdriver as I read it:

Dear Sirs
I am writing to make a formal complaint about the Chairman of Fartlebury Magna Parish Council.

In the short time I have been a councillor (nearly a year) I have received complaints from several other councillors because of Councillor Miller's style of management.

She undermines the work of other councillors and bullies the clerk. I have often had to comfort the clerk after she has been reduced to tears by Councillor. Miller.

Councillor. Miller agreed to place a web link of Fartlebury Magna Garden Centre on the parish council website without any consultation. She acted without authority and gave the Garden Centre an unfair commercial advantage and accepted corporate entertainment without declaring it.

As a veteran of the Falklands War I am aware of the need for complete "INTEGRITY" and honesty and for this reason I regrettably have to make this complaint.

Yours faithfully

David D Tripswitch

Fartlebury Magna Parish Councillor, Web Master, Web scientist, Computer Architect, Computer Technician and Youth Advocate.

I'm reeling now I've stood up from the computer. Literally reeling: jigging and jogging about, turning this way and that like one of those wooden ballerinas in a jewellery box. How on earth has this happened to me? I know I won't get any sleep tonight. My head is full of nonsense.

At 8.55 the next morning, full of speculation but empty of my porridge, I pick up the phone and dial the office. Good job we haven't got caller display. Lisa answers in a girlie voice, "Hello? Fartlebury Magna Parish Council. Lisa Purfitt speaking."

"I've just received a copy of a complaint to the Standards Board about me. What do you know about this?"

"Me? Nothing!"

"Honestly Lisa?"

"Honestly. It's nothing to do with me."

"Dave Tripswitch sent the letter to you for forwarding to councillors – like you're his PA! Why didn't you ring me up Lisa? Didn't you think your first loyalty was to me?" I dropped my voice to a more-in-sorrow-than-in-anger tone.

"It's nothing to do with me. I tried to stop him going to the Standards Board." Several pennies drop at once, like the change in a faulty vending machine.

"Well, you did know then! If you tried to stop him you knew!" My throat suddenly seizes up; I'm overwrought, overwound. "It will be a disaster for the council," I add in a squeak.

"I know. But it's nothing to do with me."

I don't know how to say goodbye so I just hang up. I've got to do something. I rush to the computer which is sleeping quietly on its desk. The fury of my fingers on its keyboard make angry clicks but Windy isn't here to rescue me from myself so he doesn't come running. I'll send an open email to Lisa and make sure my colleagues see what she has done.

From: Katie Miller
To: clerk@fartleburymagna.net
Cc: undisclosed recipients
Sent: 25 November 2004 09.03
Subject: FW: Formal complaint
Importance: High

Lisa
I think it is unfortunate to say the least that you have chosen to forward this letter to other councillors. I am surprised that you as a professional clerk have taken this stance against the council's elected chair without even discussing it with me or giving me the opportunity

to refute these ridiculous allegations. I was disappointed that when I rang you, you denied your involvement.

I do not understand why you did not inform Councillor Tripswitch of the council's internal grievance procedure instead of involving outside bodies. As you know, it would be normal practice to bring things up face-to-face and deal with them within the council before going to outside agencies. This is part of our Grievance Procedure.

I would be grateful if you would in due course let me know the Standards Board's response to the complaint. It will be a sad day for Fartlebury Magna Parish Council to have all this in the press.

In the meantime I would be glad of your explanation as to how this situation has arisen, and why you did not bring it to my attention before forwarding a complaint to the Standards Board on behalf of one councillor. I would have thought he should have done this himself, without implicating you and your 'impartiality' as clerk to the council. Katie.

From: Katie Miller
To: Dave Tripswitch
Sent: 25 November 2004 11.18
Subject: Formal Complaint

Dave
I wish you had not gone to the Standards Board with these unfounded allegations. I didn't know you had a problem with me agreeing to a website link. The first I knew about it was your formal letter of complaint. You never brought it to council. You didn't have to take it to the Standards Board. You can be disappointed with a chairperson without making up lies about them. You've made FMPC a laughing stock. I hope you realise what you've done.
Katie

From: Dave Tripswitch
To: Katie Miller
Sent: 26 November 2004 09.35
Subject: Formal complaint

I have been advised not to exchange too many emails. It is better to let the formal channels resolve the issues.
Best wishes
Dave

Windy is getting out of the car. I run out and fling my arms round his neck. It's hit me now, the raw emotion like a rotten egg thrown in my face. I'm sobbing.

"Dave Tripswitch has made a complaint about me to the Standards Board for England."

"What about? No-one'll take it seriously."

"It says I gave the garden centre an unfair commercial advantage. It makes out I took back-handers!."

"What?" Windy explodes. "As if they need the help of the parish council to carry on expanding their empire? I don't think so!"

"He's sent it to every councillor, and the clerk."

"Oh God, Katie. Everyone who knows you will know it's rubbish." He gives me a nice little squeeze that makes me feel things are not so bad. "We'll sort it out, old girl."

Two days later the local paper carries an article on page 3, illustrated by an awful photo of me they took clandestinely at the zebra crossing opening event.

CORSET DAILY POST 3 December 2004
STANDARDS BOARD INVESTIGATES PARISH CHAIRMAN
By Trixie Mann

The Government Watchdog that oversees standards of conduct in public life, the Standards Board for England, has received a complaint about Katie Miller, Chairman of Fartlebury Magna Parish Council.

The complaint was made by Dave Tripswitch, who has only been a councillor for nine months. He alleges that Councillor Miller agreed to place a weblink of Fartlebury Magna Garden Centre on the parish council website, without consulting the parish council. He alleges that she "agreed to an issue" with "commercial" implications because she agreed to place an advertisement for the garden centre on their site. Allegedly she took these decisions without appropriate technical advice. Councillor Tripswitch is the council's voluntary website manager.

An anonymous caller to the Daily Post said, "Councillor Miller has undoubtedly done a lot for the community but councillors are concerned that her style of management has become authoritarian, undemocratic and inappropriate. The correct way to make a complaint about a council chairman is through the Standards Board."

Marion Drinkwater, Managing Director of Fartlebury Magna Garden Centre, who finds herself in the centre of the row, said, "My meetings with Councillor Miller as Chairperson of Fartlebury Magna Parish Council were always completely transparent and legitimate, as have been any other meetings I have had with representatives of other local councils. Such meetings were integral to the development and success of Fartlebury Magna Garden Centre, which, following an investment of over £10 million, has helped to put this area on the map. We now employ over 250 local people and source much of the food served in our cafe from local suppliers. I look forward to continuing to work closely with all members of Fartlebury Magna parish council in future."

The Standards Board for England will now consider the complaint against Councillor Miller and make a decision within the next six weeks as to whether it requires further investigation.

Councillor Miller was unavailable for comment at the time of going to press."

Unavailable? That's a lie for a start. I've hardly moved from the spot by the phone since this haemorrhage of sense started and I can't stem the flow. When I'm a bit stronger I will dash round the village on my bike, hand-delivering personal notes to all councillors. I got the idea from Lisa who has delivered a memo to my letter box. I rip open a familiar white window envelope which has been sealed rather excessively with sellotape.

MEMO
From: Lisa Purfitt
To: All Councillors
Date: 6 December 2004

Dear Councillor
I am concerned that the Standards Board for England has been involved in Fartlebury Magna's disputes.
I would like to remind councillors that I serve the Council as a whole and my role is to look after the interests of the Council.
I advised the councillor who made the complaint to deal with this matter internally. I cannot be held accountable for advice that has not been taken.
As a Clerk I cannot become embroiled in fighting between councillors. I can only advise the Council on the procedure and keep a professional distance.

Yours sincerely
Lisa Purfitt, Clerk to Fartlebury Magna Parish Council.

CHAPTER SIXTEEN

"Everything happens for a reason, and if there's no reason, it must be tradition." *Anon*

It's St John's Christmas Bazaar today. I shall have to go and cut the proverbial tape at the village hall. I don't feel like going outside the house. If I do go out I would like to put a bag over my head. (It's not too bad – I only want to use a paper bag, not a polythene one.) I don't like the hypocrisy of presenting my calm public face when my insides are churning like a cement mixer. I could ring Hilary and ask her to go in my place but I don't want to speak to her either, not just at the moment. I'll have to soldier on. I don't know what I'm going to do yet. I want to resign, but then on the other hand – four fingers and a thumb, Tommy Cooper used to say. Two fingers to them anyway. I want to stay and sort it out. Now I'm off again, thinking, brooding, feeling too much. I should brush it off, but it's stuck to me with super-glue. It's corroding me, etching itself into me, providing an adhesion that can't easily be dissolved. I should put on a brave face and go. I can't let the church down, especially one that's so low already.

My face is actually a bit brave – it's armed with all kinds of fearful weapons, or so my children tell me. I've got the Scowl of Discontent, the Sigh of Dismay, the Crows' Feet of Anguish and the Daggers Drawn Eyes. My lips curl like cutlasses, my tongue stabs like a rusty bayonet and my teeth are grotesque grinding machines, graunching and gnashing, flashing and clashing to instil fear into my foes. My eyebrows are as hairy as those on my sister's Airedale Terrier, and they pucker up together over my nose to send off signals of gloom and doom. Oh yes, I can put on a brave face all right.

At three o'clock I pedal off to the village hall. The first person I see through the gloom is Mavis Wilson. God, no, please.

"Hi, Katie. Good turn-out. How are you feeling now?"

"Fine". I try to walk past. She puts a matronly hand on my wobbly arm.

"Don't worry. No-one else wants to be Chairman."

"That's the problem, Mavis." I think of many retorts, but I can see Thomas, the churchwarden, gesticulating to me to get onto the stage. I lift Mavis's large hand off my arm. It is like an Alsatian's front paw: big and heavy, with short digits and long claws. I make my way to the stage.

Thomas whispers some instructions and I stand poised, my false smile set on my face. I smile at Thomas. Will he be sorry I came once he knows of my fall from the heights of acclaim as Fartlebury Magna Parish Chairman; once the other councillors start talking about the dirty deeds I didn't do? Did he look at the local paper last week? Is he polite enough to ignore it? Oh, it's all more in anger than sorrow now.

From the stage I can see Mavis Wilson talking to a woman I don't know. I want to shut her up. I want to slam her mouth shut like I slam the boot of the car when I'm off on holiday. An act of finality. I smile more broadly:

"Congratulations," I say to Thomas, "I remember seeing your huge pumpkin at the Autumn Produce Show. It was magnificent."

He stares at me without returning my smile. "I didn't get a prize for my pumpkin. It was for my onions."

"Oh well. You definitely know your onions all right!"

He says, "Would you like to get on with it?" It is almost polite and he gives me a bit of a snort as he heavily descends the stage steps. I know why I got confused about the vegetables. He reminds me a bit of a pumpkin himself. He really shouldn't wear orange. I had better put on my brave face and do my public duty, but really it's a sad state of affairs if the nearest thing to a celebrity is me. I have enjoyed this kind of event in the past; it is usually an opportunity for a bit of self-congratulation, if not self-aggrandisement. Today it provides another kind of opportunity.

I shift my feet on the rickety stage and we both creak, then I blow my nose as quietly as I can. "Ladies and gentlemen." I start looking around to see if any are present. The Vicar might be called a gentleman, but Fartlebury Magna doesn't breed many. "It gives me great pleasure to be invited once again to open St John's Christmas Bazaar. At least I can get some cheap cards." This doesn't seem to have been recognized as a joke. Already children are pulling off the arms of their parents and grandparents to move them towards opportunities for lightening their purses. A small child in a buggy close to the makeshift stage renews his extreme sucking on his dummy. His action is so energetic it could be an Olympic sport next time round. My nose is itching badly. I put out my hand to rub it and somehow stick my elbow in the Vicar's face. He gives me an understanding smile, which is good because I want him to understand me.

"I expect most of you have read the stories in the paper." Quietness falls like a snowflake in June. It can't survive long so I need to make the most of it.

"The law is that until a new chairperson is elected by the council, I continue in office. I wanted to say to you today that I am very much aware that many of you voted for me and other new councillors because you wanted us to do a job. That job was to modernise the council and improve services provided by the parish council in Fartlebury Magna." I look for the sympathetic nods of agreement, but people are mainly focused on the knots in the floor-boards.

"I don't think you want me to resign, and believe me, I don't want to resign. But the actions of a minority of my fellow-councillors make it impossible for me to continue. They have made up lies about me, they have plotted and schemed behind my back. They haven't been willing to support my work in the parish. They have turned the Clerk against me. I can't work with these ..." I stop dead. What can I call them?

"..scum."

A buzz and a hum passes round the crowd and my brave face now seems more interesting than the wooden floor. The Vicar's face, always florid, is now a fetching shade of fuchsia.

"I declare the Bazaar open," I add lamely and the Vicar grabs my hand as the little crowd begins to make its way to the stalls where eager churchy ladies are waiting to take their small change. I get down without falling off the stage, or the edge of the world. Yet. But I feel as if that's where I'm going. This is a training ground for floating in space.

"Brave words," the Vicar says. "I hope you aren't thinking you should be forgiving those who have sinned against you. You can't forgive people who aren't sorry. The Bible is clear on that point. We don't have to forgive people who don't repent of their sin. Forgiveness follows repentance. Keep fighting, Katie. We are all so sorry about what's happened to you." He's got me hotly by the hand. In fact my hand is so warm it's sweating. He won't release it. It's also a bit public and embarrassing. I finally shake myself free and leave the makeshift stage much as I arrived on it, flustered, discomposed and as red as a sunburnt Grenadier guard. My nose is now dripping like the ball-cock's got stuck. I've dropped my little packet of tissues. It would be Evelyn who is there to pick it up, wouldn't it? I didn't know he could bend that far. He has always looked completely rigid to me, as if someone has stuck a rod up his back. Evelyn gives that ugly smile of his, exposing his uneven, long, yellow teeth. They rival those of the Tyrannosaurus Rex reconstructed in the Natural History Museum.

"Scum, eh?" he hisses through the gaps. He's as economical with syllables as with the truth. "You should conduct yourself with a bit more dignity."

"Look, I don't know your part in this but some of the other councillors have told lies about me. They have spat in my face. They rang the newspaper anonymously. And the rest of you have just sat on your hands and let it happen. You did nothing to stop it. You are at least partly to blame."

"Something had to be done," he shrugs. "You've been upsetting the staff, and councillors."

Hilary walks up and blinds him with a shot from her super laser gun eyes. "You'll regret this. Katie's the people's choice." That's kind of her, saying it like I'm some kind of Princess Di figure, dodging the land mines in my flak jacket.

"Maybe she is," he says, "but that's not how we do things in Fartlebury Magna. The council's not there for the benefit of what you call 'the people'. You shouldn't have gone upsetting the staff," he adds, looking at me.

He spits out 'people' – the word as well as the concept - and Hilary and I both wipe our faces. I do it dramatically with a flourish of a large cotton handkerchief that Windy's mother gave him last Christmas. She does it with a screwed-up, second-use dirty tissue. Outside there is a distraction. I can hear a sizzle and a pop and there is a barely noticeable flash, like a candle sputtering just once before expiring.

"What on earth?" Hilary exclaims.

"Christmas lights," says Evelyn.

"Had you better go and see to it?" I ask. I don't want the parish council to be responsible for burning down the village hall – especially not with all these worthy shoppers inside.

Evelyn looks at me with wide eyes. "That's Andrew 'all's job, that is."

"He's not around, is he? Would you go and take a look for us, Evelyn?"

He obviously never thought about taking responsibility before but I feel something might have been achieved on the council after all when he stumbles off towards the door.

"Lisa's over there," says Hilary with a subtle jab of her finger in the direction of the kitchen. Our clerk is out of her element, in a pair of jeans and trainers. Millie is with her.

"Hello Millie."

She looks up in great surprise. Lisa looks at me in greater surprise. It might even be astonishment.

"Hello Lisa."

"You needn't resign," she says without a trace of emotion. "I'm leaving. I can't stay now. So you don't need to resign."

This is looking like stalemate. Hilary starts looking at Christmas cards.

"I've got to go, Lisa. How can I work with the other councillors now, after all this?"

"You shouldn't resign. Fartlebury Magna needs you. It will blow over for you. But I've got to go. You've ruined everything for me."

"Me?" I've been pole-axed. How can she say I ruined everything? I'm the victim here.

Millie seems very subdued.

"Is Millie OK?"

"She's missing Dave, aren't you Millie?" she says, finding her lost smile. "She goes to his house most weekends nowadays. He's a great friend to her, isn't she Millie? And she loves Rudy, don't you Millie?"

Millie doesn't reply at all. "He's teaching Millie all he knows on the computer, isn't he Millie?"

She looks at me as if she is handing me a yellow card. "Dave's been into the school to teach the kids about internet safety. So they don't access the kind of sites they shouldn't. So they don't open themselves up to Stranger Danger in chat rooms. Hasn't he, Millie?"

I know that the cowed body language that I can now read in Millie is instinctive and not an act. She's behaving as naturally as she can but it isn't natural. I don't like how it looks at all.

"He's still on holiday then?"

"Oh yes. Getting some winter sunshine for his health. He's not coming back from Thailand until next week."

"I didn't realise he was away for so long. We need to get something in place for updating the website while he's away in future. Did his CRB check ever come through?"

"He kept trying. Things just kept going wrong for him. They sent it back because he sent the wrong ID with it, then when we tried again they sent it back because he had forgotten to sign it. I just couldn't spend the time on it. In the end he told me he would sort it out himself."

"And did he?"

"I don't know. I've had a lot of work on – thanks to you," she says with a prickle of spikiness. "But it's just a formality, Katie. I don't know why you had to make all that fuss. You made out it was a problem. You made it sound as if I was covering something up. As if he was covering something up."

Millie is staring intently at the floor.

"We weren't covering anything up Katie," Lisa says emphatically. There's a little twitch under her left eye.

Hilary decides to interrupt. "You must come and see this," she says. There's nothing I must see. It's the Church Bazaar, for God's sake. I've seen it all before and so has the rest of the village. They found the winning formula in 1954 and there's been no change since. It's 'retro' now, amusing the young middle-class incomers with its olde-worlde White Elephants, Aunt Sally and Salvation Army Band. The Vicar is the benevolent figure who strolls around Fartlebury Magna as if he owns the place. He doesn't of course, he is just playing the part, and the Diocese will move him out into a little semi on one of the new housing estates soon. That will free up the Vicarage gardens for some profitable five-bedroom houses and put an end to his life of Riley.

“Thanks again,” I say to Hilary.

She smiles kindly, “You need a lot of rescuing nowadays.”

On my way back through the throng, I see Phil Jenkins lolloping down the hall in his sawn-off green wellies. “Good afternoon!” he calls out cheerily. I show the Scowl of Discontent as he draws closer. “Tell me one thing, Katie,” he says, with a smile that cracks his face. He’s got warm walking and his armpits smell like cess-pits. “If you are innocent, why are you going to resign?”

“I don’t choose to spend my time working my socks off for NOTHING, with people who stab me in the back. You don’t expect your fellow volunteers to stab you in the back!” I whinge (but I’m glad I sound angry).

Councillor Jenkins slowly considers this. He never considers anything other than slowly. “All my working life I’ve come across people who stab other people in the back. You’ve got to expect it,” he says. He’s talking crap, as usual. That’s why the others like him. They speak the same language.

“At work, maybe,” I flash back, “but I’m a volunteer. I’m not being paid. We’re supposed to be working together, aren’t we? For the good of the community?”

He doesn’t get it. He doesn’t get much and he certainly doesn’t get the concept that the council works for the good of the community. Let alone ‘together’.

I stride off, a bit theatrically. I can’t stand there any longer watching as his silver hair turns spikier; it looks like a dandelion clock after a summer downpour. I turn and rush through the assembled parishioners parrying little greetings and social enquiries as I go.

Evelyn is still around somewhere. I can smell his trail. Pheromones attract the opposite sex so it’s definitely not that. Evelyn’s scent trail has the opposite effect. You could market it as Anti-Pheromone – the scientific product guaranteed to keep people away. It makes my eyes and nose run and my mouth seize up. His tweed jacket hasn't been cleaned since he got it - probably from an Irish labourer building the railway in the 1860s (or so I choose to believe). There's no discernible pattern on the shiny fabric. Dirt unifies warp and weft and forms a protective waterproof coating. Perspiration, grease and grime: the cheap fore-runner to Teflon. Honest sweat from manual toil binds the inside of the jacket too, apart from the holes in the lining under the armpits where it has just rotted away. When insects fly over Evelyn's head they die, giving his shoulders the interesting appearance of black dandruff. Clothing with built-in insecticide. Don't they sell that at a huge price for rainforest adventure holidays? We had it in Fartlebury Magna first.

"I don't want to run into Evelyn again."

"No, quite." Hilary makes a confident path through the crowds, her elbows as sharp as her tongue.

In the kitchen the formidable church ladies have set up a table holding china cups and saucers, dainty slices of cake and some massive aluminium teapots. An urn bubbles away behind them. Hubble bubble toil and trouble comes just once a year to Fartlebury Magna. They like to make the most of it. One of them has a nose like an Afghan hound and is looking down it at me. She is fearsome. Even the tea-cups are shuddering. "Would you like some tea, Mrs Miller?"

"Thank you. Not too milky."

She pours me half a cup of luke-warm, weak and milky tea, taking care to slop it into the saucer.

"I'll have a coffee," says Hilary quickly as she catches sight of the beige liquid not even steaming in my cup.

We take our cups to a table and sit down.

"I'm sorry you're resigning Katie." She really means it.

"So am I. But I don't know what else I can do. It's over. They won't support me. I can't work like that."

"No, I know. I don't think you've actually got any choice either." She is always honest, is Hilary. It's one of the things that makes her stand out from the other councillors.

A lump bobs up in my throat like a small poo in a hotel toilet. This is it then. I really am going to resign and no-one wants to stop me. Not even Hilary. I lift my cup to my lips and swear as several large staining drips fall with precision onto my clean white blouse.

I've had a day or two to brood now. Windy keeps telling me to keep quiet and let things die down, but the injustice of it all screams inside me all the time. Now and again it bursts out of me like the alien from Sigourney Weaver. It's intent on causing trouble.

MEMORANDUM
From Katie Miller
To All Councillors
Date: 9 December 2004

Dear Councillor
As you probably know by now, Councillor Dave Tripswitch has made a formal complaint about me to the Standards Board in which he claims I have acted improperly by agreeing without the authority of the council to a link from the Fartlebury Magna Garden Centre webcam to our website. This is completely untrue but it's the last straw for me and has finally caused the camel's back to shatter. It ends a period in which my position as Chair has become untenable.

Over recent weeks some councillors have made it clear that although they voted for me as Chairman as recently as May, they do not respect my judgment nor authority. I am even criticised for representing the council in the community. The clerk treats me with disrespect and does not share with me information which I need to keep an overview of council business. My role as Chair has now been undermined further by this complaint and it is impossible for me to continue.

I resign from the Chair with effect from the date of our next full council meeting, with deep regrets that I have been unable to do anything to stop these disastrous events from happening. I will remain as a councillor for the time being.

Yours sincerely

Katie Miller.

It falls silently onto 20 door mats and is swallowed up in a conspiracy of silence that would impress an abbey full of Trappist monks.

Now I've nothing to do except lick my wounds – and very tasty they are too.

CHAPTER SEVENTEEN

"There is no better high than discovery" E.O.Wilson

It's been a long day, a long year, and it's only two days to go before the meeting at which I'm going to resign. I am very tired. Windy has answered the phone and silently holds it out to me, mouthing, "It's Tom."

"Hello Tom." My voice is thinner than threadbare. Any once perceptible trace of enthusiasm has faded badly in the automatic washer-dryer of council life. Now I've been hung out to dry in bright sunlight.

"Look, you ought to know that although I've not been trying to find anything, well ...." He's stopped. I am too tired to prompt him because I know he'll respond to silence just as well. Sure enough he continues: "Katie – I was just fiddling around on the computer. I've found links to pornography on the parish council site."

I dash over to Tom's house. He's flushed with excitement; www.fartleburymagna.net is on the screen of his computer. The Home page looks very innocent, with its picture of the church and village green, quintessentially English. It's always spring in Fartlebury Magna, the daffodils a shining host, the blackthorn blossom hiding its vicious thorns (a metaphor for village life if ever there was one), the church clock stands at ten to three (but here they are all out of honey).

At the bottom of the screen it says:

File://F:\Parish%20Council\FartleburyMagna.net%2016th%20Oct.htm
Fartlebury Magna Parish Council copyright 2003 All rights reserved
Disclaimer.
Produced by Cam-Cam Services.

"Before I show you what I've found, look at this." Tom has printed off another email from Dave Tripswitch. The subject of this email is '*Disclaimer'*. "I was subconsciously guided to it. Somehow I just decided to click on it."

He clicks on it now. Up comes the Cam-Cam site with a list of links to webcam-related sites: *Talk to Dirty Girls Now; Teenage Sex Bombs; Live Filthy Chat with Sexy Ladies.*

"I haven't clicked on any of those," he says (and I smile because he is one person I can believe). Tom's a youth leader at Muddleton Malreward. I know being a youth leader doesn't automatically confer any kind of moral standard, but Tom's as wholesome as organic muesli.

The truth of it begins to dawn. That's why we got that robotic trouble with the Forum in the first place. The website has always had these secret links! Always!

Tom turns to the Cam-Cam site home page, clicking on its menu items one by one. They announce what is on offer from the company:

"E-Marketing: we offer a Traffic Boosting service which focuses on developing link pages by building keywords."

Tom says, "It's a trick to fool the big search engines like Google and Yahoo. When you search for any topic they list the most useful results on the first or second line, and they decide which sites have priority in their listing by counting the number of other websites linking to a site."

"What? How does that work? Even links people don't know are there?"

"That's right," Tom is calm on the surface but I suspect waves are building up and will run over at high tide. "It just gets the page highly ranked among the results for porn search terms. It doesn't matter if no-one ever clicks on it so long as Google and Yahoo index it. In fact it's better for him that no-one has found it and clicked on it because he's been able to get away with it for years."

"It's so sneaky! Is there money involved?" I feel wide awake now the adrenalin has arrived in industrial quantities.

"I should think so. Maybe a penny a click?"

"Tom, this is dynamite! Who would ever open the Disclaimer at the bottom of the screen? No-one ever clicks on a disclaimer."

"Well, that's the trick. No-one. I only did it because his email led me to it. He put '*Disclaimer*' at the top, and I thought I would look at the Fartleburymagna.net disclaimer and see what he had put in there because I had never looked at it before."

"It's always been there then," I say. It's as if the halogen spot light on next door's garage is shining through my thin bedroom curtains, and Tom nods.

"The website was always a cash cow for him."

A cash cow. Some of the farmers are going to like the sound of that. Moo.

Jim's cows, on the other hand, don't produce much cash at all. Farming seems a lot of trouble, and the neighbours don't like it either. New arrivals in the village aren't sympathetic to farming. It's probably all those muck heaps and dead animals in ditches.

"You murderer!" Mrs Baloney shouted at Jim one day when he was loading cattle onto a truck to take them to market. "Meat is murder!"

"Bloody vege-whatsits!" Jim retaliated. He didn't realise anyone knew what he was doing. Now he knows there is a witness to the crime I suppose he will have to kill Mrs Baloney too.

I'm much more sanguine. I love a bit of roast beef.

I go down to see Lisa first thing in the morning. No preliminaries. I walk straight in.

"Close the website down."

"Dave is in Thailand."

"Then you'll have to do it. Get in touch with Cam-Cam Services and make them take it off-line."

"But Dave said he owns the copyright."

"We can't just leave it Lisa. It's got links to porn sites. Teenage sites at that. Could be children being exploited."

"It's nothing to do with me Katie."

"Has he resigned as Child Advocate?"

"Youth Advocate, you mean. Not as far as I know. Hilary was going to ask him to resign before he went on holiday."

"Do you know whether she did?"

"No, but it's all an over-reaction. He hasn't done anything wrong."

She adds the coup de grace with no grace at all, "You won't be Chairman after tonight."

"Look Lisa. You must see how impossible it is for the council's website to have links to porn sites."

"I can't do anything about it Katie. Dave is the only one who deals with Cam-Cam Services."

"He pays their bills, does he?"

"No, we do but .."

"OK. I'm going to sit here while you ring them up and tell them to take it off-line."

Lisa folds her tanned and hairless arms. "Dave won't like it. He's the only person authorised to deal with the website."

"Please, Lisa, do this last thing for me."

"Why should I do anything for you?"

"OK. Do it for Fartlebury Magna Parish Council."

I'm on my feet now. I'm looking through the filing cabinet. There it is. COMPUTER – a huge file. Cam-Cam Services' invoice is on the top. I dial the number and hand Lisa the phone. She isn't smiling but she complies. "Can I speak to Tim Dodgit please?"

Tim's voice is quiet so I can only hear one side of the conversation.

"It's Fartlebury Magna Parish Council. I am the clerk. That's right. Yes. … It seems there are links to pornographic sites which can be accessed directly from our website. Yes. Yes. … Yes. … He's on holiday. … Oh did he?"

While she is engaged in this conversation, Lisa is looking at me as if I was found stuck to the sole of her boot. "We can't contact him. No. OK. I'll pass that message on to the council."

She hangs up.

"Apparently Dave gave them explicit instructions before he went away that no-one else had authority to take the website off-line. They can't do it without his authority."

She looks smug, as if she has discovered some hugely welcome secret.

"We must have an alternative."

"No. We don't. So you can go home and let me get on with some work."

At that moment Bill comes knocking on the door to the office. He must have heard the way Lisa spoke to me. His nose is twitching like a kangaroo's. He jumps in: "Is everything all right?"

"No," I quickly counter-jump. Bill has the mind of a marmoset but the body of an orang-utan. He was a rugby player once, which accounts for his bent nose and square head. He is evidence that the old saying about rugby being a game for thugs played by gentlemen is only half true. He's no gentleman but he does like a fight. I get to the nub of the problem:

"We need to close the website down. I suppose you know it's got these links to pornography?"

"Is it soft porn or is it hard?"

His eyes roll around Lisa's face just like his tongue is rolling round his mouth. "Hard porn," he adds, for clarity.

“I don’t know,” I say, “I haven’t looked at it. I just saw the list of links. That was enough.”

“What’s the problem then?”

“Lisa has rung the provider and they say only Dave Tripswitch has the authority to close it.”

“Rubbish.” He takes a couple of steps towards her. I think it’s quite menacing and she seems to be shrinking in front of my eyes, like Alice in Wonderland, and I half expect her to disappear down a rabbit hole in the office carpet. “Tell them to take it off-line.”

“They won’t,” says Lisa. Do I detect a pinch of triumph spicing her lips?

Bill grabs the phone. “Who are you talking to at their end?”

“Tim Dodgit.”

“Can I speak to Tim Dodgit please? Fartlebury Magna Parish Council. We need you to take our website off-line.” Pause. “So I understand, but he’s out of the country.” Pause. “It’s very important. I’m not taking no for an answer. You do it or you’re going to get some of the worst publicity you could ever imagine. I’ll get you shut down. You talk to him then. I’m going to call back in 15 minutes and by then I’m expecting it to be off-line.”

He presses the disconnect button with a gesture like Jools Holland.

“Thanks Bill.”

“No problem. Sometimes they need to hear a man’s voice, don’t they?” He picks up Lisa’s local paper and starts to thumb through it. I return to the filing cabinet. The fifteen minutes seem to last forever.

Bill rings Cam-Cam back in exactly fifteen minutes. Lisa is sitting at her desk, her legs fidgety behind the modesty panel. She hasn’t spoken since the last phone call.

“All done? Thanks,” says Bill and he replaces the phone on its cradle.

I've been busying myself with the documents I need to pass on to Hilary. Because she is Vice Chair, she will be Acting Chair until a new one is elected next month. I open Internet Explorer and type in the URL. A large rectangle is now obscuring the church and village green. In bold red letters it proclaims:

THIS WEBSITE IS TEMPORARILY OFF-LINE DUE TO TECHNICAL PROBLEMS.

"Oh well, that'll do," says Bill. I sigh. I need to get out of here.

"Thanks again Bill."

"No problem Katie. Any time you need a bit of muscle, I'm your man." He winks and I just manage to avoid slipping over in his slime trail as I head for the door behind him. When I get home I'm very glad to close my own front door behind me.

Not again! Windy gets up to answer the phone with a big sigh. It's never good getting a call after the nine o'clock watershed. We don't like to miss out on the strong language from the start.

It's Tom again and he's straining at his leash. In fact I think he's going to slip his collar.

"It's not really off-line!" he says excitedly.

"What isn't?" My brain is trying to catch up with my ears. "The council website?"

"Yes. If you search for Devonshire Road Play area for example, or Fartlebury Magna Basketball Club, the page for Fartlebury Magna's facilities comes up. It skips the first page, the home page, where the closed sign is, and goes straight into the page that meets your search criteria. And at the bottom of each page you can still click on the Disclaimer and get up the list of dodgy sites."

"Really?" Windy is already pushing aside a few dirty coffee cups and wine glasses and is waiting for the computer to whir into action. Whizz, whizz goes the fan. Vroom, vroom goes the second fan.

Ding ding ding dong chimes Windows as it floods light onto my virtual wallpaper. It's as slow as a slug on shingle. I must get round to replacing the wallpaper. I don't want to sit and face the council logo every time I boot up. It's really rubbing my nose in it; I shall end up making the screen dirty.

Windy types *Devonshire Road playing field* into the search engine. The page loads. Windy points the cursor straight at *Disclaimer* in tiny writing at the bottom of the page and clicks. Up pops an appropriately blue list of website URLs, underlined to invite an instant one-click access: *Naughty Girls Talk Dirty; XXX adult sites; Sexy WebCam Girls.*

"Oh my God!" I scream, "It's still there!" Windy puts his fingers in his ears. I see his eyes are bulging but I don't think that's just because of my scream.

Windy is on www.fartleburymagna.net going from screen to screen finding the Disclaimer on each page. Every click goes straight to Cam-Cam's webcam site links. He's as quiet as I am noisy, as pale as I am pink. I'm shrieking with the kind of ecstasy you get on a ghost train ride. It's the thrill, the horror, the surprise – and the sheer fun that comes from sharing those strong emotions with others.

"There is no disclaimer!" I shriek. This just shows how unimportant it is to have one. We have operated the website without one for years. "He gets money from every page then, not just every site he's made."

"So we need to get it properly off-line," says Tom, "not just put up a place-mark on the front page."

"OK."

I won't prolong the call. I can't wait to get off the phone so I can get back on it.

"Hilary? It's Katie. The links are still there. The home page says the website is off-line but it's not! If you click on Disclaimer on the other pages the links are still there, still active!"

Hilary says, "That's it. It's got to be taken down. Taken off the internet all together. And we need to tell the other organisations with websites he's made." These include Tiny Tots Day Nursery, Fartlebury Magna Scrabble Club, the Wesleyan Church and the community church. I try to imagine telling Maggie and John.

"Bill was wonderful today," I find myself saying. "He really helped. He knows how to handle Lisa, and other people too." I'm really not myself. The excitement has gone to my head. I can tell Hilary isn't impressed. She's only too well aware that men know how to handle women. Some of them know how to handle other men too.

"Do you want Bill to deal with it again then?" Hilary says. I bet her eyes are wide open with incredulity although her tone of voice isn't giving much away.

"Well, no. Not necessarily. But I was very glad to have him about."

"I've got the website now. Yes, I see what you mean. I can get into the pages direct, even though the home page says it's off-line. It doesn't seem to do it every time though. Sometimes when I click on *Disclaimer* it just goes to an innocent list of solicitors and travel agents. It's only intermittently that it goes to porn sites."

Hilary's down-to-earth attitude and lack of excitement at the latest news has shocked me. Where is her spirit of adventure? I'm so full of adrenalin I can hardly sleep. I love a scandal – or I did until I became the subject. Dave Tripswitch is coming back in the next few days and Hilary says she will ring him up and ask him to take it properly off-line.

Today is my last day as Chair. Jenny, a community member of the web team, has gone to the police. This is an achievement in itself and Windy was considering having a medal struck for her. The police aren't highly visible in Fartlebury Magna. You would think their dark blue uniforms would show up well against the green, green grass of home (and the grey concrete that has replaced it at Pratts Dell) but apparently they're not visible at all. Fartlebury Magna Parish Council has been complaining about it for months and is constantly asking for a more visible police presence in the High Street. Jenny has been looking under every stone. No stone has, in fact, been left unturned in her quest to find a policeman, but it turns out they are all hiding in the police station polishing their helmets.

She says, however, that they aren't very interested and they referred her to a service called Internet Watch. It's a bit like Horse Watch except it's easier to protect horses than it is to protect people from dodgy websites (and themselves). Jenny is keen to do something as she's worried about her involvement in the web team. She's a magistrate and she doesn't want anyone finding a link to pornography on her computer.

Internet Watch is going to look at the sites listed where our disclaimer should be and determine whether they are illegal sites.

"You mean there are legal sites?" I ask, a bit puzzled.

"Of course," she says in a voice that smacks of 'Gosh, how naïve you are.'

"We don't want any kind of pornography on the parish council website," I add for clarification. "Do we?"

"Of course not. Even if it's legal, it's sleazy, it's immoral. It's exploitative."

"And it's hidden on our website – the lowest tier of government."

"About as low as it gets, that's for sure."

Windy's police friend Mike Cannon is going to meet up with him tomorrow for a coffee. Windy's as bad as me. He can't wait to tell him the latest.

CHAPTER EIGHTEEN

"Don't be afraid of enemies who attack you. Be afraid of the friends who flatter you."   Dale Carnegie

Nobody's heard from Dave Tripswitch since he threatened legal action if we took the website off-line. It's only now since all this has happened that I realised how stupid we have been. It's all been far too loose – none of us were thinking about who owned the site. It was all done on goodwill. There was a bit too much goodwill if you ask me, and now it even seems that as far as some people were concerned their will was never very good in the first place. I wonder if he knows Lisa is leaving.

He knows all right.

Even before he's left Heathrow to come home he's on the phone to me.

"You bitch. You just couldn't wait, could you?"

I'm not sure whether to hang up or hang in there. I retain my silence and my dignity but he goes on,"You've destroyed my website."

"It was the council's website. We asked you to remove the pornographic links and you refused."

"I didn't refuse. I couldn't do it. Tom could've done it."

"You know Tom couldn't do it. Only you had authority to do it."

"Yes. But you did it anyway."

"I'm no longer Chair of the council." (I won't be after tonight anyway.)

"No. I'll be talking to Hilary too. And Phil. He always supports me, you know. He supported my complaint to the Standards Board."

I don't hear another word after that.

As soon as I'm off the phone to him I ring Phil's mobile. He sounds very surprised to hear from me. When he and I were children phones used to be attached to houses. It's a mixed blessing being constantly available on the end of a phone – often it feels as if you're on the wrong end of it. I hope Phil feels he's on the wrong end now. Phil doesn't know how I've got his number.

"I'm on the golf course," he says, by which I perceive that my call is not welcome. I get straight to the point.

"Did you support Dave Tripswitch's complaint about me to the Standards Board?"

He gets straight to the point too. "I don't think you've been fair to him. This isn't a witch-hunt. He's just a councillor doing what he thinks is best. He thought it was best for the council if you were brought to book."

I'm astonished. Brought to book? What is the man talking about? What crime have I committed?

I ask him outright, "Did you support his complaint?"

There is the slightest hesitation, like a doctor before prescribing anti-biotics. "I'm insulted that you think I would behave like that."

"Did you ring the paper anonymously about me? He says you did."

"No, I didn't."

"Did you support his complaint? He says you did."

"No, I'm telling you I didn't. He's a lying little shit."

I'm in a No Through Road. There is nowhere to turn round and a big barrier to my continuing in the same direction.

"Sorry to ring you on your day off then."

I'm not very sorry, but I've got to say something before I hit the off button.

"Bye."

To start with I believe Phil Jenkins. Surely there's just the one rotten apple. But this is cider country. Throw one in the barrel and they all begin to turn: they are softening inside, fermenting, darkening, rotting from the inside out. That's what one bad apple can do round here. Phil Jenkins must have been contaminated by the putrefaction coming from inside Dave Tripswitch. You could smell it on him, the whiff of alcohol, the sweet sour smell of something going off, the core completely putrid.

At the final meeting where I sit uncomfortably in the parish council chair, wobbling on uneven length legs and fearing that I shall fall off prematurely, I decide to go for broke. In my case, being properly schooled in the Queen's English, it's more like 'going for broken'. I feel smashed. Mashed and crashed. Bashed and gashed. Trashed.

I tell my colleagues a few home truths. I take out their dirty laundry and give it a good shake. Trixie from the local paper is sitting quaintly with a notepad and pencil, like a reporter from the fifties, making shorthand squiggles like Arabic. I am hoping she has the courage to report all the evidence I am laying before them like soiled pants.

As Dave Tripswitch is not around to defend himself I don't have to spare his feelings. I can make sure they all know what he has been up to. Some of them are completely hardened to what I am saying. Their expressions are so blank it is like sitting with a dozen dinner plates. I don't want to let them off lightly and the quieter they are the louder I get.

It's all to no avail really. At the end of the meeting, I crawl away in defeat, go home alone and watch *Murder in the Malverns* with the occasional snotty sniff. I couldn't tell you what the plot is tonight, I am having my own murderous thoughts.

The next morning I boot up slowly while the computer boots up more slowly and read another email:

STATEMENT TO ALL COUNCILLORS
WITHOUT PREJUDICE
During last night's meeting, I understand that Katie implied that I had a 'close' relationship with Lisa. You will all be pleased to hear that I would like to think that I do indeed have a good relationship with Lisa, a good 'professional' relationship. I was pleased to hear the compliment because a good, 'very good' relationship with the clerk is an essential part of our duty as councillors. Anyone who can't work with the clerk is failing in their duty at a very basic level.
Regards, Dave Tripswitch

I think he should have headed it *'With Prejudice'*. The Old School councillors have had the wool so far over their eyes that they can't see the truth when it bites them. In fact they can't see it even when it savages them and leaves them for dead. Actually, despite the kisses on her emails, and his, and the way she has him over at her house when her husband is away, I never said their relationship was 'close'. I just said it was 'special'.

Over the course of the next 24 hours I reflect on my short conversations. Phil Jenkins was quite plausible when he called his colleague 'a lying little shit' but I think it was thrown in to put me off the scent. The more I think about it the more I believe Dave rather than the two-faced scarecrow who, I hear, has ambitions to replace me as Chair of the council. Trouble is I can't prove anything.

I don't really keep abreast of national legislation because I'm so busy with local affairs but I am slightly aware of the Freedom of Information Act. I've already asked the Standards Board for England to tell me who else made statements and they refused. They don't have to divulge much under their terms and conditions so I'm making a request under the Freedom of Information Act. Brilliant piece of legislation that is.

In due course I do get what I ask for. The document has the names all obliterated with a very strong black marker, the idea being to stop me being able to read the names that I have told them I want to uncover by making a Freedom of Information request. It's a game, like noughts and crosses. Once you know the formula you have the right to put in your cross, but they always get their turn first, so they can put their nought in the box and block you getting the winning line. It's all too obvious to me who it is though. I can see the length and shape of the names of the signatories underneath. It's Mavis and Phil. In Phil's own inimitable words, they are the lying little shits.

"I can't stay on, even just as a councillor," I say to Windy that evening. "I can't work with people like that."

"Well, change is in the air," says Windy. "Mike Cannon is definitely going to retire to the States. He's been accepted."

Today I have been copied in to an email, possibly by mistake:

MEMO to all Fartlebury Magna Parish Councillors and Previous and Current Councillors and Webmaster Team Members.

Whilst I have been the Webmaster, the website team and working party have remained responsible for the site's main content and updates.
However, as I wrote the base code and created the main graphics I have retained basic copyright. This issue has been overlooked by myself and the Council for too many years, mainly due to the popularity and success of the site – even resulting in the national best parish council website award.
However, to avoid confusion and any conflict of interest, all copyright issues should have been formally signed over years ago. Therefore I formally declare that I never had or will ever claim any copyright to the Fartlebury Magna Parish Website including any source code

written or images contained on it. This includes the normal Cam-Cam Services source code sub clause 4.1 – 4.5.

Signed David D Tripswitch.
Web designer, Web architect, Computer technician, Fartlebury Magna Parish Councillor.

I can't leave this. Windy keeps telling me to stop worrying it like a terrier but IT is worrying me. It's the terrier, gnawing away at me, a terror of a terrier. Just as tenacious too, with its sharp little canine teeth. If I was a man it would have me by the balls. I've got to try to make people see. I press *Reply All* and delete Dave Tripswitch's name. It will go to all the other councillors who have email accounts. I compose a quick response telling them that Dave's latest email does need refuting. They have to see that it isn't fair to say the website team has remained responsible for the site's content and updates. It's well documented that the team were extremely frustrated by the lack of ability to update the site. We all repeatedly asked Tripswitch to update it and he would not. I also point out that he now says copyright issues should have been formally signed over years ago. It's not what he said when he wanted to keep control over it and refused to shut it down. He even threatened other members of the web team with legal action if they did anything while he was on holiday.

I don't think he can undo it by declaring it so. He did claim copyright. He did own the copyright and he is up the creek without a paddle. I tell them so but no-one replies to me. Well, I'm not a councillor now, so maybe they have just removed me from the list of people copied in. I suppose they should really. I am being tainted by this foul mess like cheese by chutney. (I hate chutney - neither sweet nor sour, with the smell and colour of poo.) I don't know whether I am sweet or sour any more either but I am beginning to suspect that I am definitely getting contaminated by the stink.

CHAPTER NINETEEN

"The first lesson a revolutionary must learn is that he is a doomed man." Huey P. Newton

Lisa's leaving soon. Our Miss Purfitt leaving us in a perfect mess. I begged her to wait until we'd recruited someone else but she just folded her arms and kept as quiet as a Queen's fart. I'm hardly on speaking terms with the councillors who are left either so I've delegated getting a leaving present to Hilary. She brought it up with councillors after the meeting last week. Phil Jenkins said we could just take the money for a bunch of flowers out of petty cash. Shows how long it is since he bought anyone flowers. We only keep about £20 in petty cash. You would like to think he romantically picks his wife a bunch of wild flowers from the farm, but there aren't any left round here. The farmers and developers can't have a moon daisy getting in the way of progress, can they? Hilary said the flowers are supposed to be a gift from councillors not from the community, and besides, it's not in the budget. They didn't seem to understand putting hands in their pockets. It's not in their nature. I suppose most of their pockets have holes in anyway.

Before Lisa's notice period is up, I decide to try once more to make it clear to councillors the role she has played in the whole sorry affair. They sit in embarrassed silence while I nervously try to get some support out of them. Bloodless stones have nothing on this lot. Lisa sits there inscrutable through the whole meeting, her colour deepening in line with the increasingly explicit nature of my diatribe to the dire tribe.

No-one gets it. Not one.

So I'm writing Lisa a letter, trying to get her to think about the good times, hoping she'll forgive me as I have forgiven her. I shall try to forgive her, although actually some of this is down to her. She really fucked up. Especially by supporting Dave Tripswitch when she should have been loyal to me. To be honest I'm not sure I can ever forgive her but I can write her a nice letter. Psychiatrists would probably say I am looking for closure. I'll seal the envelope with extra-strength parcel tape.

Dear Lisa

I'm sorry your employment with Fartlebury Magna Parish Council has ended the way it has. You have given the council and community 100% and everyone has appreciated that.
It's easy in hindsight to see where things went wrong, but I am hoping that you will be able to look back to those happy days when you and I shared a vision and worked for it. It hasn't all been bad, has it?
I'm glad you found an interesting job to go to. It will be good to have a change from parish councils.
With sincere good wishes for the future,

Katie.

We're not having any kind of farewell do for Lisa. In the circumstances I think it best if she just melts away like a lost chocolate down the back of the sofa.

Windy has decided to take me out this evening. He calls it taking me out of myself, but I don't feel as if I've escaped. You can take the woman out of the Chair, but can you take the Chair out of the woman?

We are meeting his friend Mike Cannon and his wife. Mike, appropriately enough, used to be in the army. He tried for the Marines but he wasn't quite fit enough to complete the training. Instead he chose the Royal Engineers, where he did that much vaunted thing of learning a trade while seeing the world. He has spent hours in the

Fartlebury Magna Inn talking about his life and times in Germany and sometimes I have heard something new. Mostly I spend the evenings watching Mike's wife wincing. It's not such a bad life, soldiering. Mike got to see most of the big name bands and pop idols and met his wife in Germany. At the end of his military career Mike marched straight into a police job. That is how Windy got to know him. Windy's a social worker. For the last ten years he has been training other social workers, which he enjoys much more than the raw stuff he used to deal with. Mike used to go to his classes to talk about the police side of things. They got on really well. They still get on really well.

Mike's got a side to him I don't quite care for. I can't quite put my finger on it (and I've never laid a finger on him to try). Tonight we are all in the Fartlebury Magna Inn. It is Mike and Helga's 35th wedding anniversary. Not quite enough years for a party but too many years to ignore. Mike is on form, telling stories of his army life which are almost entertaining. Windy has had five or six drinks so he is approaching the point where the dullest tale seems hilarious. Using their loudness for cover, Helga turns to me and says, "We're hoping to move to California."

"Crumbs."

"Mike can get a job over there in security. They're recruiting British ex-police officers. He's looked into it all. He can take his pension with him."

"I thought you had to have loads of money to go to the States."

"Mike's got a bit put away."

"What about you?" I ask. I would hate it if Windy wanted to retire to California. I would hate it if he wanted to retire, full stop.

"I'm sick of this weather," she says.

"Crumbs." Going to a new continent to get away from the weather seems somewhat extreme. They do have weather in California – heatwaves, droughts, storms, that kind of thing. And earthquakes.

Mike says, "It's brilliant over there Katie. You'd love it. If we get the immigration go-ahead we'll go next year for a trial holiday and look for the best places to live. You could come with us. A foursome."

"Awesome," says Windy. "Awesome foursome."

"I don't think that's for me," I say, clinking my ice cubes round and round.

CORSET DAILY POST 8 January 2005
TRUST GOES AT FARTLEBURY MAGNA PARISH COUNCIL
Clerk and Chair Both Resign
By Trixie Mann

A parish council chairman who quit her post after claims were made that she broke the councillors' code of conduct has now left the council altogether because the 'trust has gone'.

Katie Miller resigned from the chair of Fartlebury Magna Parish Council two months ago amid complaints that she was not listening to other councillors' views properly. She was accused of accepting favours from a local garden centre. No findings of fact were made by the councils' national watchdog, the Standards Board for England.

"I have worked hard for the community and established a forward-thinking council which has worked hard on initiatives to modernise the council. The complaint against me came completely out of the blue and was totally unfounded. I am disappointed but I think once the trust has gone it just isn't worth battling against other people's negativity. At the end of the day I don't have to put up with the stress of it. It's a sad day for the parish council and for the community but I hope the council can move on."

Six Fartlebury Magna parish councillors have resigned since the complaint was made public in an article in the Daily Post last July, and the clerk has now also left to take up a post elsewhere.

It's not long before Hilary phones.

"I've nailed the bastard," she says. No explanation is needed. I know who she's talking about. There is only one person we talk about nowadays. "He's as low as a worm's belly in a tractor rut."

I'm silent. What can I say? Hilary is still chuntering on.

"What's that?" I say, as I catch wind of something she's just dropped like an incendiary device into the monologue I wasn't listening to.

"The Standards Board is going to investigate my complaint."

"YOUR complaint, did you say?"

"You weren't listening Katie! Admit it, you weren't, were you? Good news isn't it? I didn't want to implicate you, but I've made a complaint about him not taking the website off-line and thereby bringing the council into disrepute."

I open my mouth but my voice is as thin as a communion wafer. I am not expecting this. I'm not really sure whether it's good news or not. I would at some point like the whole thing to fade away.

"Great," I say.

"Are you being sarcastic, Katie?"

"Of course not. It's great news." I can't manage a smile though. Windy won't be happy about it. He has told me over and over that the more you tread on a turd the wider it spreads.

CHAPTER TWENTY

"Knowledge speaks, but wisdom listens." Jimi Hendrix

Dave is not happy. He has told Hilary that he has taken legal advice.

"He just kept telling me I was out of order," she tells me. "He said all the pornographic links were to do with a search engine. Nothing to do with him. He said I don't know what I'm talking about and that he would make a complaint for malicious conduct."

"Does he know you've made a complaint about him to the Standards Board then?" I ask. I'm suddenly rather tired.

"No. I thought that would be a nice little surprise for him when he gets the letter telling him that he is under investigation. I told him I knew there was a link between his company and Cam-Cam. I told him I wasn't questioning his integrity, only his refusal to take the website off-line when I asked him."

"You had better keep your head down," I say because I want to support her. I am aware that I am something of a chocolate scaffold and if things get hotter I could melt. I'm really not sure how much I have left in me to give her now the heat is on. I don't feel much like being in a supporting role anyway. I would like some scaffolding myself – made of tungsten. "Do you really think he's taken legal advice?"

"Apparently his wife works in a solicitor's office. That's his legal advice."

"You be careful," I say, feeling like some old granny seeing a precious grandchild go off on their bike alone on a busy road.

"Well, I can't really, can I? Someone has to take the bugger on."

Tit-for-tat thoughts are seeping through my grey matter. "We could tip off the local paper then," I suggest, with a little shiver of sheer pleasure.

"Yes. Like he did when he reported you, you mean? It will be on the Standards Board website, so it's in the public domain. Why not?"

I like Hilary's response. That's it then, it's war.

I ring Trixie at the Daily Post.

"Hi Trixie, I just thought you would like to know that Dave Tripswitch is the subject of an investigation by the Standards Board for England."

"Oh God, Katie. Thanks, but I'm not sure I can cover it. I'm not sure I want to get involved again. I got into a load of trouble. We had threats from him and from his solicitor."

" or maybe someone pretending to be his solicitor?"

"Maybe it wasn't really his solicitor, but whoever it was my boss didn't like it. I got into a lot of trouble Katie."

My heart sinks again. I think it is on the way to California via the core of the Earth. He wins all round. "Can you try, Trixie? It's not right, is it, that he was able to get all that terrible publicity against me and now your paper won't follow it up? It's a great story, Trixie. He wouldn't take the website off-line. It had links to pornography. You could probably sell it to a tabloid: *Parish Council Unwittingly Peddles Porn.*"

"I know, Katie. I've got it all. I investigated it all at the time. I've got the story about the website all ready to go, but our legal people don't like it. It costs money to keep checking these things with lawyers you know. I've even got the screen-shots of the website before it went off-line. I could run a good story if my boss would let me. Why don't you write in, send a letter to the paper, and I'll see what I can turn it into. That's the best I can think of."

While I work away at a letter to the Editor in hot spurts in the middle of several nights, getting a lot of rubbish off my chest and into the recycling box, I am in frequent contact with Tom and Bill. Even Windy takes a turn looking up things on the internet, trying to find out more about Dave. Interestingly, Dave's own computer business seems to have disappeared. When you search for Cam-Cam Services, a box comes up with text:

Cam-Cam Services are no longer at this domain and will be moving to a new location and international domain shortly.
In the meantime all support contracts and advice will be provided through the normal support team online and by phone.
2002-2004 Cam-Cam Services. All rights reserved. Disclaimer. November 23 2004.

I'm thinking about that. They are a bit fond of the Disclaimer thing, aren't they? I check my emails. I keep doing that out of force of habit. I'm a bit disappointed when there is just one. I miss all the spam and adverts that I used to get as Parish Council Chair as well as all the communications from the clerk and my councillor colleagues. I feel discarded, only getting one email. Used up. Like a lolly stick in the sand. I'm hoping to be found and stuck in a castle somewhere but I'm beginning to feel it's more likely I'll be washed out to sea.

Nigel has sent me a copy of an email to Dave Tripswitch.

To: David Tripswitch
From: Nigel How
Date: 16 February 2005
Subject:

Dave
Several times in the High Street you have called out 'Hello' to me. Please note that I do not consider you to be a friend or acquaintance that I wish to be greeted by in public. Please refrain from speaking to me in this manner. I do not wish to be considered among your acquaintances let alone your friends. You are neither to me.
Nigel.

Crikey. He's no friend of mine either, but I don't think I would do that. My style is much less direct. I prefer talking behind his back, using the abbreviation DDT. Who would saddle their offspring with those initials? DDT seemed so useful, so good, but we've learned that we weren't in control; the post-war Government authorized use of the pesticide without proper trials first. Dave Tripswitch was poison. He killed off what was good and destroyed the natural balance. He did untold damage to the environment. Really he should have been banned – or tested more thoroughly in the first place. It's too late now. We are living with the fall-out.

'Well said, Nigel,' I type. I think he is trying to support me. He quickly forwards me a further email from Dave. Although it has his personal email address on it as the sender, and it gives the subject as "*Strictly Confidential and Without Prejudice*", it contains what purports to be an automated reply. I'm not convinced it is automated (or only in as much as he is not human). I think it is obvious that he has typed in the text box:

Automated Reply
Your email address has been de-listed by Cam-Cam Services because it has been identified as either sending unsolicited email or for breaking the terms and conditions set down in the hosting company's online policies. Whilst we hope that this does not cause you any inconvenience, please do not send any further spam to our organization.

We are out of toilet rolls at home. Windy's been quite good at doing the shopping while I am repeatedly trying on my sackcloth and ashes for size. I know it can't go on. I've simply got to get some fresh air and while I'm out some toilet rolls. I zip up my big raincoat and pull up the huge hood. As I approach the High Street I glimpse Evelyn ahead of me and hesitate. Can I face meeting one of the nasty old buggers? Hostilities haven't been declared against the Old Guard, but I think they've invaded Poland.

I try to bustle past him but he has seen me in one of those rare moments when he raises his eyes from the pavement. It's not just him - we all walk around Fartlebury with our eyes on the pavement. It's the only defence against dog poo. "Ah!" he says. He's trying to act normal, but he's not normal. I suppose it's hard for him because he was born that way. At least my abnormality has come upon me in stages. He must be as nervous as I am because he is talking quickly and to no purpose. My nervousness on this occasion has had the opposite effect and I am speechless. There's not much to say any more. I have got all the clever words out of my system and am just left with the stupid ones.

Evelyn's sentences rush out of his backside like diarrhoea. I couldn't get a word in edgeways even if I wanted to. "I heard you once," he says, "telling that Penny Finkless that you saw yourself as a benign dictator." He snorts. "Not so benign after all, were you?"

"I didn't do anything wrong. None of this was my fault, Evelyn."

He looks at me with utter disdain. "You didn't have to go to the papers."

"I was just responding to Dave Tripswitch's attack on me," I say, furious with the injustice of it. "I was just trying to put them straight. He told a pack of lies. He was the one who went to the papers first, not me."

"He is a thoroughly nice man." Evelyn is unjustifiably indignant. "He's done a lot to help the Scouts, and other people."

"Oh yes, a thoroughly nice man, running a website with links to pornography. More than one website, probably."

"I don't know anything about that," he says, "but I heard a programme on the wireless about Pol Pot in Vietnam, or where was it, Thailand? Somewhere over that way. They're trying to say now that he was a genocide merchant, a maniac, but he did a lot of good."

I can hardly believe my ears. I must have misheard him. He can't be talking about one of the worst tyrants the world has ever known. He can't have seen *The Killing Fields*.

"He had the right idea. Got rid of all the intellectu-rals. They're no good, intellect-urals. Farmers, that's what you want. He was all right to the ordinary people, the workers, the farmers on the land. He was only a genocide maniac when it came to rich people and teachers. Got rid of all the lawyers he did, and closed the universities. That's what we want here. He wouldn't have anyone wearing glasses, did you know? Got rid of all those people like you and your cronies, people who think they know better than anyone else. You thought you knew how to run the village. It was better in the old days before you lot moved here."

I'm standing my ground in front of him but I've nothing to say. I've gone from speechless to gaspless, as my jaw is hanging open. How can you argue with a man who admires Pol Pot? On the other hand it hasn't escaped my notice that he's lumped me into the collective title of intellectuals. I've never been thought of as an intellectual before. I've never even thought of myself as an intellectual. But then perhaps it isn't quite so flattering; I suppose it's all relative.

When I get home I google Pol Pot. Perhaps I've forgotten what he was like, or muddled him up with the Dalai Lama or something. It is a bit of an irony to read that he was educated at a Roman Catholic school and he died at a Buddhist monastery. Doing his bit for ecumenism then.

CHAPTER TWENTY-ONE

"A paranoid is someone who knows a little of what is going on."
William S Burroughs

Eighteen months have passed. They don't like to rush things in Corsetshire. We are sitting in the posh Council Chamber at County Hall. It is set out like a court-room and I recognise hardly anyone. I feel the smooth, polished wood surfaces and admire the light fittings. I can focus on the room, not on the proceedings.

Windy and I are sitting with Tom and Eleanor. Hilary and Nigel are in the row in front of us. The seats are plush, so you feel you are at the theatre waiting for the main performance. We can help ourselves to tea or coffee from an urn at the back of the room. "Hello Urn," says Nigel but the sombre mood is not lightened. No-one is smiling, no-one in the whole room, but deep inside me I feel a rare irrepressible schoolgirl giggle machine starting up. At school it was a given that I would get the giggles only at the most serious moments. I suppose this is a serious moment without compare and I think the memories of my schoolday giggle fits are threatening to re-start the machine today, even after all these sober years. I must suppress it because to sit here and laugh, or even smile, would give credence to the view that the pursuit of justice by bringing this case was undertaken lightly, or worse, that it was motivated by revenge, or spite, and that Hilary and I were in it together. We weren't. Honest to goodness, m'lud, we weren't.

The chairman of the panel is Archibald Pym. He's a pompous ass from Middleton Mire parish council who likes to flaunt his self-assumed importance and speaks with a cut-glass accent. He has studied the look he wants and wears his gold-rimmed glasses (beg his pardon, spectacles) on the end of his bulbous puce nose. This enables him to achieve the style of a distinguished judge. (I must say I perceive neither distinction nor judgment.)

Most spectators are sitting quietly in their chairs but Tom and Eleanor are noisily flicking through a file of papers they have brought with them and whispering loudly. Windy is picking his teeth (thanks Windy, glad it's not your nose). I am looking round at each new person to enter the room. I am disappointed that no-one is here from Fartlebury Magna Parish Council. They don't want their dirty linen aired in public – that's what they say. But it's going to be hung out to dry in this room today, whether they are here to watch the show or not. Their attitude reminds me of a small child putting his hands over his eyes and thinking he is hiding and can't be seen. The councillors collectively push their little fists hard into their parochial little eye-sockets, while I am shouting 'I can see you!' and they don't hear me.

The judges who comprise 'the Panel' are settled in their seats facing us, hiding behind a long table. To their right the council solicitor, the examiner and executioner upon whom it all depends, scrapes her chair, Archibald Pym reaches for his gavel, taps it politely and clears his throat. Everyone comes to order immediately. We are all ears - except Archibald himself, who is all nose.

Archibald Pym explains that Mr Tripswitch is unable to be present at the hearing because he has emigrated, but he asks each of us to follow along as he reads aloud the transcript of the interview with Mr Tripswitch conducted by the Council's Solicitor, who is also the chief inquisitor of the Standards Board. He uses the word Defendant right through the reading. I think he thinks that DDT stands for Defendant. The transcript begins with the usual trademark DDT sob story, which makes me cringe.

Solicitor

Please state your name for the tape.

DDT

David D Tripswitch. It's been very difficult for me to get here to this interview to be honest. I haven't been well. Emotionally speaking. It was a lot to deal with – earlier this year they had to remove shrapnel from inside me, a lot of it. You know, from the Falklands. They had to remove my bowel and my liver. I don't want to go into too much detail but the army doctors botched it and didn't get all the shrapnel so they only took it out this year. I found it hard to cope with emotionally. I mean I couldn't satisfy my wife. I was very worried she would go off with another man. I got so it was hard to go out. It was hard for me to come here today. I've got a bit of agoraphobia you see.

Solicitor

OK. I understand. Were you the webmaster for Fartlebury Magna Parish Council's website? I want to ask you about why you didn't take the website off-line when you were asked to. As you know, it is alleged that your refusal to co-operate with the Acting Chair of the Council breached the Code of Conduct.

DDT

I led a team of volunteers. We were all the webmaster jointly. I had the most experience so I checked it all out. There was no pornography on the website. I'm a professional. I'd have noticed if there was any pornography.

Solicitor

Right.

DDT

Besides, like I said, I was part of a team. Anyone could have taken the website off-line. The team included PC Andy Jones. When they said there was porn it implicated a police officer. I didn't want anything to do with it. All this could affect my work with the police. That's important work. Very important, not for me, I mean for the country.

Solicitor

I have an email from you in which you state that only you have authority to make any changes to the website.

DDT

Changes, yes. But any one of them could have taken it off-line. Or the Clerk could have done it. She had the power to take it off-line.

Solicitor

You created the website from a kind of template, I understand?

DDT

Yes. I used a template to make the job a bit quicker. I didn't charge anybody for my time. I made lots of websites for churches and charities. I never charged anything so I used a template to make it quicker.

Solicitor

And this 'disclaimer'?

DDT

Well, the disclaimer was hard-wired in. Of course I didn't know about it. I obviously just thought it was the usual disclaimer.

Solicitor

But when the link to Cam-Cam Services was found, you were asked to take the website off-line.

DDT

Well, yes, I was.

Solicitor

Why didn't you do it?

DDT

I was going to California. I was packing.

Solicitor

The Acting Chair of the parish council told you it was a serious matter and asked you for help.

DDT

It wasn't a serious matter. I knew there were no direct links to anything. There was nothing lurid on there. I looked. It was all harmless.

Solicitor

Oh, you looked? When did you look at it and decide it was harmless?

DDT

I don't know exactly. My boy was in hospital at the time. My wife was very upset. I was struggling with my own health problems then all this comes along. I looked at the website. I was shocked, frankly, to see how they had all let it get so out of date, but there weren't any links to anything lurid. Nothing like that at all. So I knew it didn't really matter. I've spent the last eight years... well, I've been tracing Al Qaeda with MI5 and working with Interpol tracking down pornography and paedophile teams all the way to China and I take it very seriously. I work with the police and MI5.

Solicitor

The Acting Chair of the council asked you to take the Fartlebury Magna website off-line though? Would you agree? Hilary Entwhistle, as Acting Chair of the council, also asked you to resign as Children's Champion while the investigation was going on.

DDT

She was only doing all that because she's a friend of Katie Miller's. They've all got a vendetta against me. Because I was in the army I think. Hilary's some kind of pacifist.

Solicitor

So you didn't want to co-operate with her because you saw the link to Cam-Cam Services as harmless? You didn't agree that it was important to take the website off-line?

DDT

No. Yes. It was harmless. It didn't link to pornography. Just to a list of chat rooms and stuff like that. It was more of a search engine. You couldn't get into pornography without intentionally clicking on the links. I don't know what all the fuss was about. They had been my friends. They had been grooming me then they turned against me. I was very upset by their attitude. I was very vulnerable at that time because I was really unwell with the effects of the chemo and they were really out of order towards me.

Solicitor

Did you resign as Fartlebury Magna Parish Council's Children's Advocate?

DDT

No, I didn't see why I should. Children and youth in the village were relying on me. I was going into the local schools and teaching them how to use MSN safely and stuff like that. They trusted me. I didn't want to stop. I was helping the local police. I was busy at the time dealing with a paedophile ring in China. The police relied on me to sort those things out. Not many people can deal with the kind of things I know about.

Solicitor

Hilary Entwhistle, who was the Acting Chair of the Council after Katie Miller's resignation, says she put it to you that it wasn't appropriate for you to continue with youth work while you were in charge of a website which had links to pornographic sites.

DDT

Yeah, she said that. But I don't see that. Mavis Wilson said I shouldn't stop. She's an experienced councillor. A senior councillor. She had got me some introductions to families at Fartlebury-in-the-Marsh. I was building up good relationships with kids. I hadn't done anything wrong. I was just doing my good deed for the day. Putting the council in a good light. When I went to the kiddies' homes and met their parents I always told them I was a parish councillor. It was good publicity for the council to be doing so much good.

Solicitor
And what did the clerk say about your work with young people?
DDT
She was OK about it. The clerk and I weren't having much contact at that time.
Solicitor
Why was that?
DDT
She kept nagging me about the website and I got fed up with it. I should have been more patient. Where I'm in the wrong I'll take it on the chin. I should have been more patient with the clerk. She'd got a hard job. Katie Miller drove her up the wall.
Solicitor
What was she nagging you about? The clerk says she asked you to keep away from her because her daughter had asked her to stop inviting you round to their house.
DDT
Yeah. Millie took against me. Sorry, Millie's her daughter. She must be about ten or eleven now. Well, girls of that age go a bit funny, don't they? Hormones, isn't it? Have you got any children? They can be a bit too sensitive.
Solicitor
OK. That's all for now.
DDT
When will the hearing be, because I'm going on holiday soon and I'm going to move to California next year.
Solicitor
I can definitely tell you it will be either before or after your holiday."

"The transcript of that interview ends there." Arthur Pym clears his throat. "Have you now all finished reading the transcript of the interview with Councillor Tripswitch?"

There is a lot of solemn nodding. I nod a lot more cheerfully than everyone else and turn to Windy, whispering in his ear, "He sounds a knob." This delights me.

Archibald Pym, continuing up his own orifice, begins to drone again. I see the eyelids droop on one or two of his colleagues at the top table.

"Lisa Purfitt, the clerk to Fartlebury Magna Parish Council at the time of the alleged breaches of the Code of Conduct for councillors, cannot be here either and I would ask each of you to read her interview transcript as well."

I turned the page and began:

Interview with Lisa Purfitt

Solicitor

Thank you for coming. Please state your name for the tape. You know what this is about?

LP Lisa Purfitt. It's about the complaint against Dave Tripswitch.

Solicitor

I understand you are no longer the clerk of Fartlebury Magna Parish Council? Can you tell me when you were clerk there?

LP

Between March 2003 and February 2005

Solicitor

Why did you leave?

LP

I resigned. It was awful. There was a vendetta against Dave Tripswitch and they were all coming in my office and talking to me about it. I couldn't get any work done. There was a terrible atmosphere.

Solicitor

I see. Were you aware that Councillor Tripswitch had health problems?

LP

Yes. He had terminal cancer. He didn't want other councillors to know but it was why he couldn't take on too much. He had a lot of health problems actually, and so did his family.

Solicitor

Where was the cancer?

LP

Everywhere. I don't know the details but he was really not well. He was always at hospital appointments.

Solicitor

And did you know he had had an operation to remove shrapnel he got while he was serving in the armed forces during the Falklands War?

LP

No. I don't think so. But I knew he was in and out of hospital quite a bit while he was a councillor.

Solicitor

Did you know him well?

LP He used to help me when the computer was playing up. We were both trying to save the council money.

Solicitor

Did you ask him to take the website off-line in July last year?

LP

Yes

Solicitor

Tell me what happened

LP

He was very busy getting ready to go to California – or it might have been one of his holidays to Thailand. He was away quite a bit that year. All these councillors were jumping up and down and I was piggy in the middle. I didn't want to take it off-line. He said the website was kosher.

Solicitor
What did you take him to mean, that it was kosher?
LP
I thought he meant that it was clean and good. I looked at it myself. There weren't any direct links to pornography. If you clicked on the Disclaimer at the bottom of the screen a list of links came up. Some of the councillors were making a fuss about it being taken off-line and I didn't know what to do so in the end I asked him to do it.
Solicitor
Which councillors were making a fuss?
LP
Hilary and Nigel mainly – Councillor Entwhistle and Councillor How.
Solicitor
OK. Just to be clear for the tape - Councillor Hilary Entwhistle was Acting Chairman of the Council at this time? Why do you think she and Councillor How wanted the website off-line?
LP
I think they were scared of repercussions on the council. I think they were trying to do the right thing because they were nervous about these links, but I don't think Hilary liked Dave ...er, Councillor - Tripswitch that is. At one time I thought she might be using the whole issue to get at him.
Solicitor
Did you voice that concern to anyone?
LP
Not really. I might have mentioned it to one or two in the office. Just chatting really.
Solicitor
What was your relationship with Dave Tripswitch?
LP
Professional. It was a professional relationship between clerk and councillor.

Solicitor
Was it a close relationship?
LP
Well, I saw quite a bit of him. Quite a lot actually at one time. He used to maintain the office computers so we were often in the office together in the afternoons.
Solicitor
Did he come to your house?
LP
No, never.
Solicitor
Did he get to know your children?
LP
No.
Solicitor
Did you go out for drinks with him?
LP
No, of course not!
Solicitor
I've got an email here in which you state that you can't wait to meet him in the pub again.
LP
Oh. Yes. We held a website team meeting in the pub.
Solicitor
Was anyone else present?
LP
Yes. About a dozen people.
Solicitor
Was that the only occasion?
LP
Absolutely.

Solicitor

Dave Tripswitch says you and he were friends.

LP

Yes, I had a friendly relationship with all the councillors. I saw it as part of my job to be friendly to councillors.

Solicitor

Were you specially friendly with Dave Tripswitch?

LP

Of course not. That would be unprofessional.

Solicitor

What did you know about Cam-Cam Services?

LP

Nothing. I left that all to Dave, I mean, Councillor Tripswitch.

Solicitor

Why did you refuse to assist the council in getting the website taken off-line?

LP

I didn't know anything about how to do it. I don't know much about computers. Anyway, it was a long time ago. I don't remember anyone asking me to take it off-line. I knew they were nagging Dave, I mean Councillor Tripswitch. I just wanted them to leave me alone and let me get on with my work.

Solicitor

Did you know there were secret links to a search engine for pornographic sites on the parish council website?

LP

Of course not. I was a member of the Society of Clerks! I always acted in the best interests of the council.

Solicitor

Thank you for answering my questions. You're free to go. We won't trouble you again.

LP
You're not going to ask me about his CRB check then?
Solicitor
No. Is there anything about that you want to tell me?
LP
No."

Archibald Pym looks over the rim of his glasses at the audience and I see him looking at me. I don't know if he recognises me. He says, "Has everyone had enough time to read that transcript?"

There is a lot of obedient nodding, but I am too enraged to nod. I whisper to Windy, "What a farce! Why didn't she get asked the right questions? Why did they let her off so lightly? The solicitor didn't even follow it up about the CRB check!" I'm as mad as a mint marshmallow.

Archibald Pym is giving me a hard stare, then, having got my attention, he asks, "Is Councillor Hilary Entwhistle here?"

Hilary jumps up and goes to the front.

"Can you tell us what happened when you were Acting Chairman of Fartlebury Magna Parish Council insofar as the council's website was concerned?" Silly question. Of course she can! Given the chance.

"Tom – I think it was Tom, sorry, Tom Waterman – discovered a link to a kind of porn search engine from the council website. It was sort of hidden behind the disclaimer at the bottom of the page. He told me about it."

"And did you want to do something about that?"

"Oh yes, of course. I was the Acting Chair of the Council. It isn't right for a parish council website to have links to pornography. Anyone could access it, even children might use the website to look for information, and they could come across it." Hilary was as pink as a sugar mouse.

"So, would you please tell us what you did?"

"I rang Dave Tripswitch who was the webmaster and asked him to take the website off-line."

"Did you tell him why?"

"Yes, but he was angry and started shouting down the phone at me. I had to hang up in the end."

"Why was he angry?"

"He didn't appreciate my concerns. He took it as an accusation. I wasn't accusing him of anything. I didn't imply I thought he was responsible for putting the links there, just that he was responsible for taking them off."

"Did he take the website off-line?"

"No. It was really difficult because he was going off on holiday for weeks and we couldn't get it taken off-line. The clerk wasn't that bothered and said she didn't have the authority. To be honest I don't know whether she understood the seriousness of it. It did seem a bit over-the-top. I mean it seemed far-fetched to suggest that the council's website had links to pornography, but it did."

Archibald Pym looks down his nose. I'm surprised he can see anything beyond its end, and the fact is, perhaps he can't. Maybe it's all bluff.

"Would you have described yourself as a friend of Councillor Tripswitch?"

"Yes. I thought he was a friend until he was very rude to me about this issue and point blank refused to help."

"And were you a friend of Katie Miller's?"

I prick up my own ears which are darting flames into my hairline. What has that to do with anything? I hope he's not fishing to see if we are in a plot together.

"We became friends through working together on the council."

"Did you bring this complaint to the Standards Board to take revenge on Councillor Tripswitch for the complaint he made about Katie Miller?"

"Of course not!" Hilary is full of righteous indignation. "I thought his attitude and behaviour as a parish councillor was unacceptable when he wouldn't help take the website off-line. I didn't know whether he was responsible for the links to porn sites or not, but he should have taken it off-line when I asked him to. It was a reasonable request for me to make."

"Yes," says Archibald. He is looking around him a while as if he has lost something before he asks, "What happened next?"

"The clerk wouldn't get it taken off-line either – or she didn't feel she wanted to get involved or something. In the end Bill Shorthouse rang the company from the parish council off...."

"Sorry to interrupt," interrupts Archibald. "Would you tell us who Bill Shorthouse is, and would you make it clear which company he rang?"

"Bill Shorthouse is a fellow councillor. Or he was at the time. We had to ring Cam-Cam Services."

"They provided the server?"

"Yes."

"Go on, how did the website get taken off-line then?"

Hilary is keeping her cool well for someone in the middle of a hot flush. She continues patiently, "Bill Shorthouse rang Cam-Cam Services and just demanded it. He was very assertive and wouldn't take no for an answer and they just did it, even though they had been refusing before and saying that they couldn't do it without Dave, I mean, Councillor Tripswitch's say-so. To start with they just put up a kind of notice on the front page but that wasn't enough."

"What did Councillor Tripswitch say about it being taken off-line?"

“Nothing. He had gone on holiday. I’ve got copies of the emails he sent when he found out what we had done.”

“Yes,” says Archibald sharply. “We’ve got those, thank you. No more questions.”

The hearing takes about two hours. During that time my feelings seesaw between optimism and utter, crushing defeat. It was bad enough that my own parish council would not listen. I don’t think this body of people is really listening to the evidence either.

Afterwards I promise Windy that I will now put it all behind me. I’ve got the closure I wanted. The Chair of the Board announces that Dave Tripswitch is guilty on all counts and the Solicitor says that it is the most serious breach she has ever seen. What more could I want?

CHAPTER TWENTY-TWO

"Never complain. Never explain. Resist the temptation to defend yourself or make excuses." Brian Tracy

Six months later I am sinking deeper into the quicksand of despondency. I've lost my Mojo and I feel that I will never get it going again. Life is ebbing and flowing while I sit out of reach above the tide-line. I'm happy that Phil Jenkins has been ousted from the Chair in favour of a younger (and more intelligent) woman, but she is not one of my FUC-kers. She is a complete newcomer to the council scene - a maverick. Now and again someone tries my crank handle and I sputter and make a faltering start, but it always ends in tears and disappointment. I just can't get over my ignominious defeat.

"Do you really hate that man?" my walking companion Jane asks me one day quite out of the blue, well, grey really. She knows little of my past. She's not the type to read the local papers or follow parish council websites. Not that there is anything to follow on the new Fartlebury Magna website, made in haste by the new Chair (without the help of any volunteers, I note). It has not a word about the closure of the fartleburymagna.net website. The new one has the wonderful URL www.fartleburymagnaparishcouncil.corset.org.uk.

Windy is glad I have made some new friends. Jane and I met through the Fartlebury Footpath Group (or as Windy calls us, the Fart-foots.)

"Oh yes," I say, "I hate him alright."

"Enough to kill him?"

"Oh yes. Well..." I hesitate. "No, I suppose not, but he has hurt me fatally. I can't get over it, I can't seem to move on."

We are having a nice walk together on the outskirts of Fartlebury Magna. The parish extends in all directions into former stagnant marshes where hundreds of years ago Dutchmen used their skills and experience to dig drainage channels and create peaty meadows and rushy pastures. There are willows and alders, iris and bulrush. I love it here away from the village. I love the regularity of the wet fences running straight as straw through degraded pastures. Farmers like Phil Jenkins keep it all green and tidy by constant mowing for silage. The fields are an unnaturally rich jade, kept that way by doses of inorganic fertiliser. The effect on the eye is soothing and satisfying: a grid of lime green duckweed cutting straight through rectangular blocks of emerald. The prophylactic fertiliser keeps the grass forever green and the duckweed screens the murky water. A closer look can still be rewarding too, although modern farming's heavy hand has put paid to most of the wild flowers and butterflies that adorned my nature rambles in the past. Fartlebury Magna was once home to 26 species of butterfly but it's now largely a parish full of cabbage whites. The swallowtails on the ditch edges have been replaced by hub caps and beer cans. I don't find them as pretty to look at as butterflies but the locals (those who call themselves the 'true locals') like a place to ditch their detritus. I notice that the council can't tolerate a bit of long grass because they call it untidy, but hub caps can remain for decades. And the plastic will be there for centuries.

"Someone ought to clear up all this mess," says Jane, unaware of the demon she is unleashing in me. I bite back the caustic taste of a sharp retort. I've no witty ripostes left. They have withered with my heart and done a runner with my sense of humour.

"I've been there, done that and bought the XL tee shirt," I reply wearily. I remember very well those long hot days of summers past, wielding my litter picker, filling black sacks with smelly objects of varying size and weight. Those were the days! We were indiscriminate in our selection, bagging everything from the tiny, shiny, aluminium ring-pulls, to the heavy, incorruptible, dirty nappies that disorganised child-carers had no intention of bagging and binning for themselves. They owe me a favour or two, those people! The ditch we are walking along is far from human habitation but the tipping here is authentic. I know it's proper fly-tipping because it has attracted flies. A hairy brute with bright green alien eyes tickles me pink in foreplay and I knock it away before it climaxes with an ejaculation of poison. It has brought me out of my reverie. Jane is standing by a plank which is a make-shift bridge over untroubled waters. The sluggish liquid is lying quietly at the bottom of a deep and steep-sided trench. It is a full eight feet below the plank and there is no handrail or tree to grab onto. If you fall in, it's not so much the drowning in water you need to worry about, it's getting stuck in the filthy silt in the bottom. It's made of tiny particles so fine they are invisible to the naked eye, but so solid they are very much attracted to naked skin and will cover any unfortunate dabbler in seconds with a coating that looks like chocolate and smells like nothing on earth. This foul smell lies in ambush until an excavator, or even an unwary child with a stick, disturbs the mud. The smell released is truly unique and may have given rise to the parish's name.

We cross the plank one at a time. Jane picks her way slowly and carefully, putting each foot down with conscious deliberation. I step across quickly, using my momentum to combat fear and deficient balance. On the other side we stop to look across the flat landscape to the church of St John the Evangelist, its huge, slim, tapering steeple crowned magnificently by its gold-plated weather cock, glowing in the afternoon sun. As we begin the homeward part of the circuit I feel there is a rare opportunity to unburden myself.

"I don't suppose I really hate anyone," I say, "and of course I can't imagine killing anyone." I fast-forward to the scene in a possible future where in a police interview I could be betrayed by a friend admitting that I had once expressed a desire to kill my enemy.

"Of course I couldn't kill him," I repeat, trying to convince us both. Jane's tongue is loose at both ends. I'm not going to give her a chance to wag it over me.

"I've never been a vengeful person," I add. "I don't bear grudges."

Jane responds in a low tone, "No, I know. But you are a bit obsessive about all this stuff and this guy is really under your skin now, isn't he? I think you need some therapy to help you let go of it."

Therapy? She's got to be joking!

Six months later I am sitting with my counsellor in a small room at Fartlebury Magna Medical Centre. I am subdued this evening. Most probably it's just because I'm tired and wishing I was at home watching the telly or doing the ironing. I have told her about my wound. I've picked off the scab, given it a good poke around and made it ooze poison again. She's very good about it and has offered me a plaster. It's stalemate now as I resist the application of the dressing. Now she's talking about 'people' and meaning me. God! She thinks I'm paranoid. There's a lot of truth in the quote: '*Just because I'm paranoid it doesn't mean they're not out to get me*'. I won't quote that back at her though. She's probably heard it all before, and anyway she's got no sense of humour.

"How did your mother react when you were naughty?" she is asking now, with that self-satisfied smile. (I don't think she had a mother. I think she is a robot).

"About the same as when I wasn't," I say. That is the plain truth, the whole truth and nothing but the truth. My mother was consistent only in being inconsistent but towards me she always seemed angry. I was always in trouble and that was largely because I didn't know how not to be. It was nigh-on impossible to please my mother. I always got it wrong. Now apparently I feel (the counsellor says '*falsely*') that I like other people more than they like me. This does ring true with me – I do feel as if I like people more than they like me, but what if, in fact, I do actually like other people more than they like me? There's no answer to that.

The counsellor is looking at me again but my mind has drifted off now. I've applied myself to as much of her psycho-babble as I can for one evening. I'm just biding my time waiting for the magic words: '*Time's up. That's all for this week.*'

Eventually they arrive, bang on time as usual, and as is my custom, I manage a few crocodile tears to close. I scuttle out of the door like a lobster in the light and, eyes on the ground, I sniff to see if the bad odour is from my rotting heart or from the entrails of my enemies. It's neither, as it happens, it's just that I am walking past a dog bin.

"How's the counselling going?" asks Windy kindly as soon as I get in the door.

"Fine," I say, genuinely feeling it for a moment. "The medical centre's bloody cold though and I was in that extension, the conservatory bit. You feel like you're in a goldfish bowl, everyone gawping at you."

"What? Do people walk about while you are having counselling, then? Can they see you?"

"No, not really. There wasn't anybody about in the corridors, but I just felt people could have been gawping at me if they actually were there."

Windy looks a bit knowing. (This is slightly different from his know-all look.) "Ah yes," he says in a patronising tone. I suppose he knows I am paranoid but he covers it well. "It was a stupid design, that extension. Built by Evelyn Harse's son, Dick. He's a bit off-centre."

I smile. "You would be with a surname like his. His dad's a bubble off plumb himself."

Windy gives me a nice fatherly kiss and I put the kettle on for my hot chocolate.

He has followed me into the kitchen. "You'll never guess what? I went to see Mike today. Last time I saw him I told him what I knew about our friend Dave Tripswitch and he said he would put out a few feelers."

"Mike Cannon?" I shouldn't interrupt, not least because I know very well who he is talking about.

"Yes, he's planning his retirement now, lucky bugger. You remember he said he's going to California for six weeks to get out of the cold here over the winter. He said we could go too and keep Helga company. Would you think about that Katie? Anyway, he said that he spoke to one of his colleagues who does psychological profiling of criminals and she said she would be willing to see me because what I said about Tripswitch did ring some alarm bells."

"Will you go then?" I ask. "We haven't got any evidence really – not about the bad stuff."

"I need to do something. What if Tripswitch is in California and carrying on as before? I don't want it on my conscience that I never passed on what I suspected."

"But it's been ages, Windy!"

I make my hot chocolate and without further comment go to sit down in front of the television. I haven't answered him about a holiday in California. I could do with a nice murder.

Time is passing every day since the hearing and Fartlebury Magna Parish Council has done a grand job of sweeping this whole debacle under the carpet. They don't understand what a debacle is, but they understand that sweeping things under the carpet deals with them very adequately. It's how things are done in Fartlebury Magna. I try to talk to the new chairperson, Anita, about the hearing, about the fact that Dave was found guilty on all counts, about the fact that the solicitor said it was the most serious breach of the Code of Conduct she had ever come across. Anita says she doesn't believe in airing dirty linen in public. She won't put it on the council agenda. Ever.

Anita is about forty-five. Her thick red hair is her best feature. It is young hair. It looks as if it hasn't seen the rigours and disappointments of life that show on her face. I remember as a child learning that it uses fewer muscles to smile than to frown. Anita must get very tired in that case because she works her facial muscles extremely hard to keep a permanent, unattractive scowl. When I was young we were told that if we pulled a face and the wind direction changed, we would get stuck like it. I can only think this is what happened to Anita. Must have been a gale, I reckon, in her case.

The Vicar told me that Jesus said whoever wasn't for him was against him. He was trying to comfort me. (The Vicar, not Jesus – although maybe he was too and I was too bitter to notice.) He wanted to make me feel there was a precedent for the betrayal I was feeling. I agree. The councillors who weren't for me were almost certainly against me. And the ones who didn't resign with me are those who are left, and they are all against me. Anita isn't for me either but I don't suppose she is for anybody. Possibly not for anything either. I don't know her but I know they wouldn't have elected her otherwise.

I've got to make them see what an evil little toe-rag Dave Tripswitch is. That's an insult to strips of material protecting someone's poor feet. He wasn't out to do any good to anyone and I wouldn't want to wrap him round my foot unless I intended to kick him into orbit. I would like a discussion about the results of the Standards Board hearing but the new clerk wouldn't play ball with me either. He's another autocratic little man like Newman. Male parish clerks of a certain age were made in a mould. They give a representation of a real man in the way a sugar mouse resembles a flesh-and-blood mouse. No texture, all too smooth, indistinct features and a hump back. I think about how nice it would be to bite his head off.

Of course it's nothing to do with me. I'm not really involved with the council at all now – only telephone counselling Hilary, Nigel and a couple of others who haven't yet resigned. I keep an eye on the shenanigans and now and again I pop up like a meerkat on guard and tell them what I think of them in Public Speaking Time. This is my only chance, a brief five minutes at the start of a meeting when the Great Unwashed, or 'the Public' can speak. If there was a prize for Public Speaking I would win it. I spend hours refining my speeches until each one is a work of performance art. I perfect the alliteration, the allusions and the near-truths for these speeches. I'm just trying to get a reaction out of the miserable old councillors. Evelyn once hissed *'Shame'* when I made a particularly outrageous statement, but that's the closest I've got, however hard I try to wind them up.

Have I overwound the councillors? I think I probably have because they just won't be wound up any more. I might have turned their winders the wrong way. Anyway, I keep trying, forcing them against the thread. One more turn of the screw tonight. I've worked hard on my script. I'll give it all I've got. So I turn up at 7.32 precisely, aiming to give enough time for the councillors to sit down and exchange unpleasantries with each other – the few who speak at all. They've got a few who are new on me tonight, decent people who've gone onto the council to try to sort out the mess it's in. I feel sorry for them. They have no idea what kind of people they are working alongside. But I'm going to do my best to tell them.

It's the turn of Maggie's husband John, the manic street pastor, to say prayers tonight. *"Father, your ways are not our ways. We cannot see the reason for the events in Fartlebury Magna,"* (I can.) *"But we know that all things work together for good because it says so in your Word. Help us to make good come out of the evil that has been worked here. Re-unite this council."* (Re-unite? When was there ever any unity?) *"Help councillors to lay aside their prejudice and remember that they are here to serve the community, to serve each other and to serve you."*

I open an eye. Phil has an eye open too. So has Hilary. One eyed people are kings here among the blind. "*Please Father, pour your healing oil over all the hurts and fears,*" (please don't – we had enough trouble with the water last time) "*and give us all your blessing that we may live life in all its fullness just as Jesus promised,*" (please, not the J word) "*Amen.*"

I don't feel like having oil poured over me. I'm crushed like a clove of garlic, beaten to a batter, but I don't want healing. I want revenge. I can't confide in anyone now but I feel my life has been smashed and the only way to restore it is to get even. Let their tyres down, poison their cats, that kind of thing. I suppose if I was a proper born-again believer like Maggie I would know what to do. I suppose this uncertainty would go and I would find the right path to tread. But I'm not sure of anything anymore except that I'm going to lay it on them tonight. It's my turn to speak. Anita nervously nods towards me. She keeps on nodding, like the artificial dog on the parcel shelf of her Ford Fiesta.

"Councillors, I'm here tonight to talk about the parish council's response to the Standard Board's ruling on a former councillor. You know who I mean. He breached the Code of Conduct on four counts. That isn't open to interpretation. He is not being victimised. It is not a witch-hunt. He broke the Code of Conduct. That isn't the same as with me – he made a complaint against me and the Standards Board didn't even investigate it because I hadn't done anything wrong.

Councillor Hilary Entwhistle, as your Acting Chairman, reported his unwillingness to co-operate in shutting down the website. The Standards Board said she acted correctly. If you think otherwise you are wrong. She was right to be concerned. You were wrong not to be concerned. The clerk at the time prevented her from putting the matter on the council agenda."

I am punching the air with my fist between sentences. I have taken off my boxing gloves and I am ready to bare-knuckle fight anyone who won't listen.

"You should thank the Standards Board for their decision. I hope you noticed that the Standards Board thought it was wrong of Councillor Tripswitch not to apologise for his refusal to co-operate with the Acting Chair of the council. The Board was surprised that no-one from the parish council was interested in attending the hearing. I was embarrassed when he asked if anyone from Fartlebury Magna Parish Council was there. It was the most serious breach they had ever investigated and you didn't even show any interest in it.

You can't go on pretending this was nothing to do with you. It's important to learn something and change your ways. The community needs to see that the council regrets what happened and wants to uphold decent standards."

"Get her to sit down," mumbles Evelyn just loud enough for everyone to hear. "At least it would muffle her voice."

I ignore him but I notice the new Chair doesn't even bother to reprimand him. None of them cares about me and how I feel. I'm the only normal one in a zombie movie. I'm surrounded by the living dead. I carry on, slightly less confidently.

"This councillor did the council a lot of harm. Hilary could see that. The council should now apologise to her and to the people who got caught up in his fantasy land – all the website volunteers, all the councillors who resigned, Fartlebury Magna Garden Centre for being dragged through the press twice, and all the others. You could still come out of it looking as if you know the difference between right and wrong if you say something now.

Your standing in the community couldn't get much lower, so I just want to urge you to say sorry, and to promise the community that you will take more interest in how councillors behave in the future."

I sit down, I'm very hot in the face. There isn't a peep out of the councillors. Not a word. Not even a hum or a grunt. Even Nigel's socks are quiet. Anita clears her throat and says, "Let's move on to item 1 on the agenda."

Windy is looking very pleased with himself. I know better than to ask him what he's been doing. I might get an answer I don't like, but more likely I won't get an answer at all. His favourite response is to say that he thought my question was rhetorical, but sometimes he just sighs and says he is tired, as if speaking to me is the most tiresome thing he can think of.

Later, when he is in the mood, he begins to talk about his chat with the police psychologist. He is very pleased with himself because they are going to put a note on the file. If Dave Tripswitch ever comes back to England they will be keeping a closer eye on him.

"I told them all about him, how he made things up, said he was injured in the Falklands War, said he worked with the police and social services, said he visited families in their homes, said he had been 'trained'. I told them he kept making what he called mistakes on his application for Criminal Records Bureau check- delaying tactics - and that he promoted himself as a self-appointed children's advocate, or some kind of youth worker, when in fact he wasn't really one at all with any kind of authority. I told them he was always pretending to be ill to get people's sympathy."

"That's hardly a crime," I say.

"No, but it builds up the picture, doesn't it? She said I was right to be suspicious, well, not right, but she said she could understand my concerns and shared them. He does have the kind of profile that the police would find interesting. And he's short. Small men are always under suspicion."

"Did she really say that?"

"No, of course not, but it's true, isn't it?" He goes on, "Do you remember when he wrote to the school to complain about a teacher who had done something to annoy his son, and he wrote to the school and said he was the Youth Advocate of the Parish Council?"

"And he was!" I say, although I don't know why I would want to defend him.

"Yes, but he bigged it up. You know, parish councillors don't have that kind of power, do they? What went on at school was nothing to do with him. It's laughable. He wanted to look as if he was someone."

"It's a bit lame."

"He tells lies. I told the police officer that he tells lies."

"That's not a police matter, is it?" I am still defending him.

"I had to tell her that he said he hadn't put the links on the website and he said anyone could have done it. He controlled the website so the volunteers couldn't have done it. It was only him who could have done it."

I am questioning myself now. Shining the big bright light in my own eyes. "He used to give me the creeps."

"I told her that he used to make out that he was ill all the time, walking with a stick, pretending he was at hospital appointments all the time, or that his son had cancer. He was just out to get sympathy. An attention seeker."

"He was obsessed with the clerk."

Windy smiles at me. "It's all right, don't you worry."

Now Windy has put it all like this, it seems very flimsy. Dave Tripswitch is a liar, he is short, he makes things up to make himself sound more important. He pretends to be ill. He might also have put webcams into the back rooms of pubs, and seedy hotels, but it's not a crime, is it? He likes being around young people and he messed up his CRB application. That's not a crime either.

I'm going to watch the news but I check my emails first.

From: Hilary Entwhistle
To: Katie Miller
Sent: 18 March 2007
Subject: DDT – a revelation!

I've just realised today that our Dave can't be a veteran of the Falklands War. He would only have been ten years old!
Hils x

Of course! Why ever didn't we check the dates before?

With Dave Tripswitch in America, you would think I could let it go but I am more and more obsessed with him. My counsellor has given up on me and I on her.

Tonight when I get home from WI (where I won a First for my gooseberry and strawberry jam), Windy is out and I sit at the computer, brooding about my lost life. I search for my tormentor and up it comes: Dave Tripswitch – Red Oak Pentecostal Church, San Diego County. He is being thanked in the church newsletter for all his wonderful work helping the junior church to make a film about the church, and for teaching them about internet safety. Well, he would be the man for that job, wouldn't he?

It's a couple of days later that Windy is using the computer and for some reason looks at my recent searches. "You've been looking for Dave Tripswitch," he says. "I think you need to draw a line under it all, Katie. We should have a big holiday. Let's go to California and lay some ghosts. You've always wanted to go to America and see the Grand Canyon and cacti growing wild. Let's go to America and see the Giant Redwoods and see Mike and Helga. You need to get away from Fartlebury Magna and stop thinking about all this. Maybe if we go and have a good time in America you will be able to stop obsessing about it and have only great memories of a good holiday. It would create a better association with California too."

I'm not even sure about laying the living, let alone ghosts. "OK Windy," I say, but I know it won't come to anything unless I organise it. Windy never organises anything, least of all a holiday. And I might not feel like it for years yet.

CHAPTER TWENTY-THREE

"Monsters are real and ghosts are real too. They live inside us, and sometimes they win." Stephen King

I'm leaning on the toilet wall. There isn't really room for my feet on the vile, bile-green tiles because it's a small cubicle and most of it is taken up with Windy, who is kneeling voiding his stomach over the toilet bowl. It smells bad in here and my stomach would also like to empty in protest (or in sympathy, it's hard to say which). Quite a few of the passengers are seasick. Windy is very seasick. It would have been more convenient for him to have found out in time to take some anti-vomit medication, but as we don't usually travel, we don't usually get travel sick.

We can't stay in this toilet cubicle, but Windy's clinging to the contrarily stained 'stainless' steel pan as if his life depends on it, which presumably he thinks it does. I don't think people die of travel sickness but I've never been much of a traveller. Left to my own devices I wouldn't really go out of the parish much, but here we are, on the holiday of a lifetime, not exactly having the time of our lives. I think life's like that. It rarely gives us the kind of time we want.

I'm surprisingly calm given that Windy thinks he's about to vomit his stomach up. I just keep saying, "You'll be OK," and stroking his back, as if he is a colicky baby. I want to get away from this place, get it done, get back to normal.

I try to lighten the tone a bit. "You won't die of it," I say. "You just wish you could!" I reach for a chuckle. Windy just retches. In this sick-spattered space it's no place to chuckle, just chuck up. Windy's not the only one either. In the cubicle next door another man is throwing up noisily. He's very vocal about it too, each ejection emphasised by "Fuck!" and now and again by "Fuck those oranges," which leads me to believe he has unwisely lunched. Actually I think I can smell them.

Men are coming in and out, peeing in the urinals, peering at me with amused interest. They call it a bathroom here as there are very few gentlemen in America (but there are no baths in here either. Not even a small shower.)

We see the sea-life in the end of course, from a small glass-bottomed boat on a calmer day because this is the holiday of a lifetime, and it's a requirement. We have set ourselves going on a whistle-stop tour of the must-see sights which will end up with Mike and Helga in California. The fact is, and you may know this, America is big. There is a lot of distance between one place and the next. We can't face too many internal flights so we seem to be spending too much time sitting on buses and trains, but I like it. It gives me a chance to unwind, close my eyes and dream. It's weird. You drop off to sleep in one kind of landscape, and hours later you look out of the window to find you are in exactly the same kind of landscape.

Windy has let me plan the itinerary and we are sending postcards to tell people that we are having the holiday of a lifetime. I'm not sorry we came (yet). All our stops have been planned around some 'must-do' experiences: white-water rafting, (Windy calls it 'shite-water rafting' after our experience); swimming with dolphins, mule-trekking in the Grand Canyon, Alcatraz, that kind of thing. We planned it to be very exciting, then we discussed it and decided we are too old, too unfit, too scared and we are just going to take it easy. We are having a great time. Or we would if Windy wasn't so slow in remembering to take his anti-nausea medication. I'm very distracted anyway, like a snake on speed.

One of the things that was important for this trip was looking up Windy's buddy Mike Cannon. He hasn't kept in touch with us since he came to America so I am quite interested to find out how he is getting on with his semi-retirement. And of course how Helga is liking it away from the weather. By some marvellous coincidence they are living in the same area as Dave Tripswitch. I plan to look him up too but I haven't mentioned that to Windy yet. My route in search of eternal peace has been winding about California and will end up at Red Oak for the grand finale. We will get there tomorrow. Windy has promised to ring Mike and arrange a rendez-vous.

We check into the Crystal Clear Ocean Hotel. It's pretty standard (without being standard or pretty). The décor was evidently chosen by a young man – an adolescent perhaps – as it is all moody greys and black furniture. The only colour in the foyer is the receptionist's deep tan. Her skin is the colour of my Dad's brown brogues, polished regularly for 25 years and buffed up with a brush. Even her lips are brown – she's chosen lipstick to match. She's a pleasant enough young woman, giving Windy the eye (he doesn't take it, not with me watching), calling him Sir and me Ma'am. She has a label which says her name is 'Lindy-Ann'.

We don't get shown to our room. The blonde with skin like brown leather elbow patches just gives us the magic card which hoteliers call a key and points us in the direction of a long corridor. Windy says, "We'll get plenty of exercise walking down to breakfast."

Lindy-Ann Leather-Lips smiles a professional smile. "Room service is no extra."

"Thanks," I say, with ice and lemon. "We're English. He was joking."

Our room is spacious and includes a desk where I can consult the iPad. Windy leaves me to unpack and goes to have a shower. A wave of resentment springs up from nowhere. It's a tsunami, crashing through the coastal defences and surging on, carrying long-remembered bitternesses with it. I hang up one or two of my own things angrily. I'm not going to unpack for Windy. He can unpack for himself.

I take the iPad to the desk, enter the Wi-Fi code and hey presto, directions to Red Oak Pentecostal Church.

By the time Windy comes out of the shower I'm au fait with all that Red Oak has to offer. It isn't much more than Fartlebury Magna (except a massive beach and the commercial enterprises that exist to corrupt and destroy its natural beauty).

"That's better!" says Windy, returning from the bathroom wrapped in a towel like a sausage roll. "I feel really refreshed now. Why don't you have one?"

I'm irritated by him telling me what to do but he's right. I might as well try out the shower. We might need to use it a lot if this heat continues. The local website tells me that last week included the highest temperatures ever recorded in this area. There are bush fires burning to the south and east. I'm assured they pose no risk to the houses here because the wind blows from the ocean and takes the fire in the other direction, but they reckon there's a risk to asthmatics. I wonder if there is something in prayer after all. It's been a frequent request of mine that Dave Tripswitch should burn in hell. A careless match could achieve that, with care.

Windy is giving me instructions on how to use the shower. He looks surprised and disappointed to discover that his clothes are still in the suitcase.

"Do you want me to put my clothes away?" he asks with a face as droopy as a French bulldog.

"We're only here a couple of days," I say. "Just hang up the shirts you'll need here."

That seems to have bucked him up. It must be great to be so easily pleased.

When I come back into the room, Windy is trying not to look as if he's putting his mobile in his pocket.

"You could use the iPad. There are some great photos of the beach up the road from here. It looks amazing. Coronado Beach is said to be the best in the world."

"Any emails from home?" he asks. I hesitate. He seems suspicious of my continuing friendship with Hilary.

"Just one from Hilary," I say, half on the defensive, half defiant. "I need to go shopping for souvenirs and gifts to take home tomorrow."

Windy winces.

"I'll go on my own. You hate it and I'll be much quicker without you."

Windy's face shows the same expression of relief that he shows on arrival at a toilet after two cups of tea and a long bus ride.

"I'll go down to the beach," he says. "Check out the wildlife and the bathing. I don't know how far Mission Bay is but they do whale watching from there."

I try not to look too pleased. I'm planning my trip to Red Oak Pentecostal Church. I have to. I can't stop myself.

Next day, after a lazy morning mooching about the beach with Windy, and having left him there, I turn the corner (physically, not metaphorically – I haven't got to that stage yet), and see Dave Tripswitch lurking and smirking. He recognises me at once. So much so that I can't help thinking he must have known I was coming. Dave is, just as I thought he would be, looking very well for a man with terminal cancer and no liver.

He has a badge on with his name including its middle letter. They probably like that here: John F Kennedy, Lyndon B Johnson – nobody knows what the middle letter stands for. Underneath his name are more words: *Red Oak Pentecostal Church Computer Technician.* It makes me cringe, but not as much as his very unpleasant smile. His eyes are twinkly and bright. I find it hard to look him in the face for fear of being dazzled and settle my eyes on a point just below his Adam's apple. That would be a good place to plunge a knife.

"Fancy meeting you here," he says.

I can't think of a reply so I just look ahead at his tee shirt and imagine the blood trickling down it.

"I can't think of any reason why you would come to Red Oak unless you're stalking me."

I try to find a response of some sort but I can't even produce a stammer.

"I always had you down as a bunny boiler. I'm so scared."

"Can we go somewhere to talk?" I say, finding my courage and my tongue simultaneously.

"Why? What would we have to talk about? Old times? I don't think we've much in common, have we? Me a respectable and respected computer technician, always doing things for free, you a bitter and twisted old parish council chairperson who couldn't hack it and had to resign. You, a liar and so unpopular that your council had to get rid of you. You, who bullied everyone around you."

I'm curling up inside. What if it's true?

He goes on, "And me so popular, such a hero, always fixing up computers for people, making websites for nothing." He actually winks at me. "I always enjoyed that side of my work for Fartlebury Magna. Running the website for the council all those years. They never paid me a penny, you know. I don't know how I managed financially with no money coming in; not a penny from the Fartlebury Magna Parish website you know." Another smirk at me, his sparkly eyes catching mine for a moment and then letting them go. "I spent so much time on my voluntary projects you know. Just like you, Katie. It paid dividends too. It was the glowing reference I had from the community church in Fartlebury Magna that got me the job here. I fit in well here. They give me a free rein. I'm helping with the youth club too. Well, I've always liked working with children."

Oh dear, I feel sick. I think I've been standing in the sun too long.

"We can talk Katie, if that's what you want. I'd rather not stand here outside the church. Come back to my place. Rudy is out tonight and Lorraine won't be in till six o'clock."

I glance at my watch. It's just after four. Windy won't be expecting me back for at least an hour. I nod, "OK." I want to tell him a few home-truths. That's what I'm here for. That's what I've travelled half way round the world for. That's why I risked DVT on the flight and put up with days of dodging the heat and sun. This trip's going to put years on me, wrinkling my face (and not just giving me smile lines either – a hundred crows are dancing over my face every day).

"We could go to a cafe?" I suggest, but it's too late. I've already agreed to go to his house.

"My car's over there in the car park," he says. I don't want to get in his car. That seems a very dodgy thing to do. He could take me anywhere.

"I'm not sure."

"You want to talk. I know you are dying to see my place, aren't you? Dying to see how I'm getting on. You need to come with me in my car. What do you think I'm going to do to you? You're quite safe with me. I'm not an axe murderer." I daren't look at him but I can hear his lips parting in a chimpanzee grin.

It's spine-chilling the way he said it, even at 36 degrees. I can feel his inappropriate smiling, I can hear his inappropriate breathing, I can sense his inappropriate thinking. But I mustn't let him frighten me. He's a short man, after all. And sick.

"OK. How far is it?"

"Just five minutes down the road," he says. I have no way of knowing whether that is true but I have seen the house lots of times on Google Earth. It's very modern-colonial with a veranda. I love the way the little estate is set among the trees. I know it is a stupid thing to do; I shouldn't get in his car, but somehow I just can't stop myself.

The car is a Volkswagen Golf. Mike Cannon has told me that old cars in California don't look so old because they don't rust. This one looks old. "Get in," he says, opening the passenger door with the key, flinging it open and leaving it open while he goes round to the other side. My heart is beating like African drums but without as much rhythm. I get in and shut the door. He turns right round to stare at me for a moment. I know I should keep eye contact. My submissiveness shows in my body language. I want to tough it out but truth to tell I am scared to death. No not death, I'm not going to think about death. I just want to talk to him, tell him I know about his lies and fantasies, tell him how Fartlebury Magna has suffered, how I have suffered. I try to clear my throat.

"Hot, isn't it? Want a drink?" he says, handing me a plastic water bottle. "It'll be a bit hot, because I left it in the car."

I take the soft bottle gratefully, unscrew the cap and take a big swig. "God!" I splutter. It isn't water, it's neat vodka. No comment from him. I'm glad he doesn't drink any of it. He drives off and we make the short journey in silence. I am biting the skin on the side of my fingernails so I'm too busy to talk. It doesn't feel awkward. We know each other well. We aren't polite strangers.

Dave stops the car quite abruptly outside his modern bungalow set in a modern estate which appears to be populated by modern people, because there's no-one about. In fact it looks like a film set, a façade. I follow Dave up to the porch. There are a lot of shoes in the porch. All big men's shoes I notice; mainly muddy trainers and work boots, but also some sandals. I suppose the son's got grown-up feet. Most schoolboys have. I remember the son – Rudy. Who would call their son Rudy?

The answer is leading me over the threshold into an untidy hallway. There are more shoes here and a variety of bags and boxes on the floor. A badminton racquet lies along the wall and three shuttlecocks are nesting beside it. Dave walks through to the kitchen and fills the kettle from the tap. He has his back to me and for a moment I think I could turn and run. Why would I do that? I think this is all OK, don't I? Almost normal. Almost amicable.

Dave gets two mugs out of the dishwasher and rinses them under the tap with his fingers. "Tea, is it?"

"Yes thanks." I feel I might even relax in a minute but I need to get talking. I need to purge myself.

"I want to talk about what happened in Fartlebury Magna."

Dave smirks.

"Things weren't good in Fartlebury Magna after you left. The council fell apart."

Dave draws up a bar stool and hands me my tea. I clamber up onto the other stool like a circus elephant and he shrugs a reply: "So?"

"I wondered if you had any remorse for what you did. We never talked, did we? But you pulled the council apart."

He smiles and I feel the blood rising to my neck. It might even reach my face.

"Don't keep smiling!" I say angrily. "It's about real people with lives to get on with. Some of us were really hurt. We haven't got over it."

"Aah," he says, "You poor thing."

"And others. Not just me. Six councillors resigned. I couldn't go on. I had to resign."

"How do you make that my fault?"

"Obviously it was your fault."

"I was just one of many who saw what you were doing. You were working Lisa to death. You bullied her. I had to protect her. Lots of the others wanted you gone."

I am exasperated now. Deep down I think I know that what he says is right. Further up I know that what he says is wrong. Right on top I am confused.

"You didn't have to tell lies about me to the Standards Board – or to the local papers!"

"It worked though, didn't it Katie?" he says with that smirk I want to wipe off his face (with Brillo).

"If you thought I was doing such a bad job you could have asked for a vote of no confidence." I've been rehearsing this argument to Windy for years. "Why did you tell lies about me?"

"Lies, Katie? Lies? I only told people what I knew. You and that woman at the Garden Centre were thick as thieves. I couldn't let you give them a commercial advantage could I?"

"What commercial advantage?" I bang my mug onto the kitchen worktop.

"Letting them advertise on my website, letting them put their webcam on it. Couldn't have their IT people poking around, could we?"

A lightbulb goes pop over my head.

"Anyway," he says quietly, "You told lies about me too. You and Hilary told lies about me to the Standards Board."

I open my mouth to disagree but at that moment there's a knock at the door. "Saved by the bell," he says and smiles. "But it's not a bell so perhaps you haven't been saved." He hops off the stool and goes to the door. I slide silently off my stool and nip out of the back door, slip round the side of the house and make off through the neighbours' gardens. Eventually I get back to the hotel and find Windy has got back before me.

"Had a good afternoon?" he asks. I'm non-committal with a little grunt as I walk through to the bathroom to wash away the grime I feel sticking to me.

"I'm very tired," I shout back through the open door.

"Where's the shopping?"

"I didn't buy anything."

He has followed me into the bathroom. He looks concerned. "What, nothing at all? What about the gifts to take home to people? That's what you went for!"

"I didn't see anything I liked." (That's true enough. The one 'thing' I did see today I definitely didn't like.) "What about you?" I change the subject because I am thinking of my next move. I'm not going home next week without some kind of release from the hold Dave Tripswitch has over me.

"I had a great day," says Windy and he proceeds to tell me in minute detail about his wonderful day. "Come swimming with me tomorrow," he says. "The beach is fabulous. It's much cooler down there by the ocean, too."

"No, I think I'll go shopping in the shopping mall in town. I'm bound to find something there. And it's air-conditioned."

"Oh Katie! You should come and have a nice day out. You need to chill out." He doesn't realise just how cool I am. I'm chilled right through – as cold as ice in fact.

I dream about being trapped in a building. It's a bit like the village hall. Mavis Wilson is there with Phil Jenkins, Dave Tripswitch and me. I am looking for the exit but they keep directing me the wrong way so I keep coming to dead ends or places piled up with boxes, or barbed wire. In my dream I am in a panic. I shout at them, 'Help me! Help me!' but they just smile, especially Dave Tripswitch. He's got that annoying smirk, like he had yesterday. They are not listening. They are just not listening. Mavis is laughing at me, wiping tears off her face because she is laughing so much. I look at my watch but the numbers on it don't make sense. I must have been in the building for hours. I need to get home and get Windy's tea. I'm running at the door; I'm going to shoulder-barge it but it turns into another brick wall. My shoulder and arm really hurt and I am desperate now, crying and shouting at Dave, 'You bastard. Let me out of here!'

Windy is gently stroking my arm. "It's all right," he says, "Just a bad dream. Do you want to talk about it?"

I don't, but I tell him my shoulder and arm have pins and needles from the way I have been sleeping on them. They are, of course, nothing compared with the long skewers of my inner turmoil. Hat pins and crochet hooks.

Next day Windy swallows his disappointment along with his coffee and heads off for another day alone sampling the sea and sand. I tidy up the hotel room and head out to the shopping mall in town. The sky is overcast and the heat oppressive. The shopping assistant laughs at me as I breathlessly gather up a dozen or more tourist trinkets without much thought.

"You're in a hurry, Ma'am, for such a hot day."

"The last day of my holiday," I offer in explanation. He takes the money and I run.

Back to the hotel I go and wait till Reception is empty, dash up to the room and leave the tat there, then off again, off to Tripswitch Towers. Cue the sinister music.

Dave's car is outside in the drive. That's handy. It's parked out of view of his windows. I could let the tyres down, or if I was clever I could loosen the brake pipe like I've seen in films. But I'm not clever. And I don't want to hurt his wife and kid. God knows they must have suffered enough, having to live in such a downright moral vacuum with that pervert. What if she's there, his poor wife? Shall I just pretend to be someone else? She's never met me – but she must have seen photos of me on the website, or in the Corset Daily Post. I don't want to raise any suspicions. I put my hand in my pocket. There's the little stick. It fits nicely in my hand.

I go round the back, taking yesterday's escape route in reverse. The back door is open. Dave is hanging washing on the line. I think I can make it past him if I'm quick and quiet. Into the house I dash and make for the living room. You may be wondering if I've got a plan. The exact same thing is going through my mind. I've got half a plan but plans have to be properly hatched and mine could be addled or destined for strangulation at birth. One step at a time. At the moment all I want is the element of surprise. My heart is going like a jack hammer.

CHAPTER TWENTY-FOUR

"There is no real ending. It's just the place where you stop the story."
Frank Herbert

I'm going to have to move my legs in a minute. I've been sitting cross-legged behind the sofa for hours now. I'm getting too old for soulful meditation. In my case strength is not in stillness. My static sinews seem to be preparing to snap. This isn't much like a Tai Chi work-out. It's getting very painful.

Dave is on his computer. I thought he would put the radio on, but he hasn't. It's deadly quiet. I daren't move a muscle, although they are beginning to move themselves a bit: my right leg is threatening to go into a cramp spasm. What will I do then?

Plan A: When Dave goes out I will look on his computer. I will put what I find on the memory stick in my pocket, then I'll go to the police and tell them to arrest him. And I'll drop an email to the school too and tell them what I've found on his computer. He is pretty slow to go out though, and maybe I will have to resort to Plan B. I'm not sure what Plan B is.

As it happens I get time for neither plan because Dave has plans of his own. My leg is cramping and I have to move. As soon as I make a weeny little movement Dave leaps out of his chair and pounces on the back of the sofa like a bobcat on a chipmunk. His reactions are quick for a dying man.

"Katie! What on earth brings you to my living room?"

"I wanted to talk," I say feebly, standing on my toes to relieve the pain.

"From behind the sofa? How long have you been there?"

I notice a slight tremor in my hands. I can't answer.

"Let's go and have a cosy chat in the basement," he says and grabs my wrist and pulls me out from my hiding place.

“That’s hurting.”

He knows that and he doesn’t care. He is set on hurting me a lot worse. He pulls me along and I’m just going. Why don’t I fight back? He can’t be that strong, can he? I have unhelpful thoughts, like: first, it’s common knowledge that people have superhuman strength when they are mad; second, no-one knows I am here.

The basement is neat and tidy – a cross between a store room and a living room. All the plastic boxes are neatly labelled and stacked along one wall. There must be at least thirty of them. Another wall is shelved and some of the shelves have more lidded plastic boxes and one shelf is entirely filled with DVD cases with dates and numbers on. Dave grabs a bit of nylon cord and secures my hands behind my back and to the stair rail. The way he does it makes me wonder if he has done it before.

“Don’t do this Dave. You’ll only get yourself into trouble.”

“Oh yes,” he smirks, “I nearly forgot to offer you a cup of tea.”

He goes back up the stairs and I hear him rattling cups and filling the kettle. I could do with a cup of tea, but he might try to poison me. Anyway how am I going to drink it if he doesn’t untie me? Should I shout? I didn’t see a soul about when I arrived here.

I do a bit of half-hearted struggling and wiggling my fingers as if I believe I could get loose if I wanted to, but I don’t really think it’s likely. By the time Dave comes back the only thing I have achieved is to make the nylon cord even tighter round my wrists.

“Please untie me,” I say as coolly as I can.

“Of course Katie. I didn’t intend to restrain you for long. I just needed to make sure you wouldn’t sneak off like you did last time I made tea for you.”

He crosses the room to a door which I thought would lead to the garage. He unlocks it with a big bunch of keys and pushes it open. He comes back for me, undoes the rope and pushes me forward into the next room. It is painted and adorned with wall-hangings in reds, pinks and golds. In the centre is a beautiful purple velvet couch. There is something of the art photographer's studio about it, with a tripod and camera in the corner and some fancy parabolic dishes.

"Sit down," he says and, having little alternative, I might as well. The couch must be an improvement on the patch of floor behind the sofa upstairs. I now notice a screen rolled up near the ceiling and a projector suspended there among the cobwebs. Dave sees what I am looking at.

"Would you like to watch a film while you drink your tea?" he asks, but I realise I'm not supposed to give an answer.

I'm beginning to get it. This might be a studio after all. I know he is no Walt Disney so I suspect what he is going to show me will have 'adult content'. I'm not expecting it to be *The Untouchables* but *Despicable Me* would suit the occasion.

He hasn't waited for a reply and is pulling down the screen and pushing buttons on a remote handset. A film begins. It starts quite abruptly with a title and some computer generated music. The title comes up: *Black and White.*

A young naked girl is sprawled on a dirty mattress. She looks drunk or drugged. Probably both. A big black man enters stage left. I don't want to see any more.

"You'll like this bit – someone you know."

I look back to the screen and the vacant yet imploring, innocent, beautiful face of Millie Purfitt is looking straight at me, at the camera, as the black man begins to undo his trousers in the foreground of the film. Millie can't seem to move.

"Is she drugged?"

Dave smiles. "It helps sometimes if the little ones are nervous. She was a lovely little girl, Millie. I really liked her. She behaved herself with me."

I'm silent. I need to get out of here and report him. I need to get out of here anyway because Windy says he's capable of anything. If I wasn't a threat to him before, I am now.

"Please stop that Dave, it's really upsetting me."

"Yes, well, I didn't think the kids stuff would turn you on. I'll find you something more to your taste, shall I?"

"No, please don't!" I say, taking a step towards the door. He pushes me back.

"No, really Katie, you will like this much better."

He swaps disks over and the first thing I see is still photos of the actors who will appear in the film. I want to glue my eyes shut but they keep springing open. The film is called *Office Antics* and there is the female star: Lisa. The film begins. Our heroine is sitting on a typist's chair, giggling. "You're not filming, are you?" she giggles and wiggles and wriggles. A man is speaking to her. I can't hear what is being said but she staggers to her feet and begins an exaggerated striptease.

"For God's sake, Dave!"

"Just a home movie. Are you really surprised?"

"No, of course not. I always knew you were up to no good with her, and poor Millie." But I catch a glimpse of someone else on the screen and it makes me gasp.

"Oh, someone else you know in there?" Dave sniggers.

Just then there is a loud knock on the door, and I can hear sirens in the street. It really is a good job that Dave lives in a place like this.

"Mr Tripswitch!" comes the urgent shout, "Open up! It's the police! We're evacuating the area! Open up!"

Later back at the hotel, Windy is telling me all about his exciting day. "Good job we're off tomorrow," he says. "The forest fires are getting closer to the town. You could see the smoke from the beach. There's a whole load of fires all around. The trees just go up like torches, they're full of resin, and it's so dry everywhere. This easterly wind is very drying too. I reckon we'll be able to see the sky glowing from the hotel tonight – but they reckon the wind will turn by the weekend and come in from the ocean, then the air will be more humid and it will cool down a bit. You even smell a bit smoky," he says, eyeing me steadily.

"Me? I don't think so. I haven't been anywhere near any fires. It's your imagination. You've been thinking too much about it, you can smell it when it's not there. I think you smell of smoke too. I think the whole town smells of smoke. I'm going to have a shower anyway."

"Do you want a cup of tea first?"

"No thanks. I had one earlier." I wish I hadn't said that.

"I'll just put the local news on," says Windy, "...catch the news about the bush fires."

We watch the TV side by side on the two-seat leather sofa in silence. I wonder if Windy can hear my heart pounding or notice the shallowness of my breath. There are pictures of burning trees, burning bridges, burning houses. The aerial photos show a huge area of devastation. Windy turns up the sound.

"Red Oak!" he says, "That's here! I was thinking today, I think I remember that this is the place that Dave Tripswitch moved to?"

He's looking at me even more intently now, searching my face for an answer. He knows me too well. He will notice my shaky hands and my downcast eyes but I have to continue the charade.

"Don't remember," I say lightly.

"The fires have not yet reached the extent of the fires in 2003, but today the fires around here claimed their first victim in San Diego County when a local businessman and father of one was asphyxiated in his house by smoke. Police say that they had evacuated all the houses in the area earlier in the day and it was only when firefighters entered the property to check for gas cylinders and other explosives that his body was found in the basement."

I don't trust myself to look up. In any case I am so shaky my head might fall off. "I'm off to have my shower."

When I realise my hairbrush is in my handbag, which I have left back in the other room, I open the door to go back in. Windy is speaking quietly into his mobile phone. I can't hear what he is saying. I pick up my bag and take out the brush, calmly, as if he is a cornered animal that I don't want to startle. He silently discontinues his call.

"I forgot my brush." My voice sounds quite unnatural. I know Windy will notice.

"We still haven't arranged to see Mike and Helga," I say, just to say something. "We're leaving on Saturday and it's silly that we've come all this way and we're staying so close to them and ..." I stop. Windy is staring at me. "What's up?" I've never seen him so pale. "What's the matter?"

"Nothing. Nothing at all. I've got Mike's number. I'll ring him while you're in the shower."

"Who were you ringing just now? What is it Windy?"

He looks away. The sudden failure of trust between us is like the splitting open of a tight pair of trousers when the stitching gives way. There is a real risk of being completely exposed. I've got the feeling both Windy and I are wearing dangerously tight trousers.

When I finally emerge in my towelling robe I feel much better. The traces of DDT are washing down into the Californian sewers and will make their way to the huge ocean. Windy seems to have had a similar purging experience and looks calm. He says, "That's fixed. I've cancelled our table for tonight in the restaurant here. We're going out with Mike and Helga."

I'm not entirely thrilled with the prospect. I'm not sure I want to see Mike after this afternoon. It's all been a bit of a shock and I think my feelings might show.

"I'm very tired."

"Well, we've got to eat, Katie, and as you say, we need to fit in seeing them before we go. It was one of the main reasons for our trip."

I know it makes sense. "OK, I'll go and put my glad rags on."

Actually my rags, like Windy and me, are not very glad at the moment. We've been away for weeks living out of suitcases and I haven't wanted to ask hotels to get laundry done when it's just little bits of ordinary clothes, but I've been too lazy to wash anything more challenging than underwear in the en-suite basin. It will have to be my blue linen trousers and the lacy top.

We get a taxi in the opposite direction from Red Oak. It is still stifling hot and the driver says that more areas will be evacuated tomorrow. Rain is forecast for the day after tomorrow and he hopes that means a break in the drought and the end of the fires.

"We got evacuated because of fires in 2003," he says. "It was a real pain in the butt. At least you don't get that in England, do you? It's always raining."

We arrive at a large wooden hotel called Cedar Glen. The taxi driver shakes Windy's hand and wishes him a nice evening. He will be back to pick us up at 11 pm. As we are getting out of the car, Mike appears from nowhere and greets me warmly. (It would be hard to do anything else in this heat.) Helga is in his shadow, as usual, which I suppose keeps her slightly cooler. She gives Windy a hug. We weren't on hugging terms before they left England. I smile through the metal teeth of my zipped mouth. "Great to see you Mike and Helga. How are you liking it here? Hot enough for you? It's been nearly 40 degrees ever since we arrived here."

Mike gives me a hug, a kiss and a squeeze. I feel thoroughly greeted. It's overload actually. I've never liked him that much. Helga grabs my arm as if it is a lifebelt. "Let's get a drink," she says. So she and I end up drinking together at an outside table, while the men prop up the bar inside. It seems they have a lot to talk about. Windy looks very serious. Mike looks as he has always looked: a bit of a bully, a bit of a know-all. I'm trying not to think about what I saw this afternoon.

Helga says, “I don’t know what they’ve been up to but I get the feeling Mike needs a friend. It’s great that Windy’s been here for a few days and they’ve been able to spend a bit of time together. I think Mike could be in trouble.”

“Oh yes?” I’m quite interested in that statement.

“Mike’s become quite paranoid. He hasn’t told me what’s the matter, but he goes to great lengths to hide his emails from me and sometimes I catch him on the phone and he doesn’t tell me who he’s been talking to. I’m worried there’s something going on. I don’t like it.”

“Windy does that too. You can’t read too much into it. He didn’t tell me he’d seen Mike this week. In fact he made out that he hadn’t. All men are a bit secretive.”

“Only if they have something to hide…” Helga stops abruptly as Mike and Windy join us.

“It’s great to see you both again, Helga,” says Windy. “You look well. Mike told me the other day...” Windy stops dead. He looks as if he wishes he was. “When I phoned him,” he adds lamely, but it is too late. Mike is bludgeoning him to death with his eyes, and Helga and I are sending clouds of question marks over his head. He looks at his friend.

“Oh God, Mike,” he says, “I’m sorry.” He looks as if he’s on the point of tears. What on earth has he done? It’s hardly the end of the world for us wives to discover that our husbands who are old friends have met each other.

“I understand you and Mike have already met up this week,” I say. I might as well clear the air. I aim one of the question marks right at him and he meets it head-on. “I didn’t want to bring you into this,” he says.

“She’s not into it,” growls Mike. I look right at him. I am in it, Mike. I am. I don’t know why they’re being so strange.

“We’re off in the morning,” I say brightly. “We’ll be glad to get away from all this heat. Did you see, Mike, a man even died in the fire on the edge of town? We’re catching a train to Las Vegas first thing. What would you recommend we see while we’re there?”

Mike’s eyes are boring holes into me. I can feel them like a million pin pricks all over.

“I’ve got contacts in the police,” he says. “In California - even in Las Vegas I’ve got contacts. I’m sure they would help me get you the right kind of welcome in Las Vegas.”

Windy looks confused, Helga is bemused. Mike and I know what he is talking about. It’s a threat. We are beginning to understand each other. He doesn’t know exactly what I know of course, but he’s not going to take any chances.

“That’s kind, Mike,” I say. “But I think we’ll manage. I think I know all I need to know. We don’t need to involve anyone else.”

“How have you enjoyed your time at Red Oak?” he asks. “Any surprises?”

“Oh yes,” I say, “that is the word for it. It’s a very surprising place, but on the whole I’m very glad I came. I’ve learnt quite a lot.”

Helga smiles. “You always liked to find things out.”

Mike is now the one to take my arm and he leads me firmly into the restaurant ahead of the others. I can’t take him on. I’m too tired. This has gone on too long. I’ve spent years fighting the parish council back home. I suddenly want it all to be over. I want an easy life now. I smile at him. We both know it’s contrived but that doesn’t matter. It’s what lies behind the smile that counts.

“I don’t care any more, Mike. I don’t care about what I saw at the Tripswitch place yesterday. I’ve got my closure now. I just want to go back to my little life in England. I just want to make jam and look out of the window at the view.”

Mike nods. “I’m really glad about that, Katie.” His tone has changed now he understands my position.

"Porn cocktail for starters?" he grins.

"Something grilled for the main course, I think."

"Barbecues are really popular here in California."

"Dessert is something with toasted nuts."

"Flambé, I would think. Or brulé."

Windy gives us a funny look. "Is that a game you're playing, you two?"

"Just having a chat about our menu preferences," says Mike.

"I always like a cold dessert," I say. "They say some things are best served cold."

"I like something sweet to take away any sour taste. It's really important to round things off, isn't it? You need to feel satisfied at the end of it that you've had all you wanted."

The four of us sit at the table and wait for our food order.

"Don't worry, Windy. It's all over. Katie and I have sorted it all out," Mike says, putting a reassuring hand on his arm. He raises his glass: "Here's to your return to Fartlebury Magna!"

THE END

AFTERWORD

Back in Fartlebury Magna, years have passed but I'm still an outsider here. Dave Tripswitch lives just down the road. Sometimes we exchange hateful looks. Once I stared at him until he looked at the ground. It felt like a victory, of sorts.

I miss Jim. I remember some of the things he said and realise he wasn't as stupid as I thought. (He was more stupid even than that – but he was a nice old chap.) He died last year and his cottage in the High Street has been extended and modernised out of all recognition. They even put in plastic window frames. There are no bullocks at the end of the garden now, just a modern pair of semi-detached bungalows. I don't speak to the people living in them. I don't speak to anyone much now but I make a lot of jam. This year I made rosehip cordial too. It's full of Vitamin C. I'm planning a new set of cushions for the lounge.

It didn't work out for Dave in California. His wife left him for another woman and Rudy turned eighteen and came back to live with his grandparents in Truro. Dave lives alone now. The Scouts wouldn't have him back, nor would the parish council. He seems well in at the community church. Maggie says they've forgiven him.

It was another businessman, father-of-one, who died in the fire at Red Oak. When Mike Cannon knocked on the door during the fire he only meant to give Dave a scare. He knew I was in there because he had followed me. He gave me the chance to escape through the back and I took it. Dave ran off too, so Mike thought I had finished him off. When we heard about the fatality in that area Mike and I each thought the other was to blame – or, as it happened, to be congratulated.

I sometimes cry and tell Windy I would like to move away from Fartlebury Magna. He just smiles because he thinks I'll get over it. Maybe I will, if I can find a stepladder high enough.

Lightning Source UK Ltd.
Milton Keynes UK
UKOW04f0822020915

257887UK00002B/136/P